I0699650

MAX IN THE CAPITAL OF SPIES

A MAX FREDERICKS STORY

STEVE CAPONE, JR.

CAPONE FAMILY PUBLISHING

DEDICATION

This adventure in storytelling is dedicated to the memory of Pappap Salvatore "Sal" Profeta, an engineering genius who never understood the philosophy and writing stuff but always supported my dreams.

Pappap Sal showed me all the coolest movies when I was a kid—no restrictions—and he played a strong role in saving my life while I battled a severe drug addiction and psychological collapse when I was about Max's age.

Having worked all his life as an auto mechanic or manager of other blue collar guys, Sal often wondered what I was going to do with degrees in English, Humanities, and Philosophy. I'd often say that I wanted to learn everything there is to know. I'd still say the same.

While he was on his way out of this world, I told him that I was finishing this book and that he'd like it. If I could meet him today, I'd thank him for everything.

ONE
THE SHIFT

On a Friday two months before receiving the mysterious package, Max Fredericks was scouring the Volkspark perimeter for his tutor Brady. That was when 2021 dissolved into 1965. A few moments later, he witnessed the abduction that sent him careening through Cold War Berlin.

It's happening, Max realized as the shift from present to past began with a wave of queasiness. He struggled to keep his footing, focusing on the silver Renault that had caught his attention before the world turned to static. He turned in a slow circle. The white, six-story, walkup apartment building across the street blurred. Behind him, the wrought-iron fence atop a low wall remained, but its pickets bent and wobbled. Late-November Berlin's grayish haze transformed to something grayer and hazier.

Max's 2021 perceptions disappeared inside the filter of this transition, which hit harder than any he'd experienced so far.

Max coached himself. *It's okay. You've done this before. This is why you're here. You wanted this. You can handle it.* But it didn't pass right away.

He waited, exhaling, working to ensure he didn't stop breathing as he had before.

Ugh, but this is new.

The unease in his stomach threatened full-blown nausea as the world disintegrated and then reintegrated pixel-by-pixel as though a novice photographer were bringing the world into focus. Things tilted, became firm, and then tipped again. He staggered three steps backward across the sidewalk and away from the granite curb.

He exhaled and then inhaled, counting to four for each breath. Max steadied himself, closing his eyes and leaning into the fence ringing the People's Park. He sat on the brick sidewalk, leaning hard into the concrete-and-stone ledge.

He waited.

It'll be okay.

Consciousness returned, the world's metamorphosis complete, but Max's stomach continued churning. Acclimating to a different time had never taken so long before.

Max held his face in his hands as though it would help hurry the process and stop the vibrations. He rubbed his temples and closed eyes, massaging his cranium through close-cropped hair.

The sickness passed.

He opened his eyes. His own time was gone.

He wasn't ready to stand, but he began to move one limb at a time, both checking for mobility and assuring himself the ground would remain solid while hoping against a return of nausea. Inside the ball of a fist he'd made when everything began muddling, Max felt something in his left hand. The handwritten note he clutched brought with it the memory of why he'd come to the Volkspark in the first place.

Right. Forgot.

He uncrumpled and read the relevant bits of the note for the third time: "Volkspark West. 10:15, where wolf and girl meet."

Still doesn't make any sense seeing as Brady won't write the note for decades. I guess the test—or whatever it was—is off. He shoved the note into his jeans pocket.

I wonder when I've landed...

A different, older car sat in place of the modern, French car and became the first point of focus in Max's new surroundings. The formerly shiny silver hood was now muted and faded. The hood ornament was no longer a bright silver diamond but instead had morphed into a sharp but dull "S." The Renault had been replaced.

Max recognized the vehicle parked in its place: the most famous piece-of-crap car in the Eastern Bloc. *A Trabi? I can't believe people waited for a decade at a time on purchase lists for this hunk of junk.*

He remembered a joke about that old car. "Why'd they call it a 601?" went the setup. "600 ordered it, and one arrived!" answered the punchline. Still, the Trabant was kind of cool in the way old broken things could sometimes be—as in, "Isn't it wild this old thing really existed?"

Max took stock of his new surroundings, looking for other hints about when he had landed in Berlin's history. Some times were better than others, he knew.

The sunlight seemed weaker than before the shift, now gone behind threatening clouds. Buildings were more decrepit and broken down and featured a crumbling quality. Boarded windows paired with vacant balconies replaced neat patios, and broken glass on the lowest floors revealed darkened interiors of empty shops. The color of cement had replaced any bright colors livening up the neighborhood around the park in 2021. The shift meant the world had become darker, outside the shops as well as within them.

Max set out toward the western entrance of the park, doubling back on his 2021 footsteps. He tread with care, a kind of tunnel vision limiting what he could take in at once. *Must be left over from the shift.* Broken glass littering the sidewalk crunched underfoot.

The road skirting the north edge of the triangle-shaped park had been busy with bikes and cars back in 2021. Now, a single car sputtered along the avenue. It smelled like burning oil. Another joke from

German tutoring popped into his head: "How do you catch a Trabant? Stick some chewing gum on the road."

Three men in overalls rode bicycles a few dozen yards behind the slow-moving car. The parked Trabant he'd left behind was one of maybe ten cars stopped alongside the park. Some of them even looked like they could be started and driven.

These cars are from the sixties.

This is the sixties.

I'm in East Berlin during the Cold War.

Whoa.

He'd been learning to speak German, through his freshman and sophomore years in high school. He spent whole weekends reading about the Cold War and watching spy movies. He'd been talking with Brady through his whole week in Berlin about Cold War espionage tactics Brady called "tradecraft." And here Max was, wandering around the Capital of Spies in the heat of the Cold War— the 1960s.

The daze accompanying breaking one chain of consciousness and replacing it with a fresh one began tapering.

What I've wanted since last year—since the last trip. It's happening.

Two men in weathered, gray suits rounded the corner toward the crosswalk nearby. Pausing at the edge of the street, the pair gave him a once-over, a second take, and then halted their conversation and eyeballed him as he passed them. They crossed into the street behind him. Their intensity stopped him in his tracks, and he couldn't help but to watch them watching him.

He froze, a flood of terrors gripping him.

What do they want? Why are they staring? Am I acting weird? Do my jeans stand out? Of course they do. I'm an obnoxious materialistic Westerner in this outfit. I'm not gonna last five minutes...

Under usual circumstances, this sort of anxious social interaction by itself would have Max—like many other 17-year-old boys—scurrying for safety. But not only were these far-from-usual circumstances, neither did Max have anywhere to scurry.

Then Max saw her. A brown-haired girl in tan work overalls similar to those worn by the men on bikes, looking about sixteen years old, stood facing the street. About twenty paces from him, she was waiting just shy of the corner where three streets met in a Y-intersection around the edge of the park. *What is she looking for?* She wasn't moving—just standing there.

Max caught himself. *I'm getting distracted. I'm supposed to be looking for him.*

His confusion from the sudden shift hadn't yet dissipated. His subconscious still had him looking for Brady. He stopped walking after he passed the girl, shook his head as if to shake off a mosquito landing on his nose, and squeezed his eyes shut for a breath. *Brady isn't here. But I am.*

Max's field of vision grew now to include other Friedrichshain denizens. They kept their heads down and shuffled this way and that, hurrying home, to or from markets with empty shelves, some pulling their children alongside them or pushing them in wicker baby carriages, going about their business. These people's feet echoed the sound of flattened, bruised rubber and exposed cobbling nails scraping on stone.

A vehicle trundling up the road passed Max, catching his eye, and he turned to watch. The dull-brown van was marked with a faded color print of a bouquet of flowers and a price, 20 DDM, outlined in black ink or paint.

He processed each detail he noticed: *German Democratic Republic Deutschmarks, East German money.*

Then, thoughts intruded in succession. *Do I still have euros in my pocket? Does stuff come with me when I shift back in time? Pocket litter, or whatever it was called by those spies...*

He groped for the coins in his pocket, finding the four 2€ coins he'd had when he left the hostel that morning. And his compass. *Huh.*

I wonder how much this park changed between then and now, or now and then, or whatever it was.

He entered through the iron-pillared west entrance. Rather than the neat concrete, stone, and brick patterns that had decorated the walkway in 2021, in Max's path now was only dirt. And so was everything else.

The most unusual border indicated the walkway's borders: statues, or pieces of them, lined its edges. He paused at the sight, then approached. The stone shapes were of babies with animals. Some with fish, others with horses or with birds, someone had arranged the statues by height. Full-sized adult statues were in the rear of the line nearest a fountain. Most of them were headless.

I guess when stuff topples over, the heads go first.

Thanks to age and war damage, soot and dust coated all of them, but the figures were probably once white. Rather than water, debris of cracked concrete and twisted metal filled the pool at the end of the walkway. He stood over it, trying to decipher what he was seeing. Busted lamps, a suitcase, several broken radios... all smashed and twisted, filled the fountain pool.

This is like Oz, Narnia, and Wonderland all mixed together in a real city. Only darker.

Struck by a thought, he shifted gears: *I wonder what the Wall looks like. Now's my chance.* Max turned on his heels and headed for the Volkspark exit.

Back at the Y-intersection, Max peered up and down each of the streets to get his bearings. *The wall would be west of here right? It goes around the people in West Berlin, and this is the eastern part of the city. Yeah. The park points west, I think—that way...*

He had the wherewithal not to start comparing compass to map, but he wished he could have.

A screech yanked him away from orienteering. Unlike the easterners who pointedly ignored everything about to unfold, he couldn't turn away. He was unaccustomed to ignoring abductions.

TWO

OPPORTUNITY

On a Sunday early in November, two-and-a-half months before Max received the mysterious package, an early-season snow fell heavily outside the Fredericks' Salt Lake City home. Significant snowfall was unusual at this time of year, but it wasn't unheard of. In a few short hours, meteorologists' "trace to one inch" predictions had been shattered, and the whole valley had slowed to a halt. Max Fredericks didn't think much about it.

Max reclined, hands interlocked behind his head, and wondered at textured model planets suspended over his timber four-post bed. The planets didn't fit the theme of the rest of the Fredericks' home, but 2nd-grade Max had insisted, and his parents had always supported his fierce curiosity.

When the family—Max, his sister Livi, and their parents—moved in years ago, Max's father had pushed for what he'd called a "Rustic vibe." He always annunciated the capital-R when he spoke of his commitment to making the family home feel like it belonged where it stood at the foot of the Rockies. Jeanne had been occupied at the time with her new job duties at the City-County Building and didn't have a strong opinion, so she'd gone along with Andrew's whimsy. She often did. Hand-carved banisters adorned stairwells, doors were framed with knotty pine, and each bedroom had a timber-framed bed and matching dressers. And soon after, Max's room had planets hanging from the ceiling.

Max had been lying in that spot for an hour trying to imagine himself back in time to the heyday of Virginia City, Montana—a true town of the American Wild West—when he was distracted by the planets hanging from the ceiling over his toes.

Are real planets perfect spheres? Do the people making these things know what shapes the real planets have? What would that Cosmos guy say? He probably knows. Does he respond to emails?

He paused, catching himself.

Distracted again. This is never going to work.

Max scrunched his eyes.

I have to be there.

Just as it had been since he returned from Berlin the summer before, he couldn't time travel on demand. Whether it was comics, soccer practice, or drama at school, something always interrupted his concentration, and he'd had no success conjuring the past. This time, his focus had turned to the planets, Virginia City gone, and he was still in his bedroom.

Maybe I'll never get to go back.

A throat-clearing noise brought him out of model-planet reverie. His middle-aged father's grinning face appeared between bedroom door and frame, his body casting a partial shadow in the room.

"What's up Dad?"

"I've got a ticket for you if you want to make a return trip to Berlin."

Max immediately forgot his frustration about being stuck in the present: "You have one, or you can buy one?" When it came to travel, Max was, in a manner of speaking, all business.

His father grew serious: "Just a figure of speech, Max, but I can snag you a ticket tonight when I buy mine. There's a city planning conference I weaseled my way into, last minute. Maybe a consulting job in the works for Engineering for Good. You've got a full week off for Thanksgiving break."

He waited.

"Are you in or not? I need to know right now so I can take care of some things." His features channeled hope like a laser beam.

Max sat upright, moving to the edge of his bed. "What's the catch? You're saying I can go to Germany and hang out for the week —no strings attached?"

"Yes—I will go to conference meetings Monday through Friday. I might need to take the train to Cologne Friday night, but I'm not sure yet. I may get to pitch my Tiny House Solutions idea to a firm there first thing on Saturday morning." He pauses.

Here it comes.

"Either way, I've arranged for a tutor for you, Monday through Friday."

And there it is.

"He's cheap enough that we don't have to be super rich to afford him, and he seems to know his stuff. I got his contact info from a lady I know over there. The tutor doesn't even have a website, but I've been emailing with him for a few days. He seems legit. He's old, and I'll bet he's had a lot of cool experiences. Plus he knows the area." Mr. Fredericks shrugs.

Max's face fell. "An old guy? A tutor?" He slumped backward.

"An hour or two per day is all. A bit more, if you want."

Max chortled at this.

Andrew powered on. "His name is Brady. The rest of the time is yours 'til I'm done with each day's conferences. Then we might hang out, eat currywurst, or whatever." A pause. "I've been thinking about that exhibit we saw near the Embassy—the memorial. The above-ground bit would be something to see at night, I think. And I know you're into historical stuff now, and there are a few neat museums in

Berlin. One of them has this old globe—I think you'd like it—the U.S. is just a thin coastline because the people making these things didn't know about anything past the coast. And there are sea monsters on it. Pretty cool."

Stick to the point, Dad. I hope you're more focused selling ideas to customers than to me.

Max asked, "What sort of tutor?"

"You'll like him. He's into history." He flashed a double-thumbs up, raising his eyebrows as if to say, "This is cool, right?"

You're such a dad.

Max pondered and repeated aloud, "He's... into history." *What does that mean?*

This could go one of two ways, as Max saw things: Either this guy Brady would be more like Arthur or like Mr. Ferguson.

Arthur was Max's retired neighbor. He had totally immersive stories about Julius Caesar, the First World War, and the emperor Napoleon, and Max would be happy hanging with Arthur all day, any day.

Mr. Ferguson, on the other hand, was Max's 9th-grade teacher from two school years prior, and the guy's overcooked brain seemed to be a vacant lot when it came to entertaining ideas. While Arthur managed to draw the interesting bits out of every story, Max's former history teacher did the opposite, squeezing away all the good stuff. The one showed how there was an curious side to almost every historical event, while the other worked extra hard to put off anyone who might have had even a spark of interest in learning. It's a wonder Max's curiosity had survived freshman year.

To figure which way things would go, Max had only one question: "In a classroom?"

Andrew Fredericks' grin returned. He must've known he had Max right where he wanted him. "That was the first question I asked Brady." He paused for dramatic effect. "Not a chance in hell, my dude."

So no classroom. Historical stuff in Berlin. All good stuff. Maybe I will get a chance to go back...

"Deal," Max declared. "But only an hour or two a day, and I get the rest of the time." His father nodded. Max had a few ideas for an agenda for Germany's capital city.

He glanced at his closet where his almost-new backpack lay in wait. "I'll pack now! And I've got some reading to do." He sprang from bed, heading for what he called his "go pack"—the handheld shoulder pack he'd put together after his last visit to Germany. It contained European currency notes, his passport, and a toiletry kit. Spies kept this sort of thing around, he'd learned, and he followed suit. The go pack was always ready. He checked it weekly, each time imagining adventures for which he'd need it.

His father furrowed his brow and tilted his head to the right, saying, "We don't leave for a week, bud, but suit yourself on packing, I guess. And I'm glad to hear you're reading, but you know you don't have any homework for your time with Brady, right? All you'll need is yourself and whatever is driving this obsession with Berlin and the Cold War."

"I know. I got distracted by this whole 'we-hang-everyone-we-don't-like' Wild West stuff, and I want to go back and brush up on the Berlin Wall thing." *No need to say why... Dad is not going to get this whole "I can go back in time" thing.*

Max continued, "I've read two books about the Cold War and two Le Carre novels since our trip. I really want to find a good map of the division between East and West. Last time, I had no idea what the whole deal was with the Berlin Wall, you know? But now I get it more. I want to keep figuring it out. I want to see it in person." *That's about as far as I should go...*

"Roger dodger, kiddo. Well, get on it, then." Mr. Fredericks left his son to his preparations, pulling the door closed behind him.

Max headed for his closet, grabbing the go pack and his larger hiking backpack. He set them down on the floor against his bed and checked his desk drawer for his lined notepad and favorite pens. Then, looking hard at the bags again, he moved those to the top of the bed, resting them against the wall. *No, no. That won't work. I have to sleep there.* Back on the floor they went as he turned again to the desk drawer for something... *What am I forgetting now? Oh! The compass.* He pulled it from the drawer and stuffed it in the go pack. He observed aloud, "So much to do." Fueled by nervous energy, he couldn't decide where to turn or what to pack first.

Without aim and now onto another track, he wandered to the bookshelf his parents installed for him four years ago, pulling from it some of his lately acquired books about Berlin and the Cold War, making a tower on his bedside table.

He couldn't shake the bad feeling he'd gotten when he'd asked Ms. D., his eleventh-grade history teacher, for suggestions about what to read next. She'd told Max he was "swinging at pitches above his level" and offered nothing.

Just because I'm not a typical "good student" doesn't mean I can't do it, Max had thought at the time with some anger.

Arthur, on the other hand, told Max to start by streaming the Tom Hanks movie *Bridge of Spies,* which turned out to be excellent. It was about a real-life spy exchange between the U.S. and U.S.S.R. and had featured the Stasi prominently. And the Stasi had been at the core of his "obsession," the way his dad described Max's fascination.

Missing from the stacks of interesting books and movies were his high school history and social studies textbooks. Nothing at all was interesting in those oversized paperweights. Whoever wrote them seemed to be giving Mr. Ferguson his worst ideas, sharing in his mission to suck the interest out of learning anything. At least the text-books were useful as paperweights or window props.

So what do I do now? How do I get ready? What I really need is to go back. How do I make that happen? Max realized he'd begun sweating. He was wound up.

Cool it, Max. Do the breathing thing.

He breathed in slowly and deeply, and then out in a measured way—the way his mom Jeanne had shown him after one of her Sunday yoga classes down at 9th and 9th. It actually helped.

He flopped backward onto his bed again, fixating once more on the planets, clearing his mind.

THREE

HOW THINGS CHANGED

Last summer, when Max's parents surprised Max and his sister Phoebe with their first family trip to Europe, he had no desire to go. He'd almost felt guilty complaining about something other kids dreamed about—almost.

Through his entire tenth-grade year, his focus was on getting to Michigan with his best friend Robbie for the Voetbal soccer camp. Soccer camps happened all over the place, but this camp was famous, and for good reason. Led by professional players from Holland and rumored among comp players to be the most fun and best overall development program in the country, it was all he'd thought about for months.

Max's parents used Voetbal to motivate him through the second half of the school year, and it had worked. But they'd sprung a family trip on him and his sister, informing him last-minute the promised camp wasn't in the cards for him— the family vacation would take its place. Missing Voetbal camp meant skipping the traditional midnight match against the pros, the replays of international tournaments projected on the training facility's massive interior wall, the autographs, and the independence. It was hard to give up all of that without a gripe.

Robbie had still gone to Voetbal and had a great time without Max.

After learning his fate, Max had visited his sympathetic neighbor Arthur to report on his glum circumstances. In his usual way of calming Max through related stories and compassion, the old man had helped him to change his perspective enough to give the trip an honest shot. So, while Max didn't have much of a choice in the matter, he'd left Utah in a state of mind approaching acceptance.

Max couldn't have predicted the series of events that changed him from practically being dragged to Europe to wishing for a return journey above all else.

On the Fredericks' first night in Nuremberg, a medieval town about three hours by train from Berlin, they'd dined early in the evening in a little place at the edge of the Pegnitz River. The river divided the northern and southern halves of the town, and it was dark and beautiful. Phoebe voiced her amazement at the covered, wooden footbridges crisscrossing the narrower parts of the waterway. Trees draped like low-hanging clouds over the bridges, and sloping walls of centuries-old homes lined riverbanks. The water underneath those footbridges moved slowly enough to appear still. The bridges and buildings hugging the river were, she said more than once, just like a painting.

Max compared Nuremberg with his hometown. He'd gotten a similar same-but-different feeling there as he did in the bigger city of Berlin. The people seemed to be the same as back home, just as in Berlin: they carried shopping bags, hustled from place to place, and carried their children or rode their bikes to get around town. More bikes, though, and the buildings seemed much older.

In particular, three huge rectangular churches overlooking open market squares dominated distinct parts of town.

The first cathedral, south of the Pegnitz, stood out for its two massive steeples topped with greenish copper towers. The plaza below the towers in front of the church played host to a few fruit sellers and vegetarian falafel stands. The church oversaw a modern, bustling district. Chain stores, bars, and restaurants ran the length of the street beyond the central plaza. Most of the shops were fancy and reminded Max like those at the malls back home more and were out of place in this walled city, which seemed downright ancient every-where else in town.

Max's family—Andrew, Jeanne, and Phoebe—strolled past this first church downhill toward a stone, concrete, and grey-brick bridge over the Peglitz toward the second church. Before reaching the bridge, Max stopped at a bronze statue. The sculpture, called "Ship of Fools," showed a boat containing people, a murderous skeleton, a dog, and a vile-looking crow perched on a branch overseeing the terror beneath. He heard someone say the 12-foot-tall monstrosity told about the end of the world. He shuddered and caught up with his family.

The second massive church was called "The Church of Our Lady," or "Frauenkirche" in German. Like every other big cathedral in Germany, Frauenkirche was constructed from huge stones. Unlike the first church, it featured only a single, squat, tall, and oddly trian-gular tower above its entrance. Turrets similar to the ones on the city walls were set into the building to the right and left of its entryway. Inlaid ivy tracery decorated its main metal doors, which were a dark color, hinting at centuries of maturation.

The triangular tower of the second church overlooked a massive square thick with shoppers and a vast marketplace of tents, each with its own handcrafted or homegrown specialty: produce, delicacies, hammocks, musical instruments, toys, and more.

German farmers' market, like the ones back in Utah—only more sausages. Max had chuckled.

Jeanne wanted to go inside this second church, so they did. They entered from the right side of the anteroom because the main doors were blocked off for preservation purposes.

The first thing Max noticed, beyond the astounding carvings in the foyer, was a small photograph. He got close. It showed the church as it existed immediately after the Second World War. Even to describe the Frauenkirche in the photo as "crumbling" would have been an understatement. The church in the image was demolished. All that remained were its central doors and a partial wall circumnavigating the tower at the front of the church—the way Max had just entered. The rest of the structure—as long and wide as a football field —had been reduced to piles of varying sizes of rocks and collapsed timbers. *Allied bombing.*

Max looked at the photo and then up at the church in which he stood. *How'd they go from that to this?*

The Fredericks walked along the right-hand side of the immense interior and along a row of pews, together but each in a kind of solitude. It would've been a challenge not to have been silenced by the building's beauty. Max felt drawn to the pipe organ, which boasted fifty differently sized silver pipes fitted to delicately crafted wooden framing. A man in a drab dress jacket sat at the organ bench. He began to play as Max approached. The sound stopped him in his tracks.

The ringing echo of the organ was at once powerful and benign. He stood, rapt. *Locals probably heard the same sound a hundred years ago.* As he listened, he felt a connection with the people who lived in Nuremberg before Germany and America became friends. He imagined what had happened to the church during the war and what effort it must have taken for the city to rebuild it. Awe at the sheer bigness of the church swept over him as the player struck a low note on the pipe organ. It rang out, intensifying until it was all Max could find as a focus. He closed his eyes.

The tone flattened into a deep rasp, and the source of the sound shifted to near Max's feet. He looked down. Two dogs were wrestling over a small loaf of bread, threatening one another with low, guttural sounds.

Something is happening... just like in Berlin.

Max looked up, hesitating to make any sudden moves. He was now standing in the square outside this second church. Everything had shifted.

It was dusk, and people perused the marketplace. It smelled dustier than the modern square. No hammocks for sale in this version of the plaza, but otherwise it looked similar, with steins and vegetables and toys. More leather pants on the male shoppers, but not many men around. He continued to move his attention upward, taking it all in.

Nuremberg's history struck him, triggering a heaviness like he were a led-filled tin man. Along the edges of the plaza, strung from windows and hanging on buildings, and in every place of importance or honor—swastikas. The hooked cross, death in black against white and set crimson streams.

Oh no. His stomach lurched.

He made a move to slide through the market, avoiding eye contact and working to obstruct his own view of the horrid symbols. He hadn't moved more than a few paces when a wailing siren pierced the air. Everyone around him froze for an instant as if checking their hearing to be sure they heard what they had heard and then sprang into action. Max covered his ears, watching mayhem all the more terrifying for its orderliness. People scattered, darting in many directions like human-sized ants herding and funneling into buildings.

Bomb shelters.

88mm flak guns protected by sandbags and operated by uniformed soldiers imposed on the otherwise-vacant square. Daylight-bright spotlights tore through the darkening sky, illuminating swirling patterns on the undersides of thick clouds.

Max ran to the wall of the Church of Our Lady, under one of the awful hate symbols and too close to one of the 88s.

Then came a tremendous growling, low-pitched and petrifying. He looked skyward to find the source of the tumult. The clouds had parted, and Max tracked the searchlight beams cutting through dusk and dust as they spotted airplanes, maybe five hundred of them, thundering overhead. The guns nearby shattered the world with explosions, and Max smashed his hands against his ears, his eyes watering from pressure shifts. Puffs of white smoke littered the bleak sky around the planes. Little dots fell from the group of planes like static on a television screen.

So many of them.

A cacophony of whining screams lasted for maybe half a minute, during which time Max watched one of the combatant dogs racing for cover behind bushes—the best it knew to find—followed by successive and terrifying jolts of concussion.

I can't stay here. In a panic, he scanned the edges of the square for something more substantial than a few twigs and leaves.

The dog led the way, and Max followed it between two other buildings, still within sight of the church. It whimpered. He bent and shielded the animal with his body. *A lot of good this will do.*

Buildings and parts of buildings began exploding, roofs downward, collapsing on themselves. Max twisted as the center of the church folded and its walls fell inward.

A whistling sound stood out from the din as it neared and loudened.

It was coming closer.

Closer.

Max closed his eyes hard.

And then, as quickly as the vision had begun, he was once again inside the rebuilt church, staring at the organist's deft hands. A high-pitched tone hung in the air. Andrew Fredericks tapped Max on his shoulder and whispered, "You've been standing here slack-jawed for the last ten minutes—I hate to interrupt, but we'd like to see the walls and castle."

Max blinked. The spell had been broken: "I, uh... yeah, I guess I'm ready."

They walked through the square outside the reconstructed

church and toward the third Nuremberg cathedral, which overlooked a less densely populated government district. Max felt numb. He sat outside while the rest of the family entered the third building without him.

What just happened? It was like what happened at the Brandenburg Gate, but this time it was terrifying. He was hooked, though. Other kids could spend the rest of their lives in school buildings, for all he cared. Max was going to see it all in person.

Seeing the carpet bombing in Nuremberg wasn't Max's first trip back in time on that first European vacation, and it wasn't his last. Every trip back was to a place and time different and new to him, and it was real. He'd been to those places. He'd survived that carpet bombing, had stood on a castle wall watching a final push to end a medieval siege, and he'd been among a crowd in Leipzig at a massive protest against the East German government. He couldn't explain the experiences, and he knew it all sounded crazy—but it had been real. He knew it—felt it. The experiences were too close, too big, too real to be hallucinations.

On his visit to Germany, Max had learned the Wall was built in Berlin to keep East Germans from fleeing to the West—the Eastern border guards pointed their weapons into East German territory and not outward at the people's supposed enemies. He saw with his own eyes that the Stasi hunted down all traces of pro-Western sentiment and compelled and enforced the constant loyalty of East German citizens. Max learned the Stasi were assigned this role even when it meant invading suspected pro-Western people's homes and—so far as they were able—invading their minds as well. He badly wanted to know more about the battle between East and West—the spies, their false identities, the secret disappearances, the dead drops, and the miniature cameras.

He'd spent every day since returning to the States wishing he could go back—back to Germany, and back in time. But he couldn't simply order up an international trip, so he had been trying to figure a way go back in time without leaving Salt Lake City. So far, his efforts had gotten him nowhere. If he knew how the whole time travel thing worked, maybe he could control it. He knew only *that* it worked. He needed to visit Germany, to Virginia City—or to wherever—in person.

Max hadn't expected to get the chance to return to Germany so soon. He had to make the most of it.

FOUR

ARTHUR

Following his father's invitation to make a return trip to Germany over Thanksgiving Break, Max's excitement escalated. At school, he prompted Robbie, his best friend, to be excited for him. Robbie seemed to attempt enthusiasm, but "that's cool" was the best Max could get out of him. Truth was, Robbie had listened to Max drone on about Germany for the past four months, and he'd admitted to having grown exhausted on the subject. But because a good friend always tries, and Robbie was Max's good friend, he gave it his level best. Max wasn't convinced, though.

I know Arthur would appreciate this, Max had thought to himself after that first, disappointing lunchroom conversation with Robbie. He had tests in school all week, though, so when he wasn't researching Berlin, the Stasi, and espionage, he put as much effort as he could muster into studying. This was tough, but keeping up decent grades would improve probabilities of added freedom and spending money in Berlin, so he did all he could to be prepared for school.

That Friday, with the week's tests out of the way, as soon as school let out, he passed his house on 13th South to visit Arthur, two blocks downhill to a level cross-street.

Arthur took Max seriously from their first meeting back when Max was in the seventh grade. A guy who seemed somehow to know something about everything, Arthur struck Max as kind but aloof. He tended to go on once someone got him started, so few people are willing to start conversations with him.

Max, however, liked talking with Arthur, and he often visited for help thinking through a problem. The retiree was a sort of spirit guide, never telling Max precisely what to do but instead asked questions that helped Max to process whatever was on his mind.

Max came to trust Arthur fairly quickly after first coming across him working on a sand mandala in the front yard.

"Coming across" is one way of putting it. Max had unintentionally launched a soccer ball from the street into the middle of the mandala. The ball carved a path through the creation like lava through ancient Pompeii.

Max hadn't known what the art symbolized when he'd wrecked it. He only knew it was intricate and looked to have taken several full days of work. He had thought about running in the opposite direction to avoid getting chewed out, but he decided to follow a then-recent resolution to face his fears rather than bolt from them.

"I'm so sorry. I'm not sure what to say," Max had begun.

Arthur, somehow reading Max's fear and remorse, had responded, "All things are impermanent." Standing there in his yard in flip flops, hands in his pockets, Arthur then stepped directly into and through his own work to get Max's ball for him, demolishing more of the sandworks. "No big deal," he said, tossing back the ball.

Max had been dumbfounded. He stood on the sidewalk beside the stone-and-sand-decorated property, uncertain how to proceed.

The man continued his monologue, explaining, "If I wanted to protect it from the world, I would have built it in my basement and not out here in the sunshine. But my preference for sunshine counted for more than my preference for the security of my art. And perfection, such as it exists, must be found in the world and not apart from it."

Max found himself wondering amid this speechmaking if he'd been forgotten.

The man had crossed his arms, continuing, "And had I built it downstairs, free of nuisance, we wouldn't have met." He put out his hand. "I'm Arthur."

Max offered his best serious handshake.

Arthur grabbed a rake from around a corner of the house and Max watched in mild panic as the old man turned to what remained of his mandala and smoothed over the rest of the project.

Was he angry? Max repeated his apology, "I'm awfully sorry about the ball."

"No more apologies."

Apparently not.

"Come have a sit on the porch," Arthur gestured. "Who doesn't enjoy a good sit?" He chuckled at a private joke.

Max followed him up neat, oaken stairs to the shaded deck. There, the man kept a short, round-topped table of tile and wrought iron supporting two mugs, a glass jar of lemonade, and a weather-proof container filled with ice.

Arthur shoveled ice into the cups and poured out two lemonades. He handed Max a cup, saying, "One of my rules to live by is to always be ready for a guest."

Max had a feeling the man had a book full of rules to live by.

Arthur lowered himself an adirondack chair set against the pastel-blue siding of the home and motioned to the chair beside him.

Max accepted the offering and sat, sipping his lemonade.

They talked all that afternoon—about mandalas and then about a French leader called Napoleon. Arthur moved with ease from one topic to the next, and he seemed endlessly entertained by his own stories. Max recognized this about him: it takes a certain level of ego to be so self-amused. Arthur was a good conversationalist in that he invited Max's participation and asked open-ended questions with no obvious answers. Apparently, quite a lot of Arthur's conversational fodder came from books, but he also often alluded to travels to the places where major events in human history had taken place. He'd seen quite a lot of movies, too, and he swore by them, saying, "You'd be surprised at how much someone can learn by watching a lot of movies." He was good at making history's stories not only palatable but downright fascinating.

Since that day, Max had frequently gone to Arthur to talk about history, problems with his friends or other kids at school, and about comics—Arthur seemed to have a story for whatever Max had on his mind. And on Max's visit prior to his second trip outside of the United States—his second trip to Germany—Max had paraded onto the property in high spirits, eager to share good news.

"Howdy, Max," Arthur offered as Max traipsed up the stairs and sat down against the wall of the house. Arthur kept his seat on a hanging chair. He lifted his hat from its perch on his head and set it on his lap.

"Hey, Arthur," Max began, and he dove in. "I'm leaving in a few days—I get to go back to Berlin!" He beamed.

"Quite the turnaround from last time you came down here talking about a trip to Europe. Whatever happened on that list, anyhow?" He arched his eyebrows, amusement playing across his cheeks. He'd already heard Max's story several times, with additional or differing details filled in with each retelling.

Max had described seeing the Berlin Wall, the Monday Peace Demonstrations, and the Medieval siege all coming to life. They never actually talked about how time travel, as Max had come to think of it, worked. Max didn't want to test the boundaries of fate by overexplaining it. What mattered most was that it worked.

On this Friday afternoon in November 2021, Max was saying, "You know, I've been reading up on Berlin history, and I'm thinking if I could get back there, I could see more of things—see the tanks standoff at Checkpoint Charlie, see the guard towers near the Brandenburg Gate... that sort of thing."

"What are your plans for this visit?"

"I've got a tutor for a few hours per day. I don't know how that's going to go. But for the rest of the time, I'm on my own. I'm looking forward to that part, at least. I'm going to visit Checkpoint Charlie first."

"No tanks there anymore, I'm afraid," Arthur said with a wink. "Sounds good, though. The tutor bit especially. Just you and the tutor —you can ask whatever you want. That's good. You'll find out who the real bad guys and good guys were."

Max began to ask about this—he'd always thought he had a good grasp of who was good and who was bad in the world—but he hadn't the time before Brady asked, "Is this tutor American or German?"

"What difference would it make?" Max didn't remember his dad mentioning these details when he'd introduced the deal.

"An American has certain..." he breathed, "commitments. If the teacher is German, too, you'd get a different story. It's not that this is always better or worse, but lived experience. There's tremendous value there."

Max nodded.

"If your guide is an American, on the other hand, you won't have access to that person's first-hand knowledge of Berlin's history." He looked up as though checking the ceiling of the deck for his next line. "Or, again, if the tutor is German—whether the person grew up in West Germany or East Germany would make an interesting difference."

"Huh, yeah," Max said. "Makes sense."

By the time the mysterious package would be delivered, Max will have realized Arthur had been right—that Brady had participated in or been close to many of the events that so fascinated Max. Brady saw firsthand events too dangerous to the survivors and perpetrators alike to speak about publicly or put into print. On top of all this, Max would learn that Brady didn't believe in the Good Guys and Bad Guys the same way Max did. All of this turned out to matter quite a lot.

FIVE

BRADY

On the first full day in Berlin, Max and his father breakfasted together at a little spot near their hostel in the Prenzlauer Berg neighborhood before setting out to meet Brady. As they walked along Wörther Strasse, Max was brought back to his first visit to the city six months earlier. Andrew and Max passed streetside cafés and bakeries, butcher shops and bookstores. To the younger Fredericks man, the tree-lined streets and decorative façades of the buildings enclosing the avenues were a calming oasis away from his normal life. He liked the parks, the stone-embedded sidewalks, and the tidiness of things. He liked listening to the people speak German, even more so since he had learned to follow along with their conversations. He wasn't a fluent or even conversational speaker, so people could tell he was making a concerted effort whenever he engaged in German.

"Kaffee Paradies" of Prenzlauer Berg sat one stop south on the U-Bahn #2 line, or the U2 for short, at Senefelderplatz (which reminded Max of his aunt's favorite television show *Seinfeld*). It felt like other bars, serving cafe food and coffee through the day and clearly set up to serve beer and other drinks at night. The storefront was glass-paneled, like most of the other shops in the neighborhood, with a rollaway metal screen to be pulled down at closing time. Its décor was unique from them in small ways, though. A low, dark-green bench ran along the wall under a retractable canvas canopy. Along and under the edge of this cover hung Japanese-lantern styled electric lights. Between the walking area of the sidewalk and the bench were four low, circular tables and a few tightly knit wicker chairs suitable for people-watching, very small gatherings of friends, and relaxing.

Inside, Max noted the old Hollywoodesque prints decorating walls papered with paisley blues and reds. Overhead, ancient-looking tin tiles lined the ceiling above oversized bamboo fans. Nearer the edge of the room opposite the entryway, timber beams hung lower to an alternating mix of freestanding tables and booths. The eclectic combination of styles worked, somehow.

The man who turned out to be Brady sat reading a paperback under a window and beneath unadorned timber rafter-beams with his back to the wall opposite the entryway. A drink looking like iced tea sat on a low table in front of him. Apart from this man and the bartender, the cafe was empty.

Mr. Fredericks stepped to the bar and ordered drinks: water—"with gas"—and an espresso for himself, and water—"still" for Max. Max approached the man who was reading.

"Mr. Brady?" Max ventured.

"That is me." He looked Max over as though evaluating him for the required seriousness. "Max?"

"That's me," Max replied.

Brady's face gave away nothing beyond the initial sense of stern judgment Max had felt."Excellent," he said. "So I'm Brady, and you're Max."

"Yes." Max was uncertain how to proceed.

"Yes, fine. Very well."

Brady was older than Max had expected, even for a semi-profes-sional tutor as he'd come to understand the man's job description over the course of the prior week or two. *This guy's gotta be like 70. Maybe 80.* He wore the kind of cap that made Max think about London and reading glasses balanced at the edge of his nose. A white, collared shirt, light-brown trousers, and darker-brown shoes completed the rest of his outfit, which nicely complemented his cap and spectacles.

And though Max had never been, he thought Brady looked ready for an afternoon at the dog track. He'd never been to one himself, but it was the thing that popped into his mind when trying to place for what event or activity the man was dressed.

Brady gestured to a wire-backed stool opposite him. "Have a seat, then."

A man of few words. Max sat.

The conversation was simple, straightforward, and included the character Max recognized as military order and correctness.

"Thanks." He sat.

"You're here for a week?"

"Nine days."

"And what do you expect for us to review?"

"Oh. I, uh." He floundered. "I didn't know that was up to me."

"It is," Brady answered.

Max replied after a moment's thought: "Well, not so much review... the school stuff is boring—"

—"Agreed," Brady interjected.

"So I don't know. Can I learn more about Berlin?"

"Berlin has been a city—several villages before that—for a very long time." Emphasis on the "very" here. "Just what about Berlin would you like to know?"

He probably expects me to ask about Hitler first and nothing else after that.

"I want to know about the tunnels under the Berlin Wall. I want to know how people got out and how the Stasi caught them or tried stopping them."

Brady raised an eyebrow. "Most interesting! Usually, the American kids who find me ask for one topic and one topic only. And I must admit I grow bored of it, though I realize it is of paramount importance. But the Cold War. 1944 to 1990."

Max couldn't hold back a quizzical expression at this. "Wasn't the Cold War from the end of World War Two, in 1945, to 1990?" Max thought he'd understood at least the basic idea of the thing, and said as much: "The war ended, Berlin divided in half, and the Soviets kept East Berlin and left West Berlin to the Allies—France, Britain, and the U.S." He paused. "But 1944 was before the end of the War." He was fairly confident he had the right story—at least the correct date for the end of the war—June of 1945 in Europe.

"You're right that the War ended in '45, but you are mistaken about the Cold War. The Cold War had its roots before the War ended. Long before it began, even, the U.S. and the USSR were jockeying for power, spying on each other, and each generally trying to outmaneuver the other." Max nodded. "It even goes way back to 1917 when the Communists took power in Russia."

Max interpreted. "I mean, I get we—the United States—are you an American?—wasn't really friendly with Russia from before the War, but we were definitely allies with them during... and—"

Brady waited for Max to finish.

"And we weren't fighting against each other. Right?"

"We landed troops on Russian soil in 1918, but you're right—America and the Russians weren't fighting with bullets during the Second World War."

"So which is it, war or no war? "

Mr. Fredericks approached to hand Max his water, smiled at Brady, and sat at a neighboring table.

Brady answered, "It's always more complicated than that. And I'll answer your questions. I am an American, but I've been living in Germany for quite some time now—you might hear a bit of a German accent, even, but not much. And yes—at the end of the War, even, we"—emphasis on the "we" here—"were allied with Russia. But ours was an alliance of shared common interests that concluded the day we declared victory in Europe. There was no brotherhood to it.

The United States joined the war on the Continent largely to stop the USSR from continuing their march—that of communism—all the way through France when their inevitable victory came."

Max had heard this story before, as similar to Arthur's telling as it was different from the school's heroic tale, the latter of which always featured the United States almost single-handedly saving Europe from the Nazis.

Brady continued: "If we hadn't shown up, the biggest problem for us wasn't that Hitler would have won—he most assuredly would not have—but that the USSR would have reigned, triumphant over the whole of continental Europe."

It was basically the same thing Arthur said. *It would piss off Mr. Fergeson. Not how the standard story goes.*

But Brady added some new details that helped to show why Cold War stakes were as high as they were in Berlin: "We knew the Soviets were going to take all of Europe if we didn't have an army there, so we put one there and kept one there. And missiles. The Soviet army was bigger than ours, but we had many more missiles than they did, and they believed we'd use them if the right circumstances were obtained."

This guy has a weird way of putting things.

"Berlin was the front of the Cold War as the Somme had been during the First World War."

Max began a mental drift. He watched as the wrinkle lines around Brady's eyes and mouth squeeze together and lift up and then down again.

Brady plowed forward. "Here's why Berlin was at the heart of things. In `45, at cessation of hostilities, the Soviet Army controlled about half of Germany, but its capital was in the territory they held. Roosevelt pushed for a partition—a separation into what we all called 'sectors'—of the historic capital of Germany, at least the Germany that was united since the late 1700s. He pushed for this because of its symbolic importance.

So we split Berlin, even though the Soviets controlled the rest of the eastern half of Germany, and the city was most definitely in the

East. For a year before the end of the war... essentially as soon as we knew it would end favorably for the Allies... both parties—the French, British, and the Americans on one side, the Russians on the other—were angling for getting more of Germany at the end of the war than the other side. Thus, the Cold War began in 1944."

Max wasn't bored yet, but things were headed in that direction. Max was familiar with the feeling he had at that moment—it was the same he got a few minutes into his eleventh-grade history class at the start of that school year when he realized it would be more similar to Furgeson's class than he'd hoped.

Max squinched his face, trying to maintain his focus and continue the conversation, despite his tendency against it. He wanted to move on, despite his interest in the Cold War. This was the boring way of learning it. "So we were at war with Russia—in words, anyhow—since 1944. Before the War ended." Max summarized.

"Quite right."

Not wanting to be rude, but growing tired of the near-classroom experience, he was worried. But there might be a way out. *No time like the present to be sure things will be okay this week.*

"Can we get outside, go for a walk?" Max asked. "I learn better on the spot than just talking." Andrew Fredericks looked surprised at his son's boldness, but he also looked relieved.

Out in the neighborhood, they circled a nearby park as they talked, with Andrew Fredericks trailing some distance behind. The conversation turned to the Central Intelligence Agency of the United States and the KGB, Russia's intelligence agency. He learned that the KGB actually stood for "Ministry for State Security," though in Russian.

Same name as the Stasi in Germany. Later, he learned the Stasi in Germany actually had a structure identical to the one in Russia, since it was inspired by and modeled after the Soviet intelligence service.

AFTER THAT, Brady and Max met at 10:30 each morning, always at the same café, mostly because it was easy for Max to find. And Max didn't have to repeat his wish to stay out in the world. They never remained in the cafe for long. Brady had gotten Max's message, and he made good on his word that they'd get around the city rather than sitting still.

Over the course of that week, Brady gave Max a tour of Cold War Berlin—a divided city rife with espionage and deceit, dangerous escapes, secret police, clandestine meetings, and told as well as untold disappearances. They'd visited all of the key sites in the city, taking long walks and using public transit from one end to the other to get a full sense of its tumultuous past.

They'd start in Kaffee Paradies, chat about the day's plan, and examine a map Brady couldn't have gotten at a tourist shop. Old-fashioned as it seemed, Max learned to carry and use a compass along with the map. And while they coordinated targets for the day's walk-and-talk lesson, Brady would drill Max with questions like, "Did the Wall cross at Oberbaumbrücke or at Eisenbrücke?" (the first), and "Did the TV Tower lay in the Western or Eastern sectors?" (Eastern, of course). It was as though Brady were preparing Max for what was to come, though at the time such a suggestion would have seemed preposterous.

SIX

THE NOTE

Twenty minutes before the shift, twenty-five minutes before the Stasi took the girl off the street—and nearly sixty years after Max clung desperately to a cable hanging between East and West, climbing through rain past armed guards—Max left Cafe Paradies for the People's Park looking for Brady. He did so following the handwritten instructions on Brady's cryptic note, wondering just what sort of Friday was in store for him.

Brady hadn't been so much as a moment late in the mornings before this one. The barista noticed Max looking around nervously and passed him a note. He'd slid the scrap across the bar, offering only, "He left this for you" in explanation

Though Max hadn't really seen enough of his tutor's handwriting to make a positive identification of the script, he hadn't yet any reasons to doubt that Brady had written it. He deciphered the scrawl and believed it to read: "Southernmost park bench. Volkspark, West. Where wolf and girl meet. Use caution."

Maybe it's the test he mentioned yesterday, Max had thought as he set out.

He charted an easterly course from Cafe Paradies. Max balanced hurry with particular care. Normally a fifteen minute walk, the stroll from one neighborhood to the next took Max even longer today. Using caution meant something specific to Brady. Max and he had practiced throughout the week they'd spent together, so he knew what the admonition required of him.

Arriving outside the park, Max had become distracted by a car. And then the shift happened. The nausea. The confusion. The old, concrete path with the statues.

The brown van.

SEVEN

WITNESS

The brown van pulled to a halt at a 45-degree angle to the sidewalk opposite the brown-haired girl, putting her in clear view between Max and the passenger-side sliding door. It jostled open. Two burly men in drab jackets and brown slacks moved with nimbleness one wouldn't expect from men of their stature. They hopped out of the van, onto the cobblestone sidewalk, and clambered toward the girl.

She didn't move.

My god.

Max watched the scene unfold as if he were watching a movie come alive, breath by frightened breath.

Rather than bolting in the other direction, the girl turned to face her aggressors. In so doing, she inadvertently faced Max, who stood about twenty feet behind the men. From this position, he could read her expression: eyes wide, tensed facial musculature, eyebrows drawn upward. He read this expression as one of fear but not offering a hint of surprise.

The jolt of shifting from the modern and secure Berlin into the divided and unsettling Berlin of the Cold War had thrown Max into disorientation. To put it mildly, nothing about traveling backward in time was in line with his expectation for how the world was supposed to work. This moment was icing on that proverbial cake. He stood motionless, mouth agape, eyes slightly pinched in effort of deciphering what he was seeing. The dream he had seemed to be living only a moment ago had turned nightmarish.

While she was taken off the street in front of him, all he could do was to watch in horror. The pair of goons grabbed the girl by her arms and pulled her toward the van parked at the curb. She screamed at first and began attempting to pull away. Her efforts weren't effective. The men spoke sharply to her, and she became silent and stopped struggling—this was all out of earshot, and Max couldn't begin to imagine their threats. Whatever it was they threatened, it was enough. The thugs continued pulling her toward the van, gripping inside her elbows, one man on either side. Though she'd stopped actively fighting after their reprimand, she fought passively now, her heels digging into nothing and sliding for several feet on slick stones. The men continued, unabated and uncaring.

They were nearing the open van door now.

A look of calm passed over the girl's features at first. Then, following a grimace of determination, an expressionless placidity settled there. She stopped squirming and gave up even passive resistance. She looked up at their uncovered faces and said something to them—Max once more couldn't hear what. The men permitted her to stand upright. She walked on her own power, though the men nonetheless guided her by the elbows into the open van.

Max felt her fear.

She wouldn't know where she was being taken. Her family would have no idea, either. Inexplicably, the dozen or so people who had been walking the sidewalk alongside the park had been averting their gaze and were now making their way as best they could off the street and away from the unfolding scene.

Those people either wouldn't know or wouldn't say who the captors are or where they're taking her. No one will know anything, and no one will do anything to help.

He paused.

Except me.

I could help. If these people were Stasi… I'd know more about them than anyone here. But maybe I've seen one too many boy-rescues-girl movies. Why get wrapped up in this?

Before the girl ducked inside the suspicious van, she turned slightly to the left and looked directly at Max. Her glance, brief though it was, paralyzed him. He met the pleading terror in her eyes with uncomprehending inaction. The girl disappeared inside the van. A goon followed and slammed home the door with a thud.

The abduction was much more powerful than an imaginary kidnapping as he'd seen them in movies or even in dreams. This had been different in its immersive resonance. This nightmare was real rather than imagined, and it was happening so close at hand that he had nearly felt the kidnappers' grasp on his arms, sensed their shove into the van. It was as though he were the one being grabbed right along with their actual victim.

The vehicle began to move on Landsberger Allee away from where Max stood, open-mouthed and confused.

I'm back in time, and I just saw an abduction. What comes next? Do I do something? Go somewhere? What the hell should I do?

EIGHT

WHAT GOOD PEOPLE DO IN SITUATIONS LIKE THIS

The answer came quickly on the heels of the question: *Help. I can help. Have to. That's what a Good Person would do. So that's what I should do.*

That he should help was all he could hold constant in his mind.

But there's no time.

There definitely wasn't time to think it all through. In his jumbled mental menagerie of thoughts he batted around: *Why did they want her? Why a kid? Is she supposed to tell them about her parents or neighbors? Wouldn't they ask her to come into an interview? Why take her off the street?*

Max knew enough at this point to have answered the "Who?" questions. Max's awareness grew silently from the instant the men had leapt from their vehicle. But he was afraid to bring things to their certain logical conclusion based on all he knew and what he'd seen: They were the Stasi, the East German secret police and officially the "Sword and Shield of the State." He'd seen men like them before, in another time and place. He knew what sort of treatment the girl could expect.

If Max would have taken a few moments to consider what he'd risk by getting involved with the Stasi, he'd have stayed put. He'd have settled and been still, content with marveling at time travel and at the extent to which life in Berlin had changed for the better between when he'd landed and his own era. He could have had a fine time and would have risked nothing.

And he would have had good company as a bystander: no one else went after the probably-not-a-flower-van. The people in the neighborhood had cleared the entire area with astonishing quickness. He'd have hated to think of himself as a bystander, though, in the narrative he was spinning. He wanted to be a hero. He wanted to help. So, instead of doing the prudent thing, Max did the other thing.

He acted.

I can't lose the van.

Max began jogging northwest on the sidewalk. Berlin's frigid, fall weather bit at his nose and ears. His jog stuttered haltingly into a walk, faltering through a step, caught by the suspicion he should give up the chase before drawing even more attention to himself.

I have to do this.

Decision made, he broke into a headlong run, committing to a plan he hadn't yet formulated and following the van's northbound course along Landsberger Allee.

Max had begun to sweat before he began running, and the air chilled his exposed and damp skin. He tried simultaneously to pull his cotton aviator jacket up over his chin and to maintain a fix on the van. And the not-delivery-vehicle in any case moved slowly around the corner of the Volkspark. In contrast to Max's panic, the van's driver seemed in no hurry to flee.

In his mind, Max heard Brady's admonitions to maintain anonymity—to be no one in particular at all times. For a kid on a 5'2" frame and not having the longest legs or the most efficient stride, he had to run. Running made him stand out. Everything he was doing went against his recent training with Brady, but caught as he was between Staying Safe and Doing the Right Thing, he chose the latter. Once Max determined he was the girl's only hope for escape, Staying Safe became impossible.

Anxious to avoid slipping or hurting himself on broken bottles or patches of ice, he oscillated between careful footwork and keeping pace with the van. Every time he looked up, he recalculated his speed and position relative to the van. At one of these glances, he found himself looking into the vehicle via the passenger-side mirror in time to catch a flash of the driver's face and eyes in its vibration-distorted reflection. Max couldn't be sure, but he thought he'd been made. The driver quickly looked away and back toward the road in front of him. Max stopped then and there.

Did he see me? He edged to Volkspark's wrought-iron fence at the edge of the cobblestones and sat down abruptly, trying his best to appear to be nonchalant, looking purposefully at everything but the escaping captors. *Like those people back there. If I've been made, this extraction might be over already.*

Before rising from his perch against the fence, Max waited for the van to turn another corner—to the northeast as if to make a loop around the park. Once he was on his feet again, Max moved with redoubled haste. He paid only enough mind to footwork to dodge the bigger glass shards along with larger patches of ice threatening to slow him down.

There's a saying you might have heard: "Life must be lived forwards but may only be understood backwards." Max is the one forced to live forwards, but what we're doing is closer to looking backward. Because of this, while we know that he survived Berlin (though not how), he didn't know and couldn't have known how much luck he'd need to make it back alive. Living forwards, he knew no better than to do what he did. Thinking in unambiguous axioms of do-goodery, Max acted because he wanted to help, as bold and principled as he was foolhardy and naive.

At this point, we picture Max running along a broken sidewalk, dodging ice and glass, tracking a moving vehicle. We then see Max collide full-force and as though he were completely blind into the solid torso of a larger young man in a long but cheap-looking brown jacket. At this point, we be forgiven for our surprise in learning the man had been counting on their collision.

NINE
WARNING FROM A STRANGER

Amid the chaos of the abduction before Max stumbled into the brown-jacket-wearing man, Max hadn't wondered explicitly whether or not he'd be able to interact with this older world. When he'd gone back in time before, he hadn't interacted with his surroundings. He'd been a passive observer—standing, walking, listening, seeing. That was all. This time, if he was going to make a difference, he would have to get involved. And when he'd taken off after the flower van, Max was reacting. He hadn't taken the time to wonder if he could actually do anything to help. Those men who'd given him nasty looks —they'd seemed to see him, for better or worse. And the guy driving the van.

People can definitely see me this time.

And smashing into the man in the brown jacket jolted Max to full awareness that he could interact with this past world, too.

But even knowing he could do *something* Max had no idea what he'd do. He had no plan. He'd seen enough movies to know rescuing someone in trouble *sans* plan was an unreliable way of rescuing someone. Unreliable if the hero would hope to survive, anyhow. And if his suspicions that the Stasi were responsible were correct, the danger from rash action was grave. Holding East Germany under near total control for almost 30 years, the Stasi were no two-bit outfit. They should not be underestimated.

Had he crafted a careful battle plan, though, its opening salvo would not have read, "Smash directly into solid person blocking path."

The unsurprised man took Max by the back of his shoulders and steered him into the Volkspark. This man didn't radiate the same sense of violence as the men in the van. Even as Max allowed himself to be manhandled through the park gates, he wasn't feeling the terror he'd felt watching those men take the girl. Couple this sense of comparative safety with the effects of multiple shocks to his psyche in the last ten minutes, and the result was that he was pliable. That's why there wasn't much fight in him as the man led him off the main road onto a concrete path inside the park.

Low bushes behind the wrought-iron fence ringing the park partially obscured them from the street. Hidden from those direct lines of sight, the man not-so-gently shoved Max down into a sitting position on a park bench. He stood between Max and a statue of a stoic man with a pointy beard.

The brown-jacket man was no goon, no muscle-bound ruffian like the assailants in the street. He was thin but not skinny, tall enough not to strike someone as "short," but he wasn't stand-out tall, either. He was twenty-something—perhaps 23 or 24—had cold-blue eyes, no hair sticking out from under a grey winter cap, and had no beard or mustache—but he wasn't quite clean-shaven. His face was gaunt and its angles sharp, as though he'd not had quite enough to eat this week, but he didn't appear to be sick. His gaze was serious but unfocused on Max.

He's looking elsewhere even as his eyes are directed at me, Max thought.

The man's light-brown jacket had already become an identifying feature for Max. The fabric was aged and plain but not tattered. He wore it over a beige, collared shirt. Tan slacks with brown shoes completed the image. All in all, the man wore a smart outfit that had seen better days.

If I hadn't bumped into him, I would have never noticed him.

The man carried the initiative, speaking before Max could come up with anything to say: "I couldn't help but notice that you saw what happened to that girl back there, and I saw you moving like you were going to get involved. But you didn't think long enough or carefully enough. You are lucky I stepped into your path back there."

I'm going to lose the girl. I don't have time for this. Max's sole focus remained on the abductee he was determined to rescue. He began to struggle.

The man told him, "Keep your seat," pushing him into the bench and holding him at the shoulders. He rasped, "Sit there, remain calm, and listen to what I have to say if you want to live through the day. And stop drawing attention to us. It might be too late, but it might not."

What? Too late for what? Find the girl? Stop the Stasi? Something else? Is this guy speaking English? Who is he? I'm in the East. No American should be hanging out here. As these thoughts came Max stuttered in his attempts—from the surprise of getting a warning like this, getting it in English, and realizing his attempt to force his way up and away was futile. He gave it up for the moment.

He led with the obvious question: "Why are you speaking English?" Though Max might have expected to hear people speaking English at some point, he didn't expect anyone to address him directly and so soon after his arrival.

"I'm speaking English because I can, and because I know that you speak English." The man spoke with an unmistakable German accent, but apart from this, his English was quick and seemed to come naturally.

Max narrowed his eyes in suspicion. "How could you possibly have known?!"

"Because only an American would be so boldly pig-headed and

ignorant of reality as to set off blindly after the Stasi upon seeing them pick up a suspected traitor in their own territory. Completely stupid. Asinine. If you were a spy, you'd be a pretty terrible one. Now keep your seat long enough to think for a minute. I can help you stay alive so long as you do precisely as I say."

TEN
UNDER SURVEILLANCE

The man in the brown jacket had Max's full attention, and he continued: "You'll end up exactly like her if you don't give up now. Maybe worse, depending on who she is and who you are. An American kid roaming East Berlin alone—that is something I can't wrap my head around. How'd you get here?"

Again the question hit Max like a bell being rung: *Who is this guy?* Instead of asking about the man, he couldn't get off the other subject. "Why would they want her?"

"Who knows? Does it matter?" *It's simple*, the man was saying without saying. *You don't go after someone who's been taken.* The man coughed and spat, partially turning in place in a shuffle as he looked up at the clouds.

He's checking those windows on upper stories. People there can definitely see us even if people on the street can't. Max followed his looks. Five-story buildings encircled the park. *There must be two hundred windows.*

Those buildings and their windows were closing in on the pair of English speakers the longer they sat together, indistinguishable from conspirators plotting against the State.

We need to finish this conversation.

The brown-jacket man didn't say anything about their exposure, but he didn't have to.

Maybe I can get something useful out of him before I get out of here. Max picked up the thread of conversation where the man had left it: "It matters. She's been kidnapped. She wasn't even doing anything." Max started getting up, but the man shoved him down on the wood-slatted bench again.

"Listen! Sit," the man delivered in a harsh whisper. "If you follow her, whatever she's done and whoever she is, you will not win. It's pointless to try. You're no hero. You're an American kid in the Eastern sector. If you follow her, you will lose, and losing means you won't get back home again—ever. They shoot people here on mere suspicion. The Soviets are even worse than the East Germans, if they get hold of you. You should hope that no one marked you already. There's a good reason everyone here worked so hard not to notice that scene a few minutes ago. Understand?"

Max looked at his feet and then again at the man's serious and unforgiving eyes.

"I can get her out," Max said, his doubts growing like a mental fifth-column insurgency.

"Why? What makes you so special that you will get her out of a Stasi cell? That wasn't a kidnapping—it was an arrest. And they don't arrest people for nothing around here." He paused. "Well, I suppose they arrest people who haven't committed any crime, as we'd think of it—"

We, he said.

"They always have their reasons. It's better for us to let such things go."

Max was incredulous: "How do you know what's better? What about from her point o view? She doesn't have a choice to just let it go. The Stasi won't be letting it go."

He tried thinking it through. *Maybe she broke one of their laws, just because a thing is against the law doesn't mean it's wrong—espe-*

cially here. The DDR has laws against thinking about leaving the country. There are prohibitions on collecting books from the West. It's like that book 1984, except that it's real and it's why that girl is in Stasi hands right now. Thoughtcrime. She probably didn't even do anything.

This notion sealed it for him. Whether or not the Stasi had their reasons, as long as there was a chance the young woman was innocent, or that she'd been arrested for merely thinking the wrong thoughts, Max was through arguing. *This is a waste of time.*

He said as much: "The Stasi are in the wrong here. They're the Bad Guys. And I know things," Max picked up the conversation and now directed it. "I know more than any kid my age about how things work around here. I see the cars here, I know the look of the former—er, of East Berlin."

The man examined Max, squinting at this way of putting things.

Max continued, breathlessly: "I know that if they're Stasi, they're probably taking her to the Ministry headquarters or one of their nearby prisons. I know something about where they're taking her, and I know they would probably be happy to have someone like me show up at their door."

"And how do you know all this? The Ministry's properties aren't even on maps—certainly not on any tourist maps, anyhow." The man eyed Max suspiciously. "Who is 'someone like you,' and what's an American kid doing wandering around alone in East Berlin? You still haven't answered that. The Wall went up four years ago—"

It's 1965 now, Max realized.

The man kept speaking. "It's not like anyone can get over here anymore," he said, "let alone a kid and wandering alone through city streets." He was thinking aloud, showing his surprise. "Why, just look at how you're dressed!" He waved to Max's outfit of jeans, a white tee shirt boasting an "SPQR" image, and his dark colored jacket, none of which beside maybe the jacket could have blended in with the DDR crowd.

Think of something. "I'm, uh –" Max thought rapidly—"my

father is an important diplomat." This was a lie he'd come to regret delivering.

"Who, then?"

"I'd rather not say." Max's research taught him diplomats were promised free movement in East Berlin, but he didn't know the names of any diplomats in particular. It wasn't as though he could name-drop consular officers in West Berlin. *Did State Department diplomats bring their kids into East Berlin? Probably not... but whatever. I'm going with this. Pick a lie and stick to it.*

"Okay, Mr. Diplomat's Son. So how are you going to get that girl out of detention? Going to call daddy?"

"I can do it myself." Max glanced about. "I can trade information for her."

"Oh, ho! You can trade *information*, now, can you? Are you a defector? A traitor for a honey pot? I know this game of theirs. And so your father is a diplomat—you have access that you'll convert into leverage. But whose leverage, you have no idea."

"I loyal." Max grimaced. "I won't give them anything worthwhile."

The man snorted. "How do you know what's worthwhile? Every scrap of information you hand over is a puzzle piece. The little bit you give them might complete a bigger picture that puts Americans, American allies, or Western freedom and democracy at risk. You plan to outsmart them?"

Why is he talking about freedom and democracy? What does that stuff have to do with the kidnapping? Max wondered. *Maybe he works for the West. And maybe not.*

"I'm not going to talk about it any more with you."

"Well, not saying who you are and not telling me your plan may well be the smartest things you've not said today, I'll bet. Certainly the smartest thing you've not said to me, anyhow. How do you know the West won't notice you—won't catch you in the act and think you're doing something more harmful and significant than you think you're doing? They won't be very happy about you delivering the East *any* information, you know."

"How could they know?" Max looked at the man directly now. "Are you gonna tell them?"

"I don't have to. They have ways of figuring out this sort of thing." He stopped short, and then he added: "Look. If I had observed you standing there frozen like an idiot watching them take the girl, you can be assured that others saw the same. Both sides, East and West, have spies here. Probably more spies in this city than anywhere else in the world..." The man glanced once more around the Volkspark. It had drained as the street before it, as though the locals didn't want to be seen within a stone's throw of the pair now whispering at a park bench.

"Do you have any idea where you're going?"

"Sure. I already told you I knew they're headed for Lichtenberg—the Ministry HQ or..." He trailed off. *I can't say any more*, he caught himself. He'd almost betrayed his plan of keeping mum, and it had only been seconds since he'd made up his mind not to share anything else with the brown-jacket man. Max didn't let on that he wouldn't, without the man's abrupt interference, have been certain where to go had he lost track of the van. He might have figured things out on his own, but the additional intrigue the man had inserted into an already tense situation had the unintentional effect of confirming what for Max had to that point been mere suspicion.

The man raised his eyebrows. Max read this as a tell—an revealing involuntary reaction. Perhaps he didn't believe until that moment Max knew what he was talking about doing—or where he was supposed to go to find the girl's holding place.

"You're going *there*? The Ministry itself?" The man looked at Max with an open mouth, features drawn back in disbelief.

"Where else should I go?" Max fished for more ideas.

"There are other places. I'm not really suited to give you the advice you probably need right now. You aren't my asset, and I am not your handler. I'm sure I've said too much, given too much by stopping you, and here you're aiming to hand yourself over to certain doom by going to the Ministry. You won't leave that place. You'll disappear."

I need to move. Now. He responded: "There are no rewards without risks, right?" He got up to leave, and this time the man didn't stop him from standing. "I'm going to help that girl."

"Hold on!" The man whispered, grabbing Max by the forearm even more strongly than before. "One last thing," he growled. "Whoever it is that you think you can trust, don't trust them."

Straight out of a spy novel, Max thought. Was it more creepy because it was so surreal or because its foreboding felt appropriate, given where and when Max now found himself?

"Uh, thanks. I don't even know anyone in this place," he responded, "It's not like I'm going around asking random people for favors." He dismissed the brown-coated man's advice but didn't forget it altogether. Without thinking of it, Max filed away the warning to play back to himself later.

"What's your name, anyway?" the man asked.

"I'm, uh..." Max hesitated. He thought of Odysseus and said, "I'm No One. It doesn't matter. You won't be seeing me again, I'm sure. I'm going now."

The man loosened his grasp. "You don't belong here," the man said, "and you need to leave now." With that, the conversation was over.

What does he mean saying that I "don't belong here"? Here in this park? This time? He shook his head like a dog shakes off bathwater. "Thanks," Max mumbled, not sure if he was saying the right thing. Now free of the brown-coated man's hold, he made off through the park in the general direction the Stasi van might be headed—eastward.

I could turn a corner, or just blink, and be back in my own time. Her time might be limited, but so is mine, and I don't know how long I have. If I don't act right now, there's no rescue. He picked up the pace.

We'll see how well I remember what Brady taught me about East Berlin. I'll have to get my bearings based on that map, whatever good a map from 2021 will do me. Whatever. Do I still even have it in my pocket? Without it, I'm done for—again, no rescue.

ELEVEN

ALONE

About twenty paces from where he left the brown-jacket man, Max turned. Discreet as possible, he checked his 6 o'clock, directly behind him. No one there. Whoever he was, the man had disappeared from the scene as abruptly as he'd appeared in it.

Where did that guy come from, anyhow?

Max walked on alone.

I should have gone to the sidewalk on the street. But then, they'd see me there, too. I should keep my arms at my side. That's weird. This is unnatural, and I'm walking too stiffly now. I am going to have to get used to sticking out, or I've got to find a better way of blending in. He looked down at his standard American blue jeans, plain white tee, and dark jacket. *I need some different clothes, maybe...* He continued eastward. *But how...? I have no time.* He couldn't shake the feeling he was drawing more attention to himself with every step and every gesture.

Again, the man in the brown jacket crept back into his thoughts.

Who was that guy? Why did he seem to know so much about what was going on? He could be a spy. But for what side?

The Volkspark of 1965 was the same park he'd entered in 21st-century Berlin, but it felt so different. The shape and size of the thing —they seemed to be the same. But the whole area's infrastructure— pathways, benches, stone walls, and the rest—was crumbling or had already disintegrated. The areas that had boasted lush green grasses in his own time were, in 1965, not much more than a fine dust littered with larger and smaller bits of concrete and stone.

Many of the trees and bushes from the landscaping work that must at one time have been carefully plotted had burned away or were uprooted, while those that remained were plopped down without apparent planning along walkways and the edges of the park. Concrete paths were mostly intact, while flower beds and other decorative touches were nonexistent, save for the lone, concrete statue near the bench on which Max and the man had sat in conference.

Why did he warn me like that? Why would he advise me not to trust anyone while wanting me to listen to him? He was nagged by the man's behavior back at the bench. *Why was he looking around like he was? He had to be some sort of spy. He spoke perfect English but had an accent. Who was he?*

Max could see through the fence in some places as he strode toward an east exit. People had parked a few cars here and there along the stone-block sidewalks outside the park. These cars boasted shades of mustard yellows and drab greens, with some grays thrown in for good measure. A Trabant like the one that had signaled to Max he wasn't in 2021 anymore stood out among them. Compared to his own era, the streets in '65 Berlin were pretty much empty. Not that this was an exceptionally busy quarter, but it was noticeable that there were a lot fewer cars clogging things up. Fewer parked along the sidewalks, motoring down roadways, and waiting at intersections. Fewer bikes, too. And, whatever their age in 1965, all the clunky automobiles and scattered bicycles seemed old, dented, and plain worn out.

The buildings across the brick streets between the park and the rest of the neighborhood appeared to be caught as if by snapshot in a perpetual, slow-motion collapse. Some of the bomb-impacted roofs remained concave, as-yet unrenovated structural casualties of air bombing campaigns seeming to have concluded only yesterday. Broken or boarded-up windows contributed to the plaza's ill omens. Other buildings had been weakly rehabilitated and looked moderately functional—some had lights on in the dreary afternoon's shadowless flat light. New concrete buildings stood in places where demolished others had been removed.

Which windows are of apartments used by the Stasi? At least one or two, right?

And back to the brown-jacket man: *What was he doing in East Berlin, wandering the city parks and streets by himself? There was something totally off about that guy. He was here for a reason. What was it?*

An ancient-looking dump truck of dismal pallor completed the bleak scene. It sat parked (or was it broken down?) near one of the southern entrances to the Volkspark. Near enough to be using it, two men in grey overalls were shoveling from one of the many piles of debris to an oversized, steel wheelbarrow. They were clearing some of the wreckage, overburdened with the unending task of cleaning up the Volkspark.

As it were, not a lot of resources had been dedicated to the cleanup effort, which stood out considering twenty years had passed since the end of the War.

The West already dug out and has cleaned up by now. The Germans in the East are being punished. The Soviets are going to leave it like this.

Before he reached a street exit, Max stopped.

What had put the strange man in that spot at that instant? He put himself there. He was watching. He said he was stopping me for my own good, so he saw me and decided to interrupt me chasing that van. Why? What good did it do him to stop me? Why didn't I ask any of this or at least think of it before?

He shook his head rid it of distractions. *I can't lose focus. The van is already gone.* Max began walking, at a faster clip this time, toward Lichtenberg and the Stasi.

If all he wanted was to find Stasi, though, they were right there with him. Observation posts in apartments surrounding the park meant low-fidelity video cameras rolled and cameras snapped stills from several windows. And another van, this with a state electric company logo on its side, idled at the eastern edge of the park. There, the occupants waited for Max.

TWELVE
A CHASE

Max recognized the threat as a man back of the van swung open its doors. The agent's feet appeared, and a second man in a black jacket stepped out of the passenger-side front door. They moved in concert, closing the gap.

Max's eyes widened, but everything else disappeared in the tunnel vision of panic.

He turned and checked behind him toward the other side of the park for another option.

One, two, three, four, five. He counted five more plainclothes agents closing in on and between the pathways. *Could be more at the other exits. Can't get penned in. How did I miss that?* He spun round again toward the van. *Those guys are standing there waiting for me to get flushed out.* They'd crossed their arms and made no direct move toward Max, who stood maybe ten steps from the park exit looking around in frantic hope of finding something—some other way of escaping. The closest of the two men at the van were maybe six steps on the other side of the gate. Behind him, the others were closer. If they made a quick move, they would be within grabbing distance soon.

I can't go backward. He was out of options.

Then, an object Max had subconsciously written off as part of the scenery came into focus. A rusty bicycle laid against the park fence.

A few steps. Can I get there before they grab me? Will it even work if I hop on it and try to take off? It'll be a crappy escape vehicle if it falls apart when I leap on...

He began moving with obvious caution toward the men in the van, raising his hands, speaking in German, "Yes, yes. Slowly. Slowly. I'm coming." A few more steps. "Okay," he said in English. "You got me."

The man from the front seat relaxed his shoulders almost imperceptibly.

That was Max's signal. He bolted forward. The man from around the rear moved toward the side of the van facing the park and outstretched his arms, readying himself to tackle the sprinting kid. Max used something he'd learned in soccer to feign moving to the left as he got to the exit.

The men at the van bit, leaning that direction.

As soon as he stepped foot outside the park, he parried to the right and grabbed the bike. He began running with it, hopping and straddling the seat as he'd done on his own bicycle at home. He pedaled harder than ever before, though, not daring to look back.

He heard a loud exclamation, "Scheisse!" behind him, and a team leader issued orders to the others.

Go, go, go! Max cheered himself on. *Go! Don't look. Just go.*

Van doors slammed home a hundred feet behind him as he rounded a corner, careened around a traffic control arm, zipped through a crowded hospital parking lot, and turned to the west—toward the Wall and the spot where he'd seen the girl kidnapped. He heard the van squeal into action a block behind him.

They can't cut through that lot. Bought myself a few seconds at least.

He came up with a plan as he pumped his legs, forcing the old chain to move much faster than it was accustomed as it spun around an ancient, single gear. Nearly impossible to control, the bike was oddly shaped, and his weight distribution was off-center. Something about the handlebar position on the bike wasn't quite right, and the whole contraption groaned under him.

Hold together!

Where do I turn? Can't go back to the park, and I've got to get a few streets away before I turn—or they'll see me right away.

He couldn't hear the van behind him yet, but he was worried that he would at any instant. If the van spotted him, he wouldn't be able to get away.

Max was soaked with sweat, despite the cold. *There's no time. One street down will have to be enough!*

He banked hard to the left to make a 90-degree turn away from the park, hoping the men behind him had lost sight of him before he made his move. There was no way to be sure. The bike fought him with every push.

Shouts echoed from the direction of the street adjacent the park.

An alley! He bucked the bike like a cowboy at a show back home would hold onto an angry bull, guiding the hunk of metal into an alley and putting one more turn between him and the Stasi. As he made that turn, standing up to control the bike, the handlebars bent under his weight. Max high-sided over the top and went down hard.

He rolled into a small tree growing, impossibly, out of a crack in the concrete. He scraped against stone. Struggling to hide, he righted himself, yanked the bike to a spot opposite the tree, and ducked out of sight of the main road. Max crouched behind some vines growing overtop of a dumpster.

Max peeked around the edge, nervous even to show even his forehead. *Stay low to the ground. Wait to be sure.* He waited.

God, the smell is worse down here.

The white van sped past his alley, and he held onto the ground like he would a life raft in rough seas. They'd found the street he turned on but had somehow missed the spectacle of Max's shuttering arboreal stop and disgusting hiding place.

THIRTEEN

HOW TO DISAPPEAR COMPLETELY

As he hid and did his level best to ignore the smell of the dumpster, Max thought back, mentally filing some details from the last half hour of his life.

That guy was right there when I started out to follow that van. He got in my way on purpose. The girl was kidnapped just as I was wandering around that park. Was that an accident? Was I just lucky—or unlucky? Or is there more to that? Not only this, but the timing of meeting the man was suspicious, occurring as closely as it did to the kidnapping.

He pictured everything about the strange man he could remember. He wanted to be able to describe him later, if need be. *Did he have anything to do with those other men? He was in a hurry to get out of there, and he kept looking around for agents watching us... so he's not with them. He has enemies here in the East. But which enemies? Which side was he on?*

Then there was the matter of the man speaking fluent English. Among Germany's multiple-language speakers, some people definitely spoke English. Max knew a bit about this. Maybe the brown-jacket man worked for the East German or the West German governments.

Or he could be working for the Russians. Or the Brits. Or the Americans. Agents in any one of these groups might have spoken English. Another plausible explanation was that the man had worked for or with the Allies during the Second World War, had learned to speak English and to use its common expressions then... *I just don't know enough to figure out who he's working for. It could be any of this - or something else entirely.*

Max calmed his breathing, pausing the maelstrom of thoughts about the man in the jacket and cleared the brain muddle.

Bang!

The sound counteracted his stress-management efforts, and he flinched hard, pressing with all he had against the concrete and dirt, listening for more concussions.

Nothing.

A car engine. A backfire. He'd seen that sort of thing in movies, but cars didn't really backfire anymore, so he'd never heard it before in real life.

He peered around the alley dumpster toward the side street he'd turned on getting to the alley where he now hid. It looked clear of danger.

The longer I'm here, the more likely it is they'll find me. And if they do, I'll lose any chance I've got even to attempt a rescue mission. But where do I go from here? I know it's east... the Ministry—but which way is that? What roads should I take?

The map.

As he lay there, Max rifled through his pockets.

Yes! He found it, folded and tucked into his rear-left pocket.

I will have to memorize the route and ditch this thing. It wouldn't do him any favors to be caught with it, and it wouldn't be good being seen squinting at it as he stopped at street corners to stare in confusion at signs, comparing them to the paper in front of him.

Probably not a lot of Western looking tourists in East Berlin. No tourists without supervision at all, maybe—even from the Eastern Bloc. And he couldn't just ask, "Entschuldigen Sie, which way to the Ministry for State Security Service headquarters, bitte?"

Even the appearance of being an outsider—*Really, what am I going to do about these jeans?*—would result in being reported. Citizens looking for government favors would turn him over to the Stasi.

He heard Brady's words in his mind from his tutoring—*training, it feels like*—sessions, warning him to "Always look like you know where you're going." *Maybe they'll see me dressed like this and assume if I'm confident enough that I'm doing undercover work for the Stasi. Then they'll be too scared to ask me what I'm doing. All I'd have to worry about is the Stasi themselves.*

Talking himself into false confidence was the best he could do, given the circumstances.

I'll have to do something about this wallet, too. When they search me, they'll assume I have fake credentials, and I'll look like a spy. They might even decide I'm something worse when they find post-dated, security-strip-encased, American money along with my high school ID card saying my annual birthday celebrations don't even begin for another forty-one years. I'll be a goner, for sure.

Because he had no international service and his phone was close to useless in Berlin, he'd left his phone back at the hostel when he'd left, same as every morning. So: No phone to ditch. That one would have been pretty tough to explain if he were caught here with it or if he lost it in 1965 before returning—hopefully—to 2021.

He pulled his compass from his front pocket and examined the map: *Okay, so I must be on... what is that, Pufendorf? Is that some sort of Harry Potter thing? Left on Friedenstrasse, left again on Weidenstrasse...* he traced the route. *There—the empty spot on the map east of the Frankfurter Allee U-Bahn and S-Bahn stop. That's the Ministry.* He closed his eyes and repeated the turns and street names to himself, step-by-step, six times, checking his memory the first few times through. His route from Friedrichshain to Lichtenberg would avoid the main streets by keeping to the roads paralleling the west-to-east Karl Marx Allee. Along the way, he'd best keep to the shadows and blend in with those heading home from work to eat their lunch.

The map and wallet. What should I do...?

He pulled the ID card from the wallet and dropped it in a conveniently located crack in the wall of the nearest building. He tossed the wallet into the dumpster. *I can't drop it all in the same spot.* He held onto the map to find a better spot for it somewhere else.

While he considered where to drop the map, he patted himself down to check for other pocket litter that might give him away. *The compass will need to go, too. Maybe I'll just hold onto it 'til I get to the Ministry. If I forget any of the specific roads, I can just head east and keep an eye on the main road it's near.*

He pulled the 2€ coins from his jeans pocket and wedged these into a different crack from the ID card before leaving the alley. One more pat-down to be sure, and he felt ready. Sort of.

Setting out on foot, Max implemented best he could some of the techniques for not-being-seen he'd picked up from various spy books and podcasts as well as what he'd learned through the past week's lessons with Brady.

Again: Confidence, the experts all seemed to agree, was a major part of the trick. Key rules for appearing to be assured included demonstrating that you belong and making it obvious you're not concerned about anything. *Should I really show that I'm perfectly confident if no one living here could ever be sure about anything? Everyone always has to watch what they say, do, and even think.* A ratio of one part confidence and two parts nervousness seemed about right.

As Max walked, he reviewed in his mind the street names to look out for. They'd be different in 1965 from his own time, but he was ready for that. He knew the directions of the streets, too. And then there was the compass as a failsafe.

Along his way to Stasi headquarters, Max found an open-air streetside urinal and held his breath as he ducked behind its half-wall. Max reached toward the back of the catch-all container in the oval-shaped private space in a public place, scrunching his whole face as he wedged the tourist map between the metal of the bin and the tin wall of the public toilet. Somehow, he managed not to touch anything but the map itself. The surfaces in the outdoor bathroom were... not clean.

Gross but effective.

Then he relieved himself. *It's gotta seem real, right? Anyone watching or listening might be less suspicious if it seems obvious I actually used this thing.* He had to go anyway. Public toilets like this were a thing in Europe, even in 2021, he'd learned, but never could he imagine such a thing existing in the United States, where people were too prudish to pee in public.

I get it, though. He surveyed street activity from his not-so-private privy. *No thank you.* Max was a bit prudish, too.

He left the toilet and kept to his route. As he walked, he couldn't help but to gape in saddened awe. Many war-damaged buildings dotted the avenue, interspersed with recently built Soviet-style apartment blocks. In other spots, gaping holes dotted the architectural landscape. Here and there, people in workman's clothing used buckets and wheelbarrows to remove debris falling from those not yet cleared from the area.

The stillness of desolation pervaded the entirety of East Berlin, and those Soviet tenements completed the post-War scene. These were drab, functional, and rectangular apartments slotted like building blocks into gray or brown rectangular buildings, each standing five stories tall—each identical to the last and next. Where they were most densely packed, the structures turned what might have been a lovely backstreet into a claustrophobic, concrete gauntlet. Brady had said that these buildings had been assembled elsewhere and placed into position on-site to ease and speed along the construction process.

Max left his drop spot in a hurry. In his urge to get clear of the damning evidence, he didn't pause to check for tails before crossing Bersarinstrasse with a lunchtime crowd. He also didn't notice a woman in a tattered dress and shawl approach and then investigate the urinal he'd just left behind.

He became more nervous as he walked.

He stopped repeatedly along the forty-five-minute walk to tie his shoe or to find another reason to pause, checking each time to see whether he was being followed. Each time, he found he could only be sure that he wasn't sure about anything. The immense danger—the miasma he breathed—caused time in the open streets and sidewalks to drag on, but it also seemed to race past, offering what felt like insufficient time to work out his plan for breaking the girl out of Stasi detention.

He'd stopped at a streetlight with a crowd of people at Petersburger Strasse and awaited the signal, though there were no cars nearby. Trying his best not to fidget as the working crowd pressed in around him, he stared straight ahead. Some gave him looks, for sure, and he couldn't shake a sick feeling.

They're all looking at me. If I do the math, some of these people are unofficial informants. He concentrated on The Plan and attempted to dismiss growing claustrophobic terror.

The light had clicked audibly as it switched to a "walk" signal—a small green man with arms in an "I'm walking" position, frozen in place and time in a traffic light. *Hey. It's Ampelmann.* Just like the keychain guy he'd gotten at a shop near Potsdamer Platz. He walked with and then worked to get ahead of the crowd using all the grace he could muster.

The streets had grown busier in the afternoon bustle. *They'll probably have a much easier time following me than I'll have spotting them. Maybe the crowd will hide me. Or will I stand out while someone tailing me blends in with everyone else?* There were no obvious solutions. *Followed or not, I have to keep moving. No time to waste.*

After walking a while without spotting anything suspicious, Max had to wonder at his skill, luck, or whatever it was that explained his easy passage. *Am I getting lucky? Doing everything right? Are they letting me go where I want, just observing to see what I do?* He made it all the way to Lichtenburg and the Ministry for State Security without interference.

FOURTEEN

MAX'S TOTALLY BRILLIANT AND HEROIC PLAN

Max now stood across the street from the same concrete-walled, rectangular-perimeter building complex he'd toured on a Wednesday in his time. So many windows.

...these Ministry buildings have eyes.

He wanted to run the other direction, but he needed to stay to follow his plan, so he stayed. But he didn't approach the building, either.

The truth was that most folks stayed away from this whole block, and absolutely no one stopped outside the MfS headquarters and stood there staring. *Hopefully, they'll take one look at me, figure there's no way I could have found my way here unless I knew where this place is and figure me for a defector with information to share.*

Three uniformed guards who had been standing with purpose a moment ago turned toward him and marched around the red-and-white striped gate at the entry checkpoint. The pole had been removed by the time he and Brady would see this spot a few days and fifty-something years into the future, but the rest of the building will look the same. The men neared, heels clicking.

Here goes nothing.

A short time earlier, he'd worked as much of it out as he could. As he'd walked from his hiding spot near the Volkspark toward the MfS central buildings, Max had remembered a legendary Spartan refrain Arthur quoted in one of his best stories: "Come back carrying your shield or upon it." Max had already come to terms with the possibility that he might be facing as deadly a fate as did the men who'd trooped, double-time, to face the menacing Persian army at Thermopylae. Hopefully, he'd have a more successful outcome than the Spartans—they had been slaughtered to a man, their country soon to be overrun. For them, bravery had made no difference in their end other than to hasten it. They died for their cause, though, and there's something to be said for their sense of duty and bravery.

He pinned his hope on the notion that the Stasi might be over-confident in their power over him and so might screw something up. The Plan wouldn't work without that mistake. And the Stasi were nothing if not meticulous. Max found small comfort in this hope, as hope was all he had.

The 4km or so walk from the People's Park gave Max time to work out The Plan, including his backstory. As he figured things out, he wondered repeatedly at a question with no obvious answer. *Who am I?* He didn't yet have a name for himself.

The rest, though, was settled.

New field agents are apt to make mistakes, and one of the catastrophic errors they might make is in generating a backstory that's too complicated. An unnecessarily complex story is tough to remember. Beyond this, true stories aren't confusing, unless the storyteller is a confused person—and also not trustworthy. If he weren't trusted, The Plan would fail.

So Max developed a simple backstory. If he appeared to be confused, they'd know he was lying, or they'd judge him untrustworthy. At the same time, the story had to have some details that'd be attractive to them—something to grab their attention. He needed the handler interrogating him to worry about getting fired if he were to ignore the opportunity Max would offer.

The podcasts and field handbooks he loved so much had touched on the point about simplicity repeatedly, but there was more to it than this: *An agent in the field always has a simple backstory—but fitted to the purpose.* So, what were his purposes? If he weren't clear on these, The Plan would fail.

He needed to get the Stasi to release the girl, and he needed them to trust him long enough to for him and the girl to make good their escape. He needed them to think the girl is key to something that benefits them in the West. But what? If he didn't figure this out, The Plan would fail.

So it came to this. He'd offer to spy for them. *I'll offer them what I supposedly know, in little bits and pieces. I'll draw on what I know is true.*

And the best thing I can do for them is to fit in west of the Wall, so I'll offer to meet one of their agents in the West. The authorities over there wouldn't have any reason to suspect me—that's both true and useful. I'm a total nobody anywhere west of East Berlin. Maybe I need the girl with me for some reason. Or I'll need her for future missions. Maybe we're supposed to be boyfriend and girlfriend in our spy lives.

Cringe. He shook his head with vigor as if to rid himself of stupid daydreams.

This is serious, Max: they could kill her. They could kill us both.

But who am I, and what can I offer them? Why do I need her to go with me? Max thought back to his conversation with the brown-jacket man, realizing that what he'd told the man wouldn't work. *Diplomat's son is too easy to check out and prove false. They have people with lists of diplomats. Heck, I'll bet the West reports who their diplomats are to assure they get the right access when they want to cross the border.* The diplomat's son fable wasn't right. As he passed under hanging street lamps, walking east, he worked hard at stepping with one foot in front of the other, trying to pass for normal.

So, who am I?! Max was getting frustrated.

Then it hit him.

Instead of being a diplomat's son, Max would claim to be the son of an American military attaché—a military advisor to the American ambassador serving in the West-German capital, Bonn. Max was accompanying his father on a short trip to Berlin, where his father had military business and related social events to attend. That story would take more time to prove false than the other story, and perhaps the East Germans and Soviets didn't have an up-to-date list of all advising attachés in the West. *And probably no record of attachés' kids. And it's 1965. No internet. No quick search.*

In addition to the story being difficult to disprove, being a son of an attaché might also put Max in a position to know something about American attitudes towards the Berlin controversies. He might know his imaginary father's private thoughts, and as his father was the military attaché in Bonn, his opinions had importance for the politics of Berlin. *They'd value that, he thought.*

As for the "puzzle pieces" comment the Brown Jacket Man had made, Max had some ideas. *I can use this way of thinking to my advantage. They're looking for scraps they can assemble. So maybe I feed them some bogus scraps.* Maybe the Stasi would be interested in some true pieces of intel that any curious person would know in his own time but the East Germans had no way of knowing during the Cold War itself.

Whatever he knew, he would know only incidentally, of course. The Americans attempted to take security seriously, despite the Stasi's continual successes at placing agents (or recruiting them) in high places in the United States' government, so his father wouldn't likely be broadcasting intimate details of troop placements or anything of the sort to Max or to anyone else. So the Stasi probably wouldn't expect him to know specifics about the American military, and he reasoned that this expectation perhaps rendered it less likely they would terrorize him in hopes of him revealing details they had no reasonable expectation of him knowing.

That wouldn't stop them from asking, of course. Maybe asking twice. And maybe not asking so nicely as the first two times when they asked a third time. The East Germans would know the score and so wouldn't press him too hard. Then again, who knew what they'd do when they had him under lights in an interrogation room?

He closed his eyes and shook his head. *Get back on track. Let's go. Only a few minutes' walk left.*

Whether or not he was questioned about military intelligence—troops, missiles, whatever—he promised himself he wouldn't invent details they knew he wouldn't or couldn't know. He could cause a catastrophe if he said the wrong thing—suggesting that the Americans were taking immediate precautions and making preparations for nuclear war, for instance. And he'd be toast if he invented specifics about troops or big guns—the Stasi knew about that stuff from their higher-ups both in East Germany and in the KGB, the Russian spy service.

They'll spot those lies a mile off. Rule number one: No giving the Stasi good reasons to throw me out or send me to one of their Russian friends' gulags.

But why would an American military attaché's kid appear at their gates offering to spy for them? Or be in the East at all? This part of The Plan was the trickiest bit.

Maybe I'm mad at my dad and looking to get back at him? That would maybe get him to the East, if he was extremely angry and knew where father would forbid him to enter.

But the part about helping the Stasi? No, that kid stuff was too menial to induce treason. *I've got to be turned against the whole system in the West.* From everything he'd learned in his reading and from Brady, the communist East was obsessed with a war against the West's system of capitalism—of free trade, of rich and poor, of class divisions—of materialism—buying, selling, and owning stuff—Max could take up that mantle.

That'll work. I've had a change of heart about the way of life that surrounded him in the opulent West. I never had a choice about being born in the U.S., and coming here is part of growing up and following what I know is right.

Max knew there had been many defectors to the East. And for

those who weren't motivated by ideas alone, the East Germans did not pay exceptionally well, but they did pay for information on occasion. The USSR's KGB had been known to pay a great deal of money for intelligence if the source was highly-enough placed to warrant the expense and ideological motivation wasn't enough to move the asset in question.

Max wasn't going to ask for money, though. *I'm a true believer.* And if that wasn't enough, he was going to demonstrate his terrible need for their help. *Make myself look like I'd do anything. They'll want to use me as an asset.*

He worked once more through the American attitudes about Berlin. What were they, again? Better get it straight before showing up at the Stasi's front door. He had always been a good thinker, but back in Leipzig, he'd seen a Stasi interrogation. Thinking back on that drove home the absolute necessity of being crystal clear on everything within his control.

The Americans are secretly glad the Wall has gone up. It reduces tensions at the border. Tens of thousands in single days had defected to the West through East Berlin, which increased tensions—that was curtailed now. The President and military leaders had been happy enough to leave the Eastern sectors of Berlin to the Soviets entirely. They still worried about blockades stopping the flow of necessities into West Berlin. The whole city sits inside East Germany, after all, with only a few ways in and out to the West.

It was easy to bring life in Berlin to a halt once before by closing the ways into the West. Even though Eisenhower had found a way around it, airlifting millions of pounds of food and supplies was not a permanent solution. This was especially now that the Wall was up, surrounding the entire western half of the city.

The Americans are most concerned with keeping things calm and stable. No more blockades. And no more tank standoffs at Checkpoint Charlie. Because of the politics of keeping things chill, I guess, we don't love it when people try to cross the border without permission or scale the Wall. At the same time, we're glad when we can publicize that people don't want to be in the communist East.

And the tunnels! The West builds tunnels, unofficially, to help people escape more quietly. We look the other way when tunnel plots unfold.

The Stasi know a lot of this already, so if I talk around these issues, I won't be giving away anything precious. I've been around my parents' dinner table and hear about the escapes that have been in the news. The Stasi will believe that much. And I can only give them a little bit at a time, promising more to come if they help me by letting the girl go with me. But why should they let her go? That remained the sticking point.

That he would refuse the money, Max was convinced, made his story more believable. And the fact that it would cost them relatively little if he failed or turned out to be lying might make them more likely to release her to his supervision.

This plan will work. Maybe. He would ask them for help in releasing their captive only to serve their own purposes—a "help me help you" situation. If they didn't buy it, The Plan would fail.

The guards were approaching him from their side of Ruschestrasse.

And who am I? What's my name?

As he'd worked out the other details, he toyed with several options, nearly settling on several borrowed pop stars' probably-also-invented names.

As he'd scrambled to decide what to call himself, the approaching guards' shoes made a noise altogether different from the scraping of the cheap-leather trappings worn by the commoners at the People's Park. From these men's shoes issued the sounds of soft but determined footfalls—a clap-clop of black, leather, standard-issue soldiers' shoes. These three men's shoes were not disintegrating under their feet.

In the critical instant when he found himself standing on the Stasi's very doorstep with guards approaching, he had a moment of clarity. He realized the unnecessary risk he'd be taking by inventing a codename he'd need to remember along with his just-invented story.

It hit him at the last possible second. *I'm me.*

That was it.

I'll be me. It's easy to remember, and I haven't been born yet. They don't know if my father, Andrew Fredericks, is or isn't a military attaché. No record of me or my dad exists. Max Fredericks it was, and so Max Fredericks was the name he spoke as the trio approached.

As the Stasi officers addressed him directly, he reminded himself to remain flexible, recalling a German military leader's warning, "No plan survives contact with the enemy."

FIFTEEN

THE MINISTRY FOR STATE SECURITY

Wanting to seem forthcoming and helpful, Max spoke first. Speaking first would also let the guards know straight away that he was an English-speaking Westerner.

Maybe they'll call someone out who speaks English. If the Stasi got first crack at questioning him, the situation might get away from him.

As the men approached, he held out his hand as though introducing himself to a school principal: "Hi. I'm Max Fredericks. I'm here to see the Minister, Herr Mielke." He didn't smile.

Two of the three grey-uniformed guards looked at one another, flummoxed. The third seemed to be ready for this exact situation and turned immediately on his heels.

Ummm... that is unexpected.

The man hastened to a call-box behind him, removing his flat-topped hat as he entered the booth. That man had some sort of gold-bordered red stripes on his shoulder and collar, and his subordinates had no such insignia. The others' surprised looks didn't last long, as they adjusted their manner to match that of the third. They stood, jaws set and faces without expression, staring hard at Max.

Guard One, Guard Two, and *Guard Three,* Max named them.

The cement-jawed men both did the same thing, though. As Guard Three telephoned for instruction, each of the other two raised his pistol and commanded "Halte!" as though Max weren't sufficiently halted where he stood motionless. Cautious, Max opened his palms and raised his hands, compliant.

Time slowed to a crawl, and he was sweating. A coppery taste took over his palate. He tried to do what his mother talked about: he breathed in calmness, breathed out nervous energy.

In.

Out.

He thought about his facial muscles relaxing, softened his shoulders.

In.

Out.

It wasn't working. His chest tightened the way it did before he had to give a presentation in class. He focused harder on his breathing, listening for the sounds around him—a few dry leaves drifting across the empty street, a distant streetcar—anything to bring him away from his anxiety.

The man who'd gone to the booth held the telephone receiver to his ear, eyes firmly fixed on the American. He nodded almost imperceptibly every few seconds. Meanwhile, Guard Two circled Max and patted him down for weapons. As he did this, Guard One kept his weapon trained on Max's chest.

Max's mouth was dry, and he swallowed. *This isn't part of the plan, but I guess I should have expected it.*

So they didn't welcome me with a hug and a handshake—be flexible. He waited.

At least I've got The Plan and I got rid of all the incriminating stuff. Probably just as dangerous to have a tourist map and student ID from a much more modern America as a pistol or knife at this point. They'd probably shoot me right now—or interrogate me for the next five years—one or the other.

The man searching Max seemed satisfied and moved to face him, loosening handcuffs from his belt as he altered his stance. He paused and gave a look that Max read as, "What the hell are you wearing?" and then bound Max's hands with cuffs. Max dropped his head and shoulder posture, hopefully as a clear message of accepting his fate. *You are in charge*, he thought at the guards.

Guard One, still maintaining his unflinching aim at Max's center mast, shifted position, edging sideways, to maintain a clear shot past his partner.

Max was under arrest.

He repeated the breathing exercise, inhaling calmness and exhaling nervous energy. *More focus on the breath. I can handle this.* This time, he began to feel his chest loosen. *Okay. What next? This still works.* He raised his head again, keeping his eyes forward and awaiting instruction.

Another thing he noticed had changed about the front of this building since his own time: prison-like bars surrounded the underpass entryway, blocking much of the access to the inner, central courtyard for the Ministry for State Security. Things were locked down.

Once they take me in there, I'll have to talk my way out, 'cause that's the only way I'm going anywhere.

Guard Three hung up the phone, saw that the other two had the situation well in hand, and called to them in German that Max understood: "Move him over here," indicating the underpass beside the call box.

The pair nodded curtly, not for an instant taking their eyes off of their captive westerner.

The two men directed Max roughly into the same passageway Max and Brady had crossed in their own time, stopping him again about halfway to the courtyard.

He easily distinguished the clatter of a nearby door out of his field of vision opening and swinging closed. All three gatekeepers remained behind him as he waited, terrified of making the wrong move, facing forward. He stood still as possible and listened carefully to everything.

The three original guards remarked to one another in inaudible tones. A fourth pair of footsteps appeared in his aural landscape, increasing in volume as the wearer gained ground. The crisp echoing off stone in the alcove made more distinct what would have otherwise been a confusing muddle of sound. The fourth man's boots were different—the man had a different uniform than the others had.

The newcomer's new voice inquired in stiff and staccato German, pausing for equally terse replies. The whole group broke out in sudden laughter.

Guards One and Two deferred to Guard Three as he offered what must have been a coded explanation to the unseen superior officer.

All Max could make out were the words "Amerikaner" and "Westler." What else the men might be saying moved too quickly for Max to track, so he had to imagine: "Some idiot Westerner just showed up at the Ministry's gates... He's speaking in flawless English. American! He wants to speak with Mielke." Then the laugh and— Max understood this part: "Ja, Ja. Alles klar"—"Yeah, yeah. All clear."

Footsteps departed. The door opened and closed again.

Then, nothing.

Am I about to be shot? They wouldn't do that here in sight of the street... not that they couldn't come up with a story to explain their 'defensive measures' against an enemy spy. But they don't know who I am. They'll want to at least listen to my story. They have to... another moment passed. He heard crunching footfalls behind him, oscillating, but none that came closer. The men were pacing—waiting for something.

About three hundred paces ahead, a long, tarnished-white car pulled out of the concrete-block alcove concealing the entryway to the main building in the echoey courtyard at the heart of the Ministry for State Security. Its diesel engine issued sounds that filled the court-yard. As would surely happen in a movie, a group of birds lit out from a standalone tree in a corner of the open space and beat a path of escape.

Max recognized the car from photos he'd seen. *A Volga. Cool.* The old—new, actually, at this point—Soviet standard turned down the lane and motored toward him through afternoon shadows. It stopped short. The driver kept the car running but parked it in the middle of the courtyard road.

More waiting.

Max could make out a man sitting in the front-passenger seat, shuffling through some papers before exiting the car. The man who climbed out was shorter than Max's father, whom he knew to be about six feet tall, and he labored somewhat in the cold, taking a moment to reposition his gray—*Does everyone at MfS wear gray all the time?*—overcoat, look up at the buildings above Max's holding place, and nod at a someone or a group of someones watching from a place Max couldn't see.

Maybe it's the other guy who was just here.

The man coughed into a handkerchief and folded it. He was clean-shaven and well-put-together. He deposited the used hanky in his jacket.

Gross. Max wondered if he was surreptitiously taking a photo with one of those hidden-camera devices spies used in this era. The man had no need for subterfuge, though. *They've got all the power. They can take my picture right out in the open.*

The clean-cut Stasi man wore black-rimmed glasses and a cap like those Max had seen in old images of American businessmen dating back to the fifties. Shadowed creases in his face joined puffy cheeks to soft nose. He looked Max up and down, pausing to study Max's eyes.

Max did his best to return the stare with confidence. *If I look like prey, I'll be treated like prey.* He recalled his beloved *Calvin and Hobbes* comics, thinking in Calvin-like narration: *Spaceman Spiff stares down the alien commander.* But this adventure was different than any of Calvin's. Much more dangerous.

As the man moved closer, Max was again glad he'd thought cautiously enough to have ditched his personals and pocket lint.

"Max Fredericks." It was a statement, not a question.

"Yes."

"American, yes?"

"Yes. My father is –" he began.

"We know all about you already," The man cut in.

Max said simply, "I don't think so."

"We know everything."

"No. No you don't." About this, Max could afford to be completely confident, and his tone conveyed his certainty.

The man's eyes narrowed. "So it may seem to you," the man returned. He called to one of the guards that had arrested Max and had kept him standing in the passageway, frightened for his life, for the last five minutes.

Only at this point did Max dare to turn his head to look at the three. Guard One casually scraped his shoe on the curbside. Guard Three, the one with the stripes, intently observed, smiling without warmth. Guard Two was back to his post out front but kept looking back to see what was going on with the foreigner. They were amused.

Max returned their interest with a scowl. They'd caused him confusion and anxiety, and they seemed to enjoy it. *You are bad people*, he thought to himself, *and I'm the Good Guy here to do what's right.*

The man from the Volga nodded at Guard One. Despite Max's withering looks, that man smiled slightly and stepped forward to unlock the clasped handcuffs binding his hands. He hadn't realized that the cuffs were hurting him until he was free of them—he rubbed his wrists where they had bitten into his skin.

Max's bubbling terror surfaced again at the Stasi agent's last comment—"So it may seem to you." *What could they know? I've been here for maybe an hour and a half. Have they been watching me already?* Max recalled the maps and videos he'd seen in 2021's Building One at the MfS headquarters. In particular, at this moment, he pictured the wall-sized map of Berlin with red-dot stickers indicating the known apartments the Stasi had used for intelligence-gathering in the 1980s. He didn't know whether or not they had already been renting apartments for the purpose at this point in time. *If they have all those apartments now, they definitely know at least that I don't fit in… they might know I saw them take the girl. Does this change anything? What should I say?*

Stick with The Plan, Max. He said nothing.

Perhaps his moment's self-doubt showed on his face, because the Stasi man standing opposite Max smiled with a satisfied smirk. It was the same vacant smile Guard Three had issued a moment before.

They've got practice with this intimidation thing.

They probably practice this kind of thing to put a suspect on edge or at ease, depending… That's what I am now. A suspect.

Max was suddenly quite sure they'd been tracking his movements from the Volkspark to the Ministry. His awkward pauses to tie his shoes, his shifting glances at intersections… his stop at the public toilet. Maybe even in the alleyway that he'd thought he'd escaped into. He forced himself to stop thinking right there. *Stay in control, Max. I have to focus on the here and now. Like Arthur's mandala.*

Max was drifting into calmness when the agent interrupted. "You're a brave boy to come here. But all the same. Of course, what we do here is the same as you do in the West."

"What I do?"

"Excuse me. A way of saying. Your comrades. What we do here is security. You are at the head offices for the Ministry for State Security."

"I didn't find it by accident."

"Hm. We'll see. You say you know where you are." He paused. "But why are you here? I'll admit, westerners do not come here unless we bring them here."

"We should go inside. I have some information for you. And I need your help."

At this, the dark-rimmed-glasses man chuckled. "So it may be," was his reply. "The entire West requires our help, though they do not seem to know it." He chewed on nothing, and then said, "Perhaps we can help you." As he turned toward the car in which he'd arrived, the man waved for Max to get in first.

Max did as bidden, ducking into the front passenger seat of what counted as a luxury car in the mid-6os East.

The man with black-rimmed glasses and the soft nose climbed into the bench seat behind him, breathing heavily.

SIXTEEN

MAX'S FIRST INTERROGATION

The ride under darkening skies through the courtyard of the MfS was agonizing. The Volga moved at a snail's pace.

While they covered the 200 yards from the gate to the covered entryway, the Stasi man introduced himself in as threatening a way as he knew how: "So, Max Fredericks, let us be clear with one another. We know all about you, and here's why: I am a deputy minister for counter-espionage. It's my job to know when someone poses a threat –" he met Max's eyes in the rear-view mirror and nodded toward him "– has entered the German Democratic Republic." He paused for emphasis. "Please, call me 'Sam.'" Another hesitation. "Like your famous uncle!" The man calling himself Sam chuckled.

Clearly not a real name. Did some informant see me appear, materialize, or whatever it was? Max narrowed his eyes and nodded. *Yes, I understand everything you're saying,* he wanted to communicate.

The Volga crept into the portico camouflaging the central entrance to the Ministry for State Security Building Number One.

Max followed the man's lead—*I'm a guest, not a captive*—leaving the vehicle and climbing a few stairs toward the MfS's foreboding doors, the man asked, "Do you know what counter-espionage is?" Max studied his face. The black-rimmed glasses on his clean-cut face reminded Max of a character from an Indiana Jones movie. Max thought, *He's one of the bad guys—but a bit pudgier.*

Not waiting for a response, Sam answered his own question: "I deal in halting the most harmful elements that creep their way into our workers' and peasants' state—outside agitators and foreign terrorists, mostly, but others as well. Anyone who is a threat to our way of life is my business."

Which do they think I am—terrorist or outside agitator? Or both...

Sam held the lobby door for Max, and in he went—into the belly of the beast that was the Ministry for State Security, or MfS. Two guards stood at strict attention outside those doors, barring exit and entrance alike.

If things weren't serious enough before... this is it.

A female attendant sat at a desk on the right-hand corner of the room closest to the front of the building. *Right, that's all they let women do here. For all the talk people in the East did about equality of the sexes...*

A balding man seated at a small desk behind the woman didn't even look up as the deputy minister led the American through the lobby.

What is he doing, monitoring the secretary? It's bad enough they don't give women jobs other than this—but they're watching her, too? He paused. *So who's watching the desk guy?*

Max examined his surroundings as best he could using peripheral vision. The atrium looked much as it would on Max's visit fifty-plus years in the future. A businesslike mood of efficiency prevailed in 1965, though, rather than the somber one that had dominated perception in 2021.

Suit-wearing men crossed to and fro on the balcony of the first floor above the lobby. A lot of concrete and opaque glass were the standard decor, and wood paneling was as fancy as things got. Max observed no women in the space apart from the secretary at the front desk.

A man wearing a black tie sat in an uncomfortable-looking chair in a corner at Max's seven o'clock. He gave the appearance of reading a newspaper—"Neues Deutschland" ("New Germany").

He's not reading. He's watching me.

Max's escort, effectively his captor, led him across the large room without comment to the receptionist or to anyone else. He drew back the elevator's metal accordion gate and held out a hand, palm open, offering Max a gracious opportunity to step into the tiny space first.

Like a dignified guest. Not that he had much choice, Max nodded and stepped inside.

Sam followed, cutting off any chance of escaping the metal tomb. He snapped closed the gate with a clang.

Max shuddered in surprise and prayed to the gods it wasn't noticeable.

The man gave no indication either way and pressed a panel button marked "2." The car jolted into motion.

Barred from accessing the old-fashioned elevator during the self-guided tour in the modern era, Max now found the view from inside its cabin mesmerizing. The interior of the elevator shaft laid exposed to the naked eye. The metal gate that had so startled him in its closing was the only thing between the passengers and the walls of the cave through which the elevator moved. He watched the lobby disappear below as they crossed the balcony. A man's legs slid by, then his torso, and then his face and hat.

Floor one.

For the moment, Sam did not speak. Max watched the world slide past, listening to the clunking of the elevator cables and contemplating the danger that increased the higher he shuttled inside the building.

I'm inside the brain of the Stasi, he marveled. Sam continued to stare deadpan straight ahead. *Or is it the heart? They control people's desires and thoughts from this place. This is like that central intelligence place from the Madeleine L'engle book... except it's for real.*

They arrived on the second floor—*third floor in the States,* Max thought as though he were watching a documentary tour of the Ministry headquarters.

Sam led Max to the right.

Max did his best to hide his relief in sighing at escaping the shoebox elevator. It was the first he'd exhaled since its door had closed—he hadn't realized he was holding his breath.

"Here," the man said, and directed Max into a room whose door was marked "206" in copper.

Inside the cider-brown room were three simple chairs and a T-shaped arrangement of two tables. The two chairs situated on either side of the "T" boasted pale upholstery and thin metal legs. The third chair, a more substantial seat on wheels, was set at the table crossing the "T." A frosted window permitted fading afternoon light into the room from behind the bigger chair. The two table surfaces were utilitarian dark brown and spotless. The floor and walls, too, were pristinely kept, though aged. Several mirrors made up the majority of one wall—

Probably one-way mirrors so they can watch interrogations.

The interrogation room itself wasn't any bigger than Max's small bedroom back home. Overhead fluorescent lighting aided dim natural sunlight through clouded glass. Heavy, dark olive polyester curtains were drawn most of the way closed. The tabletop served only a beige-and-white intercom and manilla file folder.

"Sit now," Sam said, gesturing. His tone belied neither bark nor bite. Instead, his matter-of-fact flatness masqueraded as reporting mundane facts, rendering orders unnecessary.

Taking a seat in one of the yellowish cloth-bottomed chairs, Max tried with his posture to convey bravery balanced with compliance. He noticed that, high in the corner, a video camera the size of a small microwave monitored his reactions. *Best to put on the right show.*

"So, Max Fredericks," Sam said, exhaling as he took the seat opposite the boy. He leaned back slightly in the chair and did not touch the file folder.

Something's in there, but what could they possibly have on me? Been here only a few hours.

The man calling himself Sam placed one leg across his other knee and clapped his hands together, rubbing, and then opened his hands in a gesture saying, "What can I do for you?"

"What can I do for you, my Western comrade?"

Stick to The Plan, Max reminded himself, and he told his story. "First, I want to say up front what I am after, so that you know there aren't any tricks. I know you are suspicious, and I understand that." He waited for a sign that he should continue. Receiving none, he proceeded: "I saw you take a girl from the street beside Volkspark earlier today." Max waited for a reaction.

The man raised his eyes and shrugged his shoulders.

Is he confused? Is that like "So what?" Max tried to read Sam but got no clear sense of anything useful. *Just keep on, Max.*

Sam motioned with his left-hand pointer finger, giving the universal sign for, "Get on with it."

Max continued: "I saw her taken"—a quick nod of the head from Sam—"and I want you to release her to me."

Sam smiled.

"That is the first reason I am here. The second reason is not for the girl but for the good of the Democratic Republic of Germany."

"My friend. Max. You're what, sixteen years old?"

"Seventeen."

"Hmm. A young man. And an American. What interest have you in the good of the DDR?"

"Well, as I'm sure you already know, my father is a new military attaché in Bonn. With army intelligence."

Sam nodded curtly.

That's a different look from the one you gave when you really knew something. When you don't know, Max realized, *you pretend you do.* "He doesn't know that I'm here, of course. I won't be missed until tomorrow night, when I don't show up to a dinner party at the Mayor's residence. I'm supposed to be visiting with family friends tonight, but those people are so busy that they won't even notice I'm missing."

Max had been prepared to ham it up and to really pour on the distaste for all things capitalism. He tore into it: "But that's just it. The dinner parties, the materialistic extravagances. The private school I go to—it's expensive. Not everyone gets these things, and it's an unjust system. In America, people go without jobs –"

"Everyone in the German Democratic Republic has a job," Sam interrupted.

Max had heard of this commonly pronounced fiction before, and he shook his head in vigorous agreement. "Exactly. But not in the U.S.A.. Even the people that have jobs in America have to choose sometimes between having food and having healthcare. My family has an easy life and possesses a lot of material goods most people can't afford. Everyone is so busy looking at what their neighbor has—their possessions—that they don't care for that person. The rich build their wealth, pass it on to their kids, and the poor people get poorer. All of society suffers. It's a disease, and it's unfair. It is the wrong way." Max took a breath.

Was that too much? But he was really winding up now, so he carried on: "And I don't know everything about socialism, but I know it cares about the people—" this bit actually went against quite a lot Max had learned so far about the DDR, where the government and party officials lived lavish lifestyles, despite contrived appearances of being equal citizens serving working-class people—personal habits hidden from so-called comrades. "Things are not right in America."

Sam nodded in a muted way but offered as fervent an expression as Max had yet seen from him.

And here comes the pitch! Max thought in a mock baseball-commentary. "So I am here to help you—to help socialism in the East and the West. I want to do my part, though it will be a small part. Yes. I'm still in high school, but I can help. I have to. After all, how many

Americans get the chance I have by living so close to the East and knowing what I know?"

"Everyone does what he is able," Sam replied, "and gets what he needs."

Got him.

Max said, "I want to get the girl out, yes. But if there is anything that I can do in exchange, I want to do it for the people—not only for the people in the German Democratic Republic, but for the people at home who I'd help by aiding the worldwide revolution."

Sam looked satisfied. He said, simply, "And you also want to help our prisoner?"

Max winced. "Yes."

"You understand that we operate according to the law here? If she's broken the law, we cannot just let her go because you're offering favors. This isn't America—"

Have I gone too far? Max worked to maintain a straight face, but this worried him.

Sam continued, "where people with connections walk free."

"That's actually something we've got in common," Max thought but didn't say. "Understood," he said instead.

"Wait here, Max. I must discuss this matter with my superior." The man calling himself Sam stood and left by way of the door they'd entered, leaving the file folder on the table.

For the next three hours, Max was left to wonder if he'd be brought on board, incarcerated, or taken out back and summarily shot as a Western spy. He played out in his head any number of ways things might go, none of them particularly reassuring. He pictured East German headlines: "Americans stoop to new low—children used as spies"—in German, of course. He'd make for an effective East Berlin's poster boy in a new propaganda campaign.

He had to do whatever he could, though, despite the risks. Maybe the girl was guilty of thoughtcrime, but that was no reason for her to be locked up.

All the while, the folder called to him. *What do they have on me?*

Photos? Reports about the chase, maybe? He reached forward, putting his hand on the cover, opening it.

Something stopped him. A feeling. *They're watching me right now to see if they can trust me.* He didn't turn to look at the mirror behind him. Prudence won out. He sat back in his chair, folding his hands, sometimes moving them to clasp his knees. He managed patience without comfort.

Had Max been a fly on the wall in the next room over, number 208, he would have observed two men standing for the first twenty minutes and watching a boy sitting uncomfortably on a simple chair. They watched Max through a one-way mirror, sometimes looking more closely at his face via their video feed. The muscles around his mouth twitched every twenty or thirty seconds. His eyes and his eyebrows shifted. Like many Stasi agents, these men had been trained as human lie detectors.

A fly on the wall would've seen them analyzing Max shifting his weight. Now and again, they'd comment aloud or hand-scribble a note on a small pad, but mostly they only scrutinized. The fly would have watched them sit at a small table in that darkened room, keeping an eye on Max but also discussing the case in hushed tones. In Room 208, Max's immediate fate was determined.

Max did not speak fluent German in 1965 Berlin any more than in 2021 Berlin, and so even with a perfect view and with perfect audibility of the conversation between the agents, he might not have understood the substance of the conversation in Room 208. Had he understood, though, this is what he would have heard:

"Are they using him?" the first said to the second.

"Does it matter if it turns out we can use him to our own advantage?"

"Perhaps he's a spy, lying to us. We have to assume so."

"Perhaps." A pregnant pause. "Well, he's already inside the building. If he's a spy, he's already gotten this far. If he were a spy, it would be... problematic, to provide him with any more true information. We could feed him misinformation, though, and offer the appearance of helping."

The first asked, "Can we check on his background? What else do we know? Can we make use of him? If he is a spy, and we can confirm this while maintaining secrecy from him, perhaps we can use the knowledge to our advantage. We can be the tail that wags the American dog."

The second man possessed the air of authority that often accompanies a higher rank, though neither of them wore uniforms. After all, these were agents of the Hauptabteilung II, the counter-espionage arm of the MfS. They worked for the deputy minister, and not only were they rarely uniformed, they often dressed in Western outfits for operational purposes.

The man of authority said, "Of course. We will find out. We need another hour to develop leads. If he's genuine, the possibilities are endless. A confidential informant in a child living in the home of an advisor to the ambassador? No one would suspect it. But, of course that works only if he's genuine."

"What are we doing to confirm his story?"

"Well, you heard him. His father is a military attaché, he declares. A new one—that may make things difficult. Check the lists. But the bit about the dinner party. Have Günter in West Berlin check tonight's agendas and look into social events. If we cannot confirm his claims, maybe we catch him in a lie. We might prove false if we cannot prove true."

The first man nodded. "I'll look at the most up-to-date list of staff.

We'll contact Günter at Brandt's about the dinner party. Anything else?"

"We'll have to let Wiegand—er, Sam—know of the boy's demeanor and whether or not he peeks at the folder. We could show him what we have after he waits a while longer to measure his reaction. And he can be useful even if he's working both sides. Let him sweat, though, and see what he does..."

After that, the conversation dropped to the level of murmur, and even fly-on-the-wall Max wouldn't have been helped by an interpreter. They whispered as though the walls had ears, and someone standing in the same, tiny room wouldn't have been able to follow the discussion. The second man made then two phone calls.

Following this, the two men whose names we don't know took shifts watching Max on a viewing screen and through the glass. They noted all telltale signs he was becoming agitated, worried, or otherwise departing from his sincerity. At slightly greater comfort than Max in Room 206, these men waited. When the return call came, they understood Max a little better and decided to make their move now. Otherwise they'd risk retribution later for failure to act on what would seem in hindsight to have been reasonably clear intelligence. They called the Deputy Minister himself to confirm.

EIGHTEEN
THE DEAL

Meanwhile, Max reviewed his story in his mind again and again, committed not to speculate about his fate and considering all knowable contingencies. While he thought, he counted the dots in the ceiling tiles. He examined the folder on the table as best he could without touching it. Assuming he was being watched, Max leaned forward, hugging his knees. He allowed his eyes to drift as he straightened again and pressed his left hand into the small of his back, bending and twisting, working both to alleviate the pain he was feeling from sitting stone still and to provide an excuse for looking at the folder. *How is it so thick already? I've only been here a few hours. Maybe it's full of someone's laundry receipts and is stuffed so full to make me think they've got a file on me. But they can't, right?*

A few times in those hours, he stood to flex and stretch, reaching for his toes. The first time, he half-expected a Stasi agent to burst into the room, yelling for him to be seated—but nothing happened. He paced. *I am really on edge.*

Toward the end of his wait—and he didn't know it was the end of his wait, of course—he fought with himself again and nearly opened the folder from the table. *Why would they leave it here if I'm not supposed to look at it? They want me to see it. Fine, then. I'll look.*

Then: *No. I don't want them to think they've won. I still hold the cards. They don't really know anything.*

Before Max was overcome, Sam returned and sat as though he'd left Max for only a few moments. He began speaking as if to continue a conversation only recently paused. "Max, one one thing we wanted to ask you. Where again did you say that dinner party was tomorrow? I apologize for asking you to repeat the information, but, you know the expression—nobody's perfect." He shrugged and smiled.

This is nonsense. No one misses anything here. It's a setup.

And then, Max panicked. *What if they can check on the mayor's schedule? I made that up. Can I say I don't know now? That I'm not sure... What happens then?* He prayed the abject terror he felt in his core didn't show on his face. To combat the possibility, he scrunched his face like a kid trying hard to remember something his father had told him. Not such a stretch for Max in terms of acting.

Max looked upward and recalled, by associating action to memory, Mr. Ferguson reminding him that, "The correct answer is not on the ceiling, Max." He looked back down at the table, stifling a laugh.

This behavior didn't go unnoticed, and it earned a glare from Sam.

He pieced together the background: *The Embassy is in West Germany—in Bonn—not in Berlin. My dad isn't in Bonn, but he works there. Where do important people have dinner if they're in West Berlin? I should just stick with what I said. The mayor's house.* He was second-guessing himself, and it did him no favors that he was waffling now, though it was all internal. "I have to be honest. I don't remember. I think it was... the mayor's house? I think?" He concluded his sentence with a bit of upward inflection he hoped would indicate he was drawing from hazy memory.

"Ah, yes. Mayor Brandt. He's hosting a dinner for dignitaries tomorrow evening. He's been moving up the ladder, you know?

Looking to be Chancellor, we suspect." He paused, and then added, conspiratorially: "You know, we'd like that," and he winked at Max. "We have more than a few men on the job right now. An advisor has done particularly well, specifically. Perhaps it will turn out to be something you can help with? Maybe you could keep an eye out tomorrow evening for us? See if you pick anything up at that event."

They can't be planning to shoot me if they're setting me up to spy at a dinner party in West Berlin. Not shoot me today, anyway. Max withheld expressing joy as best he could. *They're gonna go for it. I can get her out and get myself clear of the East.* "Absolutely," he said.

"And what time is the dinner set to begin?"

Shit.

Germans in Max's own time often eat dinner later than Americans. Restaurants in 2021 Berlin seemed most crowded around 9pm. But he had no idea what would be the norm in 1965. He only knew he'd found himself in what was to him a black-and-white era of completely foreign culture. In the `60s, people in West Berlin tried to go on living normal lives, despite the fact they were in the crosshairs of a nuclear war that might kick off at any instant. West Berliners avoided compulsory military service by living on a kind of island, surrounded as their neighborhoods were by East Germany and cut off from the western half of the country. But Max had no earthly idea when average people ate dinner.

More to the point, he hadn't the faintest idea when Mayor Brandt would be hosting dinner tomorrow night. If this man Sam had a contact in the West, and if Mayor Brandt were actually hosting a dinner party, the Stasi agent would have more information than Max could possibly invent from whole cloth. *I'd be screwed.* The more rope he handed them, the more secure the rope they'd use to hang him with might be. *What am I supposed to say?*

He heard Brady in his memory. "Keep it simple."

Keep with the literal truth of 2021 and remember less fiction. Like using my name... when no lie is necessary, tell the truth.

So he stabbed in the dark, hoping to wiggle out of being specific about the party itself: "I'm to be home by seven-thirty. I'm not sure when the dinner begins, but I am supposed to be home by then. If I'm not back, my father will be impatient with me whenever I show. If he has reason to suspect I've rebelled against his rules, he'll go without me and I'll miss my opportunity to help." *Yes—give them more reason to release me when I'm through here. I'm useful in the West!* "It would make things... difficult. But I can explain it to him if I get there by seven-thirty, or even by eight." *I'm rambling,* he realized, and he stopped speaking abruptly.

"Thank you, Max. Your candor is appreciated."

Sam left Max alone again, and this time he noticed a lock click into place after the Stasi officer pulled the door closed.

Did they lock it last time? What's going on? I'm done for. For the first time since arriving in Room 206, Max noticed the heat, which from then onward would be impossible to ignore. A bead of sweat dripped from his brow. Another seeped down his back. He couldn't have said whether the heat caused the sweating or if his captivity screamed at his body to cool him however it could—it was probably a bit of both.

Doubts whirlpooled.

This whole idea was stupid. Why did I think I could outsmart the Stasi? Did I say too much? What are they doing? They've obviously looked into my dinner story—do they know something about a real dinner happening? They must. The way they asked me about the Mayor... Brandt. Brandt. Willy Brandt, I guess? That sounds right, but I hope they don't want me to confirm anything else about him, since I really only know the guy's name and that I think he was the Mayor of West Berlin...

A chain of bad thoughts rapid-fired and stuck like spitballs targeting a spot labeled "worries go here" in his mind. The whole mass threatened to crush him at any instant. His worried compounded, brick upon brick, for an an indeterminate, seemingly interminable period of time.

WHEN THE YELLOW-BROWN door to the interrogation room swung open again, it was not the man calling himself Sam returning. Instead, the man who unlocked the door, knocked twice—as if Max could refuse him entry—and entered softly was a skinny man with a dark suit-jacket and black tie. "I'm Ernst," the man calling himself Ernst said, and he put his hand out to shake Max's hand. "Operations. I'm assigned to your case. I'm here to help you."

At least this guy has a German-sounding fake name. He shook the man's hand.

Under one arm, Ernst carried a manilla file-folder identical to the one on the table. He crunched an apple between bad teeth. He placed the new folder underneath the one from earlier and seemed to forget about it immediately, placing the apple on the table beside them both. The apple wasn't fresh and would've been the sort he'd pass on in any other situation and on any other day.

Ernst checked his watch, casual as a lazy Saturday, and only then seemed to notice Max's longing. He looked at the apple and then removed it from the table, wrapping it in a handkerchief and putting it in his pocket. "I'm sorry, Max. It seems you have been here for some time. It's nearly five in the evening. I'll get you something to eat. We'll come up with something, but let's talk about the mission first."

Can't show weakness. But being hungry is normal and natural—it doesn't make me weak, does it? He was beginning to drift before steadying himself internally. "Yes. But the girl is part of the deal. Where is she?"

"You must mean the young woman Elsa. Yes, I have been informed of your interest in this suspect. We will get to her soon enough. But first, you must agree to perform a task on our behalf. To prove your loyalty to the socialist revolution, you might say. It is a simple thing, really. And then? The girl can go with you."

"What do you want me to do?" Max was prepared to be told to do something he'd have to turn down. Even if he were willing—which he wouldn't be, he imagined—he wouldn't be able to photograph top-secret documents, to record conversations with his father and his father's associates, or to assassinate anyone. How he'd say "no" to the Stasi was something he hadn't yet thought through.

Ernst continued with the same level of concern he might show reading the box scores of an unimportant match, waving his hand as he spoke. "Right. As I said, it is a simple thing. You are to cross into the West, and you will meet our man at the border. He will transport you to the main part of the city, where you will receive information at a predetermined location."

Max allowed a sigh of relief but awaited the rest of his orders. *How can I do this without harming the West? And without the East seeing that I'm holding out?* He said, "What will I do with it?"

"Bring the package back to us at what is called 'Checkpoint Charlie,' at Friedrichstrasse. And we'll need to discuss Elsa's arrest so that you understand what you're dealing with. We assume that you know her personally already, yes?"

"Arrest," Max repeated, though he spoke the word with a tone that didn't follow the pliable attitude he was hoping to maintain throughout his contact with the MfS. "Arrest—of course," he corrected himself, and after a pause, he continued. "I'll need more details. I apologize. I do not know her personally. I only wanted to help her because I saw her taken—it startled me." *You're talking too much, Max. Redirect this thing so he is on the right track with you.* "I only wish to help the state."

Ernst was letting him talk as long as he was going to keep running his mouth.

"She hasn't done anything too serious, I hope," Max continued. "Maybe she can help the state as well, and she owes it to the people, if she's really done something wrong. We'll both work for the GDR." *I'm rambling. Get back to the mission.* "I'll need careful instructions about collecting the information you need."

"That is the purpose of my presence here with you, Max," Ernst assured him.

So this is my handler, Max understood.

"Now, in the generalities, do you agree to the arrangement? You retrieve the information. We release the suspect Elsa and you together."

"Okay. I agree. Assuming I can do this thing you're asking, I am here to do it. I work for the socialist revolution and will help a person I think might be innocent."

"Ah, innocent." He shook his head as though Max were lost in hopeless confusion. "More on that in a moment. One additional detail. You may be called upon to do some work for us in the future. That is a part of the deal."

Max didn't foresee staying in 1965 for much longer than it took to free Elsa. He nodded. "Absolutely fine," Max said. "My desire to help the German Democratic Republic began long ago, and it won't end tomorrow."

"Very well. It is decided. Elsa's temporary release is being negotiated right now in Building 15, and after you complete your task, she will be released to you. But I must issue to you a warning, for your own, uhm, well-being." Here, the fact that English didn't come naturally to Ernst leaked through his Western façade.

"A warning?" *Because of course.*

Ernst leaned forward and rested his elbows and forearms on the table between them.

Like he's my friend.

He dropped his voice. "I had not known you lacked a prior relationship with Elsa. This speaks better of you, believe me. So take note, and this is important. I do not lie: The girl is dangerous. You should not take her with you at all." Ernst frowned, giving Max the look of a stern but concerned father. "It's obvious why you've come here. You've joined a childish infatuation with the misguided western obsession with heroism for a sex you've predetermined is weaker, always needs a man's aid. But you westerners are foolish. You might be killed, spending time with her. She is a spy for the West, and she is involved with—we have reason to believe—pro-fascist activities.

Possibly violent actions." He leaned back again and spoke at a normal volume. "She is harmful to socialism and therefore the people, in general. We arresting people with only proper reasons, and we do not make mistakes. If she is here, she is not, as you say, innocent."

Max had an answer prepared in case the Stasi were unwilling at first to let Elsa come with him, but he wasn't mentally prepared for them to release her with such apparent ease, albeit with heavy warning. He couldn't help but to wonder at this last part. *How seriously should I take their warning? Maybe they're trying to get in my head… I guess it's working.*

He gave his scripted response, though it had been prepared expecting an alternate set of circumstances: "I need her to appear to be less suspicious in my work for you. Afterward. In the West. The girl will help me to blend in."

To this, Ernst merely shrugged, and Max had no way of knowing whether or not his reasoning had been accepted.

Max added, "And if she is a risk, we can get her to a safe distance from the Republic and use her for intelligence-gathering, whether she knows it or not. I'll take responsibility."

"It may turn out that you are correct. But take heed in my warning is about Elsa and her… associates. I say again: we do not just pick people up off the street in the DDR for nothing. This person is a known associate of terrorists and fascist sympathizers conducting anti-state activities.

We will have to monitor her after she's gone, and that means monitoring you even as you work for us. Elsa is young, as you are, but she in particular has a great potential to become a leader of harmful activists. Our job is to prevent harm to the people and cut out any infection."

Though this last bit was put Max on edge, Ernst had a look of genuine concern. Max considered that sincerity and misguided beliefs weren't always mutually exclusive—both could be true.

He worked through what the Stasi man was saying. *To them, anyone from the West is a terrorist, probably. And the Wall—they call it the Anti-Fascist Defensive Barrier... so almost anyone on the other side is supposedly a fascist like the Nazis were. If she was picked up for anti-state activities, it is more reason than ever for me to think she's a political prisoner fighting for what is right, and what is right deserves everyone's help.*

And Elsa is not a distressed damsel waiting for rescue. Ernst was right about that—but however strong she might be as an individual, she won't be breaking out of prison on her own. Anyhow, this whole mission is not just about her. If I can help the activists she knows, I can do a greater good while helping her get out.

Max had talked himself into even more righteousness. A lot of thinking in just a few seconds meant there wasn't much of a delay before he acknowledged Ernst's warning with a nod and an "Okay. Thanks for the warning." He got back to business. "Assuming I fulfill my end of the bargain, when will she go free?"

"I fear I must repeat myself. When she goes to the West, we have to keep watch. If she contributes to the destruction of our workers' state from the West, we will have to act once more in self-defense. We must protect ourselves. We are the sword and shield of the state, after all." In other words, Elsa will never be free.

"I understand all that. When can you release her, even if she's monitored?" *Maybe I can work out some sort of asylum deal with the West. Maybe, if we can show her life is in danger in West Berlin, she could even be—what was the word?—exfiltrated to the States. Stasi will have a harder time operating there than right in their own back-yard. I'll get her to the U.S.*

At this moment, Max revised his plan: *Elsa could trade her East German connections—access to common people and so potential assets—to Western spies. She could be useful to the West and win her freedom.* He counted on this hope for the puzzle pieces of The Plan to fit together. After all, without Western cooperation, he'd be simply dropping Elsa from prison in the East into homeless destitution—and continued Stasi harassment—in the West. So the plan setting her up with a career of intelligence-sharing or an escape to the U.S. was key to her escaping the Stasi's grasp.

"I get all of that," was all he said to Ernst. "So give me the details. Where must I go, where must I be, and what must I do—be precise, please."

"But of course." Ernst opened the folder that had been sitting on the table from the moment Max entered the room some four hours earlier. From it, he withdrew three black-and-white photos of Max, who could not at that moment hide his shock. His mouth dropped. Ernst placed the photos on the table, each meticulously placed in chronological order, and snapped them down on the plastic-like table surface.

The first image had been taken from street-level and featured Max standing outside the Volkspark next to a Trabant and staring at it, his face in a state of pale confusion. The second street-level photo showed Max looking, transfixed, at a girl in the background of the photo—Elsa —who was out of focus but in frame. The third offered an aerial perspective and showed Max seated on a park bench facing the brown-jacket man. The photo was taken from an angle that showed only the back of the older man and kept Max's face in clear focus. Max's eyes widened as he examined them. *These guys don't miss a trick.* The three were all from different angles—the last from a height of maybe three stories. *How many agents were watching the park when I appeared next to it?* Ernst then withdrew a final photograph—of Max leaving the street urinal, head down and looking like he was hoping not to be seen.

Max swallowed hard. There were more documents inside the folder, but he couldn't make them out—typed reports of some kind.

"As you can see," Ernst began, explaining the photos in calm narration, "We know everything about what happens in our workers' state, and we notice every out-of-place person. If you do not do as you promise to do, you will finish your evening tomorrow in a cell beside Elsa's, and neither of you will see the light of day again. I want you to understand what is at stake. If you do not do as you agree, no one will know where you've gone." He closed the folder with resolution. "And remember: we have agents in the West as well. We are... international." One more threat—this one explicit—to go along with the the day's implied threats.

"I understand the consequences," Max said. "I want to help."

"Good," Ernst replied.

They are in charge, now, even if my plan is a good one. In Max's mind, the capital-P had dropped from "the plan." All was all in doubt, now. He worked to control his breathing.

Ernst gathered the photographs from the table, replaced them inside the first folder, and slid from underneath it the folder he'd brought with him a few minutes ago. He didn't open it and instead placed it between Max and himself.

He removed a dull silver watch with a burnished leather band from his jacket pocket and placed it on top of the folder in front of Max. "Here. So you know the time."

Max put it on his right wrist. It was 5:46 in the evening.

Ernst remarked, as though in passing, "People tend to lose perspective when they don't know what time it is. We wouldn't want you to lose your perspective about any of this."

More threatening reminders, Max thought. *But he's right: At least I know what time it is.*

"We'll need to get you some different clothes. As badly as you stand out here, you will also attract the attention of Western agents. We know they're here in the East, and we know where they operate here and in the West. It would be best if you become invisible to them. We'll know where you are, of course, so don't you worry that we'd lose track of you." He wagged his finger as he said this. Then he added, "The clothes will take a bit of time to select. They'll be brought to you in your quarters."

"My..." Max began.

"Temporary, of course. You will notice that the operation cannot begin until tomorrow morning as it will take us some time to reach your contacts in the West as well as with our man in the West Berlin mayor's office. The information you'll be collecting is from that office, but we must signal to notify our man with instructions to bring the package to your target location." He waited for this all to add up for Max. "So you'll be spending the night here."

Max raised his eyebrows. *This isn't part of the plan. Not part of the plan. Breathe.* He worked to maintain composure.

It'll be okay. Dad doesn't expect me back til tomorrow, and who knows how time works here anyhow... if time is passing at home, I can get home tomorrow without causing any worry, since Dad is away for the night. If time isn't passing, then I'll just get back to 2021 at the same time as when I left—again, no problem. If time works some other way... well, I can't worry about that.

"Max?" Ernst pulled him out of his time-travel hypothesizing. "You aren't speaking."

"I follow."

Ernst drew from the slim folder between them a single-page, typed document. He placed it down facing Max. "The action." He paused as Max began to read, and then he added, "Memorize the contents of this page. In ten minutes, you go downstairs. In the morning, we will brief you on any remaining mission details or updates before you depart."

Ernst left Max alone again, locking him in once more.

Ten minutes, Max thought. *A schedule.* He hunched forward in his chair, lifting the document a few inches off the table and beginning to read, furrowing his brows slightly in concentration. *I'm holding mission orders from the Stasi.* It was hard not to be impressed, as anxious as he was feeling.

Council of Ministers of the German Democratic Republic
   Ministry for State Security

Department / Department / Division
    <u>Main Directorate for Reconnaissance</u>
<u>Division A IX and Hauptabteilung II,</u>
<u>Counter-intelligence</u>
   Regional Administration / Administra-
tion <u>Berlin</u>
   Case Officer <u>Gen. H. Vogel</u>
   Telephone <u>_[- - - -]</u>.

Operational Orders for Action Code-Named
"Canary"

0600 Mission Briefing Review
   0615 Depart MfS
   0700 Arrival at Glienicke Bridge for
crossing into Western Occupied Zone.
   0705 Meet contact across G bridge in W
Berlin. Passenger to central W. Berl.
   0755 Arrive at Zoologischer Garten
Berlin drop point. Check for, drop any
surveillance.
   0915 Collect dropped item. Option 1
Placement: beneath green wooden park
bench inside ZG 100 paces east of
entrance. Option 2 handoff at lamppost.
Option 3 walking handoff at exit.
   0940 Walk to Checkpoint C at
Friedrichstrasse.

```
     1015 Cross border to Democratic Berlin
at Checkpoint Charlie. MfS Pickup.
     1105 Debrief at MfS.
     1300  Release  of  [-  -  -]  to  Little
Sparrow
```

So much could go wrong. Max almost spoke his fears aloud. There were places where he could mess things up, or factors beyond his control could skew the plans. And if he didn't get it right, Elsa would become one more victim of the Stasi, disappearing into semi-permanent interrogation for years. Or she'll be shipped to the East and left to rot in a gulag, forgotten by everyone but her family. And none of these worries took into account the danger to Max himself. The risk was extreme.

Ten minutes.

TWENTY

LITTLE SPARROW

I have to memorize it.

And he did. He mumbled it aloud to himself, closed his eyes and called it back to mind, speaking it aloud. He read it over and over again. To keep the whole thing straight in his mind, Max began to think of its stages as "Approach," "Acquisition," and "Return." It was a simple enough schedule, since between 0700 and 1015 there were only four steps to remember.

The most important elements in his mind were that he'd be dropped off at 7am, would need to lose anyone attempting to follow him when he reached the Zoo, and then he'd pick up the dropped intelligence before making a walking break for the East at Checkpoint Charlie. *About a twenty minute walk...* He calculated as he ran through the steps.

Ernst and Sam interrupted Max's analysis, knocking, unlocking, and entering the interrogation room turned operation briefing room. Sam held the door and stepped aside, leaving a clear path to the hallway. The pair remained standing and addressed him:

"Max," Ernst said, "it is important at this point that you consider whether or not you have been completely honest with us."

Max began nodding.

Before he could respond verbally, Ernst added, "Think carefully. The door right now is open without penalty. If you have told us a single lie, you absolutely must use this door to leave, head directly to Oberbaumbrücke and cross back to the West. You had no papers upon your arrival here, which is suspicious and perhaps worthy of investigation on its own—but on assumption of your good intentions we will provide what you need to cross the border remove you from our concern."

A few seconds passed, and Ernst continued. "Also: If you are too frightened to carry on, you must use the exit now. We will not stop you. However, if you remain here and you've lied or intend to deceive us in any way or fail to follow through on your end of the deal, you will not return to the West. Ever. Now you must choose."

Sam added, "We can make it easy enough for you to return to the West, Max. Maybe you should go now. We'll drop you at the bridge crossing to Kreuzberg." Ernst and Sam waited.

It's not a real choice. Max said nothing for a moment, hoping to look like a person contemplating his life. He was, after all. *This is another test. They'll never let me leave here without doing what they ask.*

A person any less committed than Max at this point probably would have balked, hesitated too long in responding, or wouldn't have given the right sense of serious contemplation and genuine concern. And for other reasons, a person less devoted to Doing the Right Thing would have attempted to abort the mission right then. Someone less aware of what the Stasi were all about would have failed at this point or sooner and would have been sent to a gulag to be worked to death in Siberia.

Max's predicament offered only one possible successful outcome, at least insofar as getting out of MfS was concerned. His only chance was to stick to the revised plan and never waver. He demonstrated his thinking with his facial expression, and inside thirty seconds, he responded with a confident, "Yes, comrades." When he had an uncomfortably long night to think about everything that had gone down so far, the "comrades" bit he thought had been a nice touch.

What might pass for a smile in another context crossed the man calling himself Sam's usually impassive face—a kind of upward curl of the lips—and then it disappeared. He sat at the head of the "T" table arrangement, and Ernst sat across from Max in the other floral-patterned chair. The man calling himself Sam was deadly serious. Clear beyond any doubt was the chain of command in this room. "Very well," Ernst said as he took a seat. "You've reviewed the schedule? You'll remember?"

Sam looked on, evaluating.

Max replied: "As you instructed. I will remember and will do as ordered."

Sam added, "Also: you're forbidden to carry anything unessential to the action of the mission. You must agree to this, as well,"

"Understood. I have a few questions, though. I need some clarity."

"We'll answer what we are able," Ernst responded in a helpful tone.

"First. Who is my contact? How will I know it when I see this person?"

Ernst replied, "Your contact will be in a car on the far side of the bridge. The man driving it will be someone the BND—West German intelligence—would not suspect. In any case, he'll arrive when you do, so the four guards usually at that station won't have much time to respond with a telephoto lens, and they want to keep up the appearance that the West and East are one country, so they won't interfere with your crossing or his picking you up on the other side."

"Uh huh," Max said. "Won't the BND receive a report of my crossing and a photo of his car?"

"Certainly, but he won't use the same car next time, and they have no reason to distrust him. Quite the opposite, in fact." The Stasi men shared a glance.

"Other than that he'll be picking up someone who was just

dropped off early in the morning to cross into the West at a disused border point," Max voiced aloud. "They'll at least take note and report it up the chain of command."

"We've considered that, too," Ernst said. "Officially speaking, you are being expelled from the German Democratic Republic in the morning, and your later crossing will not be noticeable by the BND, given that you're still a child—"

Max bristled.

"—and that crossing will occur at a different border checkpoint. In any case, by the time they have time to act on any suspicion of your arrival, you'll be gone. For your return to us at 1015, you'll have proper paperwork, as far as our border patrol is concerned. You will be checked and double-checked as you cross back into the East. On a Saturday just before noon, there is significant border traffic at that checkpoint, and you will blend in if you do your job properly. So there will be no suspicion there."

He's talking a lot, but he's not saying anything. "Okay. So, second. What method of delivery will be employed at the pickup?"

A straightforward reply, for once: "An American coin. A half-dollar with the former president's face on it."

"A Kennedy half-dollar?"

"Yes. A simple thing."

"Okay, but how will I know it's going to be at that location or the backup, and can we get precise about what I'm looking for along the way?"

"Glad you asked. It's good to know that our newest asset is detail-oriented. We were going to go over this bit tomorrow, but you're asking all of the right questions. You must also memorize the following for operational success," the operations officer explained. "To the left-hand side of the iron entry-gate to the animal park, you'll find a small mark on the wall. A three-centimeter scrape of stone on the red brick at about waist-height."

Max nodded.

Ernst continued. "No one else can notice, so be cautious. This waist-high mark tells you it is safe to proceed to the drop area. Then you'll enter the park, walk directly ahead one hundred paces, and you will then look for the next sign. This will confirm the next steps in your mission.

"The signal on a tree to your left at that point will be small and unnoticeable except to you and the person who leaves it—another operative—and it will indicate one of three possible options.

"Option one is the best because it is easiest. One downward mark on the tree indicates that the coin will be at the bench forty paces ahead.

"Option two is the backup plan and will be indicated by two marks. This second option is for the object to be handed off at a lamp-post on the southern end of the park's central plaza—near the beer garden.

"Three marks on the tree mean the third scenario is in effect. These indicate you should hurry to the southern edge of the park to meet an asset in person for a brush pass near the exit there. The person would approach you, so you needn't know what she will look like."

"She?" Max inquired.

"She," Ernst confirmed. "The BND, Brits, and Americans don't use women for operations, so our female agents are easily overlooked. The West overlooks women, to our benefit. But please, Max, do not become distracted by these ideological details for the moment. This next part is as important as the rest."

Max again nodded.

"If there is a diagonal slash on the tree, you will know that the operation we've described so far has been aborted, and you will proceed immediately to a safe house at 12 Anhalter Strasse near Wilhelmstrasse. This is near the crossing at Friedrichstrasse."

That's Checkpoint Charlie, Max recalled.

Ernst continued, "A clear safe house will be marked with a white shirt hanging from a balcony planter. You are to knock and identify yourself by name. Then remain there until a contact informs you of the next steps in a revised action. If there's no such signal, you're on your own. Let us hope things don't deteriorate that badly.

"If the drop carries on without cancelation and following options one, two, or three, you are to proceed afterward to Friedrichstrasse checkpoint to be reacquired by our agents when you're safely back in the DDR. And listen, Max. If the drop proceeds at the bench or the lamppost, it will be placed haphazardly on the seat of this park bench as though someone had lost it. It is critical that you arrive at the animal park to follow our plan at precisely the appointed time—"

"9:15 am," Max interjected.

"Right," Ernst continued. "9:15. If you must waste time, do so without attracting attention. If you are behind schedule and someone else were to collect the intelligence item, the consequences for us would be minimal, but the consequences for you will be most severe."

"I follow," Max affirmed. "What's in the coin?"

"That's not for you to know."

A dead-dropped coin. Probably hollow. "Third question. Why wouldn't the Western border guards interfere at the second checkpoint?"

The man calling himself Sam took this one. "Those in the West like to pretend to the public that the border is not closed, so while they will advise against your crossing, they will not prohibit it. And you will not have any DDR identification with you, in case you are stopped in the West, but you will carry a coded message. State Security manages the checkpoint on our side, and our men will place you under arrest."

"Arrest?!" *Getting arrested was not part of my plan.*

"Look. For all practical purposes, you're already under arrest. But you're here freely, and we have made a deal with you to allow your departure when the mission is complete. Perception is all that matters. If the observers in the West see you arrested, they won't have reason to suspect you when you return later. They'll think you're someone gone wrong in the head who's decided to cross unauthorized into the DDR. We'll allow them to think so."

"Okay. I get it," Max said. *Can't argue with that.* He paused. "Fourth. Why is Elsa's name removed from this document?"

"We have internal reasons for redactions," Ernst answered. "Her name is not to be recorded on paper. This is not a discussion we can have."

"But why—" Max began, but he was cut off.

"This is not negotiable," Sam interrupted.

"And Elsa will be released as soon as I've finished?"

"After you've completed this action to our satisfaction, yes," Sam replied.

"Fine. Last question. I'm assuming that I'm the Little Sparrow? What's that about? Can't I name myself?"

"We don't pick the names in this room," Ernst explained in a curt non-response. "Is that all?"

Max checked his watch. *6:10pm.* "Okay, so where do I sleep? And can I get some food? I'm practically starving."

Sam: "Your quarters are in the holding corridor." He smirked.

Max cocked his head and looked to Ernst's facial expressions for clues, but the man's self-regulation was effective.

Ernst continued, "One more thing before we address that element. If you are picked up by the BND, they'll hand you over to the U.S. Mission in West Berlin rather than interrogate you themselves because you appear to be American. It's the arm of your government from which operations are staged and where your army administrators do their imperialist work.

Sam leaned in. "If they take you, you won't complete your mission—if only because of the time it will take for them to release you. If you have to answer questions, give them something true and believable—but don't tell them too much. Just give them enough to satisfy, and perhaps they'll let you go."

Perhaps? Max thought. *Stay on track.* "Okay. What's the holding corridor?"

Ernst answered. "In another building. You understand that, for security and until we complete further investigation of your case, you will be blindfolded while in transit. Other prisoners will neither see nor hear you. This is a necessary, standard procedure."

"Other prisoners? Necessary? Is it, really? I've been agreeable. I am working for you, now."

Ernst, again: "We will see it as a sign of your devotion to our democratic cause. A sign that you are serious. You want to work for the common people's revolution? You will sleep like a commoner sleeps tonight. No soft, bourgeois mattress for you. Maybe a life lesson. How do you say..." Ernst trailed off for an instant before finding the expression. "It builds character. You will receive a meal, and—as I said—suitable clothing will be brought as well. This is much better treatment than one of ours would receive in the West, I can assure you."

"Okay." Max swallowed hard. "Okay. For the cause, I will sleep however you wish for me to sleep. I'm hungry. Can we go, now?"

Max followed instructions and stood beside his chair as Ernst waved to no one in particular.

The mirror, Max remembered. *My file has probably doubled in size with notes about my facial tics since I arrived. And the seat.* He glanced at the seat cushion. *Removable. Probably going to save my scent for the dogs.* They could track him later if needed.

The door opened, a uniformed guard, and he stood behind Max to cover his eyes with a black, cloth blindfold.

Max didn't fuss as the man secured it.

The man patted down his pants pockets and removed the only thing in them—the compass.

"He can keep it. He may need it," Sam offered, and the man replaced the item.

"This is where we, er, see you off, Max. Pardon the expression," Ernst said. He had to be grinning.

By now, Max easily distinguished the two men's voices.

The operations officer Ernst spoke again. "In the morning, I will check back in with you and review the plan one final time before I put you in the car to Glienicke Bridge."

Max's anxiety spiked as he was pushed toward the door. The blindfold held tightly, constricting and at the same time expelling all comfort and confidence from his body. *Just get me out of here.*

TWENTY-ONE
CAGED

Max began to panic, being pushed like that, but he didn't flounder for long. The guard took him by the shoulder and led him out of the room and through a series of hallways.

Max tried to memorize the turns, but it was too much under the circumstances. He was hungry and exhausted. He did his best to make a map in his mind's eye as the guard led him into the deepest parts of the Ministry for State Security.

Right, left... long hallway, right, right. Long corridor. Stairwell. Three levels down, maybe—maybe. Hold the railing! Left at bottom. Right-hand turn again. Another long hallway. By the time they looped and doubled back on their footsteps for what Max believed was a third time, he'd completely lost the nonsense pattern.

Eventually, they halted.

I suppose I'm at their mercy. If I leave, it will be because they've let me out. If he had been let into the heart and brain of the Ministry, he was now trapped in its bowels. *The smell fits.*

A now-familiar feeling of existential panic rose once more as the guard nudged Max firmly into a room off the echoey hallway, saying, "Take it off, now."

Max pulled off the blindfold to reveal a room much different from the one where he'd been interrogated and where he'd cut his deal. This space was much cooler, for one thing—*Not more than twenty degrees Fahrenheit above freezing. Must be underground.*

An overhead bulb protected by a wire frame lit the room dimly. A 24-by-12-inch bit of clouded-glass high on the wall opposite the door. This window, if you could call it that, was criss-crossed with thin bars preventing anything passing through, were the glass to be broken. The cement walls boxed in a room about twice the width of and the same length as an old-fashioned dining room table.

The only things in the cell—that's what it was—were a low bed and a seatless toilet that Max hoped to ignore for the rest of the night. He examined the bed, which was affixed to the wall and cornered some 24 inches off the floor. *More like the world's most uncomfortable beach recliner, sans beach.* No mattress. Tightly arranged wooden planks formed the surface of the bed, and had a slight upward bend near where the head of a typical adult would rest. Max was not adult-sized, though, and it wouldn't have been very comfortable to recline on if he were. *Fat chance of me falling asleep on that.*

He sat down heavily anyhow and remembered a map he'd seen during a tour in the defunct MfS with Brady: *I'm probably in House 15—where they do counter-espionage—and I was interrogated in House 1, the main building. That's where they'll do the tours...* but a visit by the public to this place was far from seeming real, from where Max sat at this moment.

Before the guard can leave, I might as well ask. "Where's Elsa?"

"I don't know who you're talking about," the man replied as he closed the door, "but communicating with other prisoners is strictly forbidden. If you do it, you will regret your choice." The door clanged shut.

Max started nervously.

The guard slid open a panel to finish his thought: "It will be added to the list of any charges already against you, number 75."

Number 75? I'm a man, not a number!

"You'll have the assigned items in a few moments. And food." The guard chuckled as the metal panel slammed home.

Oddly enough, what Max noticed at this point was a whirring sound that he tracked to the tiny sink beside the toilet. The white noise seemed to emanate from the drain. *So we can't talk through the pipes.* He'd heard about this countermeasure.

Rather pleased with himself for catching onto the Stasi's tried-and-true methods for controlling prisoners, he realized quickly that it did him no good knowing this fun fact about the prison hallway in which he found himself. He removed and placed the watch and compass at the end of the bed meant for his feet. *6:30pm.*

He tried to relax by lying back. *Hmm. Firm.* He folded his hands behind his head as he often did at home. *I guess that's a little better.* The light pierced his eyes. He tilted his head and stared away from its daggers.

A few moments later, the panel in the door opened, and a kind of makeshift tray was lifted into place on the other side of the door, as a metal plate appeared and didn't tip or fall when it seemed to be placed in the opening itself. It hung there.

Potatoes and some kind of mystery meat. He grabbed the plate and began tearing into the slop. *So hungry... I don't know what this is, and I don't care.*

The person on the other side of the door forced a string-tied bundle of clothes through the opening, and it fell to the cell's floor. "Plate goes back here when you're through. I'll return to collect it in eight minutes. Change clothes tomorrow when you wake up—not before then, though. There is no need to smell of toilet." The voice belonged to the same uniformed guard from before.

"Don't worry, comrade," he offered. "We'll turn out the lights for you. Enjoy your dinner."

"Don't you normally do that anyhow?" Max wondered aloud. The man only chuckled again softly and departed, his clapping footsteps echoing in the hallway.

The closed door had changed Max's perspective, closing him off from the whole world. A small keyhole-like opening at about an adult's eye level was covered by something on the outside of the door.

Despite his numerous misgivings and intense discomfort, Max did fall asleep on the bed in the cell, but not before spending a full two hours wondering how he came to end up in this place and asking himself what a fool he had been for an obsession with rescuing the girl—Elsa—the girl to whom he still had not so much as spoken a single word and who might well enough be an actual criminal in the East.

Someone switched off the lights from outside the cell at some point soon after he checked his watch for the last time that evening, which he did at 8:55. He shivered his way through a broken slumber, but once ensconced in complete darkness he managed to disappear into sleep. An inkling of the reality began to sink in. A quarter-million other prisoners would feel it as their constant mode of existence: fear.

Before drifting off into that ineffective night of in-and-out-of-consciousness rest, he had a final thought: "I guess I'm a spy for East Germany now." Even as other incoherent thoughts came, this one stood out among those memories from a lost reality. All else became shadow.

TWENTY-TWO

MORNING BRIEFING

From vivid dreams of bombers over picturesque Nuremberg and a family disembarking from a train amid a thick crowd at Oranienburg, and out of hazy and bleak memories of a public abduction, light exploded overhead. Flashes that began in his mind as aerial incendiary bombs burned through his eyelids, and he forced open his eyes, shielding his face with his arm. A coruscating flicker of an overhead bulb added to the dreamlike surreality of Max's cel. He knew just where he was, though for a moment he wished he were somewhere and sometime else. He remembered his mission and the Stasi's mission, in that order, and willed himself to accept his fate, however awful or heroic it would turn out to be.

He grasped for the watch received during negotiation—or was it interrogation?—the evening before. He squinted at the hands on the aged timepiece: fifteen minutes prior to six in the morning. *Mission briefing at six,* he recalled from the document whose contents he'd memorized. *The Germans do tend to be punctual,* he noted grimly.

A key rustled from a collection of keys outside his room. The heavy clank of a key sliding into place and unlocking the cell door offered one more reminder that he was at the mercy of an oppressive arm of a tyrannical government. The Stasi were, as per usual, in control.

Max had been counting on them believing they were in control, though. *So far, so good, on that front.*

He was foggy and rather groggy, still half-submerged in the night's dreams and doubting the reality of his perceptions. Sliding metal awoke him from reverie once more as the door opened six inches outward into the hallway.

It was Ernst, and he was smiling. "Guten Morgen, Comrade Maximilian," his voice intoned with upbeat gentility and sternness surprising in their confluence. "Do not forget—the clothing. Or you will stand out as a beacon to the West as you did to us yesterday."

I almost forgot. Max had been using the clothes as a makeshift pillow, which had helped. He shifted into a higher gear, sitting upright and working the clasp on the watch. He unwrapped the pants and shirt combination and stretched them out to have a look. Common cotton trousers that were dark grey and a simple—surprise! —greyish-white shirt with a simple but wide collar. Brown jacket, leather with cotton at edges of sleeves and thinly lining the interior. *Standard issue clothes that won't stick out in West Berlin or in the East. Smart.*

"Tick-tock, Herr Fredericks. We must go—you have a job to do. Unless you've changed your mind, of course. You could stay for lunch... and dinner."

"No. Almost ready." He pulled the shirt over his arms and buttoned it in front. He replaced his American jeans with the slacks —*I guess I was an enemy just for wearing these things.* He dropped the jeans on the wooden-plank bed. "Okay."

With quiet efficiency, the door swung outward the rest of the way. *Get me out of here,* he thought as nearly scrambled into the hallway.

"Apologies for the precautions yesterday," Ernst said. "No blindfold this time. We trust you."

Weird, Max thought. *Weird and suspicious.*

Stepping into the wide-by-comparison hallway made plain his cell's cramped size. He gave another look—*hopefully my last look*—at the beige room where he'd slept. *It's different looking at it when they close you inside.* This hadn't been like the tour he'd taken—would take—in 2021.

The man calling himself Sam stood in the hall with Ernst, and he greeted Max with a curt nod. A guard in a grey uniform was already departing down the dimly lit corridor of House 15. His keys jangled as he disappeared around the corner.

Since Max left the MfS lobby yesterday, that guard had been the third person Max had seen. *Where is everyone? Doesn't anyone else work here? And what about the other prisoners?*

At this moment, he recalled from his visit to Hohenschön-hausen Prison Memorial that, when one prisoner is on the hall, no other suspect or prisoner is permitted to move—no eye contact, no human contact of any sort, for that matter, for the prisoners whom the Stasi sought to dominate. Max caught sight of the red light, now illuminated, over the hallway gate, indicating to the staff that no other prisoner was to be moved while prisoner number 75 was in motion.

Max followed Ernst and Sam past the other cells—dozens of them—and up the stairs, perhaps retracing his blindfolded steps from the night before. *So many cells. The other rooms—they could be totally empty or 100% occupied. Who knows how many people they have in here right now and what those people supposedly did to hurt the so-called workers' state.* He scoffed under his breath.

As Max followed Ernst, with Sam following closely behind, he focused on the timeline he'd memorized. Their march was silent, apart from the three's footfalls. They walked first dead-ahead through two buildings' basements and then to the left along a city-block-long passageway, and again to the left—*This isn't how they brought me—* this time neatly following the map he remembered from the 2021 exhibition of MfS headquarters. They were leaving the counter-espi-onage section, and the men were leading him back into the heart of

Stasi operations in the DDR and the site of the prior night's investigations: House 1.

Ernst, the operations officer, spoke again as they reached what the windows in the stairwell told him must have been the ground floor: "Are you prepared for your briefing, Max?"

He looked at his watch. 5:59. *Impressive.* "Ready," he replied.

Fueled by adrenaline and other neurotransmitters preparing his body to fight, freeze, or flee, Max was wide awake now. There was no flight path available to him, and so he would fight, in a way. His handlers must have noticed the growing strength in his eyes. Hopefully he wouldn't freeze.

Why didn't they blindfold me this time? Max couldn't help but to wonder again as he climbed the stairs to the central corridors of East German power. *Is that a good sign or a bad one? What's about to happen? They wouldn't be talking about briefing me if they were going to throw me into a van and take me to a work camp or a prison, right?* Sure, they'd so far continued talking this morning as though presuming a final briefing, but Max can't be faulted for doubting them.

The main corridor, he thought, as they entered a place he recognized the lobby. They took the elevator again, packed this time quite tightly with three rather than two people inside—to the third level above the ground floor. *Glad we're not headed to 206. Not so glad we are going to the administrative level.* The higher levels of the central building of the MfS were reserved for more important officers and their staffs.

Max stood at attention and kept his eyes facing front as they arrived at the third floor, and so he was able to take in the full shock of seeing the shoes, and then the torso, and then the face of a man no one in the West apart from Max could have positively identified in 1965.

Markus Wolf, "the man without a face," Deputy to the Minister for State Security, met them stiffly. He boasted a double-chin and a wide nose. He wore his brown hair parted and combed neatly to the left, covering that side of a slight widow's-peak, and his wasn't quite a military cut, despite his status at MfS. His sideburns reached down to his earlobes. The lines in the deputy's face that were a product of his already-given years of service presented a circle around his wide mouth, accentuated by a small mole below his left eye. Wolf wore a knit-fabric suit, dark-beige in color, and a wide, striped tie knotted tightly at the neck. The intelligence in his eyes couldn't be denied and the eyebrows above were thin and neat. Everything about him communicated control. However, the man had a soft countenance, all considered—markedly kindlier than the men calling themselves Sam or Ernst, anyhow.

This is B.S., though. This man is monstrous. Max saw through the facade.

As the trio opened the accordion door of the lift, Wolf waited patiently, half-smiling and half-grimacing, with hands crossed calmly in front of his trim belly. He greeted his subordinates with a slight nod and Max with a handshake and a slightly less-reserved smile: "I am Herr Markus Wolf, Deputy to the Minister for State Security. I'm glad you're here, Maximilian. I understand that you're here to help—to help us and your friend. We're here to help you."

"Well, sir, I don't really know her, but that's why I'm here."

"We can manage if you can manage, comrade," Wolf replied congenially.

"Thank you," Max replied.

"Sam and Ernst have briefed you thoroughly, I imagine. One last review. I wanted to thank you personally for your service. Viel Gluck." He turned smartly and left Max with his agents-in-charge.

*Are they going to kill me now that I've gotten a good look at him? No one is going to know what he looks like in the West for years... It does help that someone more important than these two handlers—*thinking of Sam and Ernst—*knows the deal and approved it.*

He allowed himself to feel optimistic. With handshake agreement in hand, Max's mind was put somewhat more at ease. The other two men appeared to be middle-management and operative types, respectively. But Wolf was not just one among many deputies. He was deputy to *the* minister—Erich Mielke, the dreaded and, it would turn out, permanent director of the Stasi. The deputy's word meant more to Max that of the underlings. Perhaps it shouldn't have.

He checked the time again: 6:05. He didn't need a briefing to remind him that he was supposed to be leaving in ten minutes' time.

This time, Sam led the way. Max and Ernst followed. Sam entered a conference room at the southern end of the hallway. A large emblem of the DDR hung on the wall behind the center point of a long, massive, wooden table. A map and several photographs of key places were spread on the table.

The one calling himself Sam slid from one end of the meeting table a posh-looking, fabric-covered chair, indicating that Max should sit there.

Max sat.

Sam sat across from him, and Ernst remained standing near the head of the table. "We leave in nine minutes," Ernst began. "Now, listen closely."

We?

The briefing included a more detailed runthrough of the order-of-action for the intelligence operation code-named "Canary" than they'd provided him the prior night.

To the timeline, Ernst added the Ministry's border clearance details. He'd receive the necessary documents and an explanation for how to use them before Max and Ernst would arrive together at the East German side of Glienicke. The change in plans was confirmed.

Max didn't question it. What could he say? What would he ask, exactly, what wouldn't insert new doubts or confirm old ones? The more he said, the worse things would get.

Sam reiterated that any failure to meet the specific demands of the mission, whatever its complications along the way, would constitute a breach in Max's agreement with the Stasi. Max would be held responsible for any variances or failures during the mission, he explained. Of course, the Ministry would be responsible for any of its successes. Max would be rewarded as promised if he accomplished their goals.

Sam and Ernst issued more warnings, but Max's mind drifted. He was thinking instead about Elsa. He remembered what she looked like: brown hair, beyond shoulder length. Prominent eyes, also brown. Taller than Max. Sophisticated, despite her East German clothing. The skirt was a sign of protest, probably. *The little things matter here.*

When Sam rose from his seat, Max stood as well, not really hearing Sam's words. Ernst had remained standing throughout the quick discussion that had mirrored the printout from the day before. He pointed to photos as he and Sam went through the mission phases: drop-off at Glienicke, dead drop in the Tierpark, walk to Checkpoint Charlie, report to the Ministry for State Security after pickup at that location. *Maybe not as easy as it seems simple,* Max observed presciently.

Conversation paused for the slow elevator ride back to the ground floor. The man calling himself Sam left them at the lobby door, saying to Max, "See you when you've finished. Don't forget what's at stake." He had turned after that and headed for a ground-floor hallway without so much as another glance back at his newest and youngest communist operative.

TWENTY-THREE

THE BRIDGE OF SPIES

The Volga must've been too conspicuous for the mission, so Max and Ernst rode to the Glienicke Bridge in a Trabant P50.

A Trabi!

The ride turned out to be less than stellar. Max's feet threatened to crash through the floor. And until he got used to the feeling of the ill-padded seat and hard edges around him, he grimaced at every bump. Without any seatbelts in the back, he hoped the driver knew what he was doing—and, given that there was no fuel gauge, that he'd fueled up before leaving the Ministry.

The driver, a plainclothes man with greying hair despite his obviously young age, must already have been informed of the route's particulars—or perhaps he'd driven it before? The drive took every bit of the forty-five minutes allotted and not one moment more. Few cars were on the roads.

Ernst asked Max to review the plan by recounting it aloud.

Max did so without hesitation or error. *I got the idea, anyhow. We'll see what happens when the plan meets battlefield conditions.*

The Trabant bumped and rattled as late-50s Soviet vehicle tech met 1920s road construction, and it skirted the Wall and circled around the free island of West Berlin. They tracked it from eastern to western edges along its southern border, going from city neighborhood to country lane. They passed Schönefeld airport, driving right under a silver, two-propeller airplane. Max could just make out the East German flag on its tail and the letters "I-N-T-E-R..." in block lettering painted onto its fuselage.

The plainclothes driver was silent for the ride's duration, and Ernst left Max to his thoughts after they'd recapitulated the operation, giving Max plenty of time to ruminate.

He kept a shudder to himself as they passed one after another of the more than three hundred guard towers. He couldn't yet see into West Berlin.

That's how they want it. No one can see what's happening there, or people might be corrupted with poisonous ideas. That's the home of the imperialist fascists that are so threatening to the workers' and peasants' way of life, according to the DDR.

Before this trip back to Germany, he'd wondered how the Stasi and other arms of the government in East Germany had been so successful keeping hold of the thoughts and actions of easterners, but he was beginning to see how it was possible: every state action and every design was aimed at what they called "stability" and "security."

Keep the people frightened. Make sure they don't trust one another —even in their own families. Crush all opposition immediately—even in thought, like with Big Brother in that Orwell story.

His thinking never really brightened during the ride, and he lost awareness of the route—city streets with tenements blended gradually into hovels and thinly arranged buildings. They left the Wall behind for a time, too—out of sight, but not out of mind. *Just like it is for the people who live here.*

"Anti-Fascist defense barrier," Max thought with sardonic distaste as he spotted the Wall again on approach to the Glienicke bridge. The Wall itself terrified Max, and he was glad that at least for now the Stasi, who controlled it, were going to let him through. *Unless they're not,* he couldn't help but to think. *Maybe they'll wait*

for me to start across and then shoot me. The Western border guards won't be able to interfere. I'll fall and lie there, dying. He put the image out of his head as the car slowed on the East German side approximately one hundred paces west of the DDR control fencing and out of direct eyesight of West German border watchers.

Ernst shifted in his seat, looking at Max directly for the first time since departing the Ministry. He removed three documents from a jacket pocket and handed them to Max. He explained each in turn.

The first was a slip of folded paper embossed with the mark of the Minister for State Security that was to be Max's pass to depart the east without interference.

Second was an expulsion paper indicating that Max had no paperwork but was clearly a U.S. citizen who had no business in the DDR, which would be his passport to the West.

And the third—ha!—a tourist map of the western sectors of Berlin. Max put the map safely in a rear pocket and held the other two papers tightly in his hand, terrified of losing them.

He immediately realized he had more questions. *More questions I should've asked but didn't. At least they seem to want to protect their asset for now.*

Ernst had one final warning couched as advice. "When you get over there, remember Max: these people are not your friends, and they not only don't want to help you, but they couldn't do so if they were to try. They will lie to convince you to serve their greedy aims. Do not trust anyone. At least, not before you're safely back in Ministry custody."

Hmm. Ironic. Max nodded. "This is it," he remarked aloud. "See you at 10:05."

The man didn't respond, instead turning to face front. He was done with Max, for now.

Max slid across the bench seat and climbed out onto the grey-brick road. Driver and passenger alike kept eyes forward, and the Trabi kicked up leaves in its wake on the desolate road as it kicked into gear. The deadly silence following the car's disappearance was not one of calm but was instead pregnant with foreboding. This was the silence of death and decay rather than of peace.

Max checked his watch. 7:01. He turned to face the bridge crossing the strait between Glienicke Lake and Jungfernsee ("the Maiden Lake"). The border installation itself stopped him dead in his tracks.

Concrete pillars about two feet by three feet and twelve feet long had been laid on their sides in an interlocking pattern so as to prevent unwanted vehicular traffic. *No one crosses this way anymore except for Stasi-approved foot traffic.* Diagonal red stripes painted near where he was about to cross commanded him not to do so.

He looked to the right and left as he approached the bridge's disused road across. Large concrete guard houses—big enough to contain bunks and all other necessaries for extended shifts—flanked the bridge stanchions marking the entrance to the crossing. Towers were built into these buildings. Glass windows gave guards on the top of each tower a vantage point protected from the elements, and steel balconies provided a place for marksmen to stand prepared to shoot anyone attempting a crossing.

Metal traffic-control arms blocked two lanes astride a narrow, one-man police box situated at the center of the road between the two bunk houses and towers. A soldier at this box was keeping a vigilant watch not toward the border with the West but rather toward the DDR's interior. *A lot more concerned with enemies within than from the outside, despite what they tell the citizens.*

Max held out the paper with the Secretary's mark.

This guard in particular saw the paper but then seemed to look right through him, giving no acknowledgement besides not shooting him or screaming at him to stop right there. Two more guards stood somewhat casually on the balconies of the guard towers. All three seemed intent on not noticing the Stasi car or the passenger who'd just been let out at the closed border crossing they were detailed to protect.

It was 7:02am, and Max approached the DDR guard at the

police box, walking with purpose toward Glienicker Brücke over the river Havel. Still an hour from sunrise, there was no light to glow meaningfully on the horizon or to illuminate the divided city. In 1965, in the DDR, there was not a lot to be hopeful about. Back in the USA, people anticipated the end of days from nuclear apocalypse. Here in Berlin, the world had already cracked apart.

TWENTY-FOUR

CONTACT

The East German guards continued ignoring Max, who handed to the guy in the box what might have counted as the Cold War version of a hall pass. The man wore a characteristically gray military coat and a DDR-insignia-bearing fur hat that looked positively comfortable, and he carried what Max knew from the movies to be a Kalashnikov automatic rifle—an "AK-47," in pop terminology. The young guard looked quickly at the paper and made a telephone call from inside the box. After mere seconds, he waved Max into the zone between the two halves of the city and continued ignoring him.

Max, who wasn't about to stand around wasting time on ceremony, marched forward and didn't look behind him.

As he crossed the trussed arches of the windy and silent center portion of the bridge, Max began to wonder at the contexts for his two crossings: to the West from the East and to the East from the West. *Why would the Stasi want me to cross at a spot and time with no possible public notice or fanfare in the morning but then cross at a well-known place at midday?*

He was caught amid these thoughts and snapped back into heightened concern when two of the West German guards on the far side of the Glienicke trained their weapons on him while a third seemed to be examining him from afar as he closed his distance to the American sector.

One foot and then the other, he told himself, trying to settle an onset of nerves. *It's not illegal to cross into the West. Remember: they want to pretend that Germany is one country. I could reasonably be a refugee... one who the East Germans didn't shoot for some reason. A Stasi saboteur would worry them. But they let me cross without trouble out of the East...*

"Hello, I'm an American!" he called as he got within what he judged to be reasonable range. The men with guns lowered their arms slightly but were surely ready to change tack if he made any wrong moves.

"Hands up!" came the response from a stiff, American-accented. He heard a curse word in a that same voice as though the man were saying, "An American? Only East Germans come from there."

Max hastily complied, holding the second document he'd received in his right hand between thumb and fingers. He kept a good grip on this lifeline. It would do him no good if it blew into the icy Havel below. "They kicked me out!" he shouted.

As Max made steady but slower progress toward the guard—in West German garb—the American voice came through again, calling, barely loud enough to be heard. It came from around the corner of the guard post: "Hand your paperwork to the guard on the left."

Max spotted him, clean shaven and serious, and halted several feet from the armed soldiers. He did as instructed using obvious and careful movements.

The German called "Alles klar!"—"All clear!"—after a cursory look at the expulsion notice.

The American, dressed in a smart dark suit with a black tie, emerged from what had served as a hiding place—from behind the squat, yellow-brick building. He stepped toward Max and the guards slowly but with firm footsteps that spoke volumes of his authority. The guard handed this man Max's paperwork.

He looked a little closer at Max's pleading expression and didn't even glance at the paperwork. "You can put your hands down, kid," the American in the suit said. "The border here isn't closed to entrance—we only keep guards here to shoot back if they shoot at anyone on this side." He gestured across the bridge to the DDR guards.

Max lowered his hands, still careful not to make sudden movements. He also looked back at the East German border guards who were facing their own territory again.

"Hang on a second," he said, and he walked back into the low building on the north side of the border-crossing road.

Max waited for what felt like hours but was more likely fifty or sixty seconds. The clouds broke overhead, though the sky was still dark. Not even the Moon was visible at this time of year.

A second American—a man in American military garb—exited the building. Pulling down his cap over his face, he strode toward Max—on a mission of his own. He was bearded—unusual, Max thought, for the American armed forces back in the 60s.

Maybe he works for the man in the suit?

The suit-wearing man did not reappear.

He held onto but did not hand over the paperwork and said with unmasked suspicion in his voice, "I'm not sure who your friends are, but someone up top is glad you're back. You will be debriefed by our people in the near future about what you've seen and done in the Soviet Sector"—*isn't it part of a country now and not some Soviet zone?*—"and you must check in at the U.S. Mission in Berlin for a briefing and to reacquire a passport and proper documentation." He paused, seeming only to remember at this moment, "So, yes. I'm not sure who your friends are, kid, but there's a car waiting for you. He's one of ours. He'll take you the rest of the way."

One of "ours?" Whose? Be confident. Be okay. Be calm. He didn't quite believe his own coaching. "Thanks," he said.

This exchange was positively confounding to Max, who hadn't anticipated the Americans or the West German guards knowing anything about his arrival. Sure, he'd known there'd be a car awaiting his arrival in the West, but it was supposed to be a Stasi contact. *I guess they'd have to know there was something odd to this crossing. But "one of ours"... I thought the contact would just be a civilian or some other agent for the East. Or at least someone friendly to the East... and why is he still calling it "the Soviet Sector"?*

His thoughts disappeared as he realized he'd been standing there for fifteen seconds in silence with the American soldier facing him, staring inquisitively at Max's response. He looked beyond the serious-faced man to the car that Max only now noticed was idling twenty steps further into West Berlin territory. He nodded to the man and he set off in that direction.

The car was an old Fiat—a two-seater that would have passed for a sports car if it weren't so beat up.

The man at in the driver's seat of the little car did not leave adjust even to remove his hands from the wheel as Max crossed through the headlights. He must have struggled to see through its windows, frosted as they were from the cold. He kept his eyes straight ahead as Max climbed in the Fiat's passenger seat. Only then did the driver acknowledge Max's presence, turning in his seat to face the boy in his cab. Max recognized him instantly. The Brown Jacket Man said, simply, "You haven't been completely honest with me, Max." He put the car in gear and started down the cobblestone street.

"I told you who I am." Even as he uttered the words, Max knew he'd been caught in one of those spur-of-the-moment inventions he'd offered the morning before. True, he hadn't lied about his name—he hadn't given it—but everything he'd said had been complete fiction.

"No," the man said. His declaration was straightforward and without a hint of anger, but he said it like parents say, "I'm not mad—I'm disappointed."

"You have not been honest with me," he continued. "You didn't tell me your name, Max,"—*he knows my name*—"but you also claimed to be a diplomat's son. And you claimed to be a loyal American, besides. Now I learn you're working for the Stasi?" He tsked. "Shame."

"I told you I was going to help the girl they took off the street," Max was terse. "I even told you how I'd go about it, and I did what I said. "Who are you working for?" Max thought but didn't say. Instead, he asked, "What are you doing here?"

The man ignored the question: "My contact told me your name is Max Fredericks and you're actively working for the East Germans. Now is the time to tell me who you really are." His voice softened somewhat, "Things will go much better for you if you tell me everything."

Max thought hard. *I can't tell him "everything," I know that. But what can I tell him?*

The Brown Jacket Man drove on.

Where is he taking me? Is he working for the Stasi or the West? I have to know—at least what's going to happen next. If this guy takes me to the U.S. Mission, the mission is done for, and so is Elsa... Truth is, Max had begun thinking he needed to accomplish what he'd set out to accomplish to be able to get back home.

The man grew impatient: "Are you going to tell me what's going on, or what? I'm trying to help you, kid."

Max was by no means prepared for an interrogation by the Brown-Jacket Man, but the men calling themselves Sam and Ernst had briefed him about what to say to any West German or American agent who should happen to give him trouble. *How can I give something without giving everything?*

"Okay, so I wasn't honest. My dad isn't a diplomat." He waited for a response but received none. "I told the Stasi my father is a military attaché—newly appointed."

"That's a bit better, I might suggest, than the nonsense you gave me the other day," the man advised, and he narrowed his eyes slightly. "But it's also a lie."

"Yes. That's what I told the Stasi. The truth is that he's a nobody."

"What were you doing in East Berlin?

"Wandering."

"No one simply 'wanders' through the Eastern bit of Berlin."

"Well I was."

"How'd you get across the border? They don't let just anybody in for any purpose."

"I crossed with my father. As tourists."

"They let you through?"

"Well I was there, wasn't I?" Max actually had little idea of how a visit to East Berlin would have gone for a tourist—he just assumed it would have been possible, if the proper paperwork were filed and visas acquired. *They'd probably let us in, but we'd have to check in with the Stasi and would probably be under surveillance the whole visit.*

"Well, why wasn't he with you?"

"He decided he'd have a drink. And then he had three. I didn't want to watch him. That's the truth." Max did his best to appear disconsolate. "He's probably still there, too. He won't miss me."

"Someone will. What of your mother?"

"She's dead." *That'll stop his questions*, Max guessed wrongly.

"How'd she die?"

Things were turning distinctly worse for Max. Things were getting more and more difficult to track. *Keep it simple. Stop complicating the story.*

"Childbirth," he offered falteringly.

"Okay, Max. So you say your father's a drunk and your mother died in childbirth. Those are more interesting lies than the ones you told me yesterday, but they're still lies." He paused. "You have one last chance. We are nearing the Mission."

What is he going to buy, if not what I already told him? He's a spy, so maybe...

"Look," he began. He took a measured breath as if steeling himself to reveal the *real* truth. "My father is a communist." He held his breath in wait. *If this doesn't work, I'm cooked.*

The intended effect achieved: this was a startling revelation. The man pulled the car over to the side of the road between two cars dripping in melted frost. Neither Max nor the Brown-Jacket Man noticed the vehicle a block behind them slip into a spot to mirror theirs.

The man turned his head, looking Max squarely in the eye. This was it—a lie befitting the era. He was stupefied. "A communist?"

"Yes. He's a member of the party back in Salt Lake City. You know how those Mormons are."

"Actually, I don't."

"They're all about community, working for the good of the hive—you know, the state symbol is a beehive. It symbolizes collective work. There are a lot of communists there, though they'd deny it."

"Huh. Learn something new every day, I suppose." The Brown Jacket Man was thoughtful for a moment.

"Anyhow, he's an advisor in a manufacturing plant back in Utah. New plastics. The DDR promised him a good life here if he'd advise them about their facilities. The Russians don't care if the East Germans are happy. They still want to punish them for the war."

The man nodded.

Sprinkle in some truth, Max thought.

He continued: "They don't want the country to fall apart and show how weak their whole system is, but maximizing productivity is not exactly their forte, you know? They make a lot of plans, and then they lie about the results when production is lower than expected. It's the same for manufactured goods as it is for food. So the East German government brought in my dad to look at things. Maybe they'll make plastics in their factories. 'Plastics for the people' is his motto."

Now it was the Brown Jacket Man nodding.

"He might actually stay, but I really hope he doesn't because him staying means me staying. This place is terrible. It's no way to live. Constant surveillance from the Stasi and all..." *Pretty, pretty, pretty good.*

"And your mother?"

"Divorced." He tried to look sheepish about having lied before, like now he's an open book. "You know communists don't care much about holy matrimony, but it's a bad look for the family unit, so Dad thinks he might marry an East German woman if we move here."

The Brown-Jacket Man checked his mirrors, not responding directly to Max's new pack of lies. "I've been instructed to take you to the Zoologischer Garten if you told me the truth."

Instructed by whom? Max had to wonder. *Are these Western or Eastern handlers who directed him to drop me there? If it's the West, maybe they want me to finish a mission, and he's reported to them. If it's the East, maybe they were testing my lies... And they told me their man was meeting me in a car on the far side of Glienicke Bridge—so this should be him. Is he working for both sides? Who is his actual master, if he is?* A torrent of thoughts raced—a cacophony of worries, some more and some less reasonable, crowded out Max's rational thinking.

The man put the car back in first gear and pulled out of the parking spot. He continued onward through the quiet streets, heading toward the Sun in the East.

"I'm not sure what to make of you, Boy Who Calls Himself Max Fredericks." He looked again in his rear-view mirror. "I can't tell yet for certain if you're being honest. I do know you're being followed, and that's not one of ours"—he nodded at the mirror. "And if you're being honest, you might be an interesting asset for us."

Who is "us," Max wondered again. He also checked the mirrors but didn't see whatever it was that had caught the man's attention. "So," Max drew him out, "I went to the Stasi headquarters."

"You are better informed but stupider than I first thought," the man spat.

Max ignored the insult. "I wanted to do the right thing, and the right thing was using what I know to help that girl. I knew where they might take her—my dad told me all about it to prepare me for my visit to East Berlin." *Is he buying this?* "He knows I like to wander and told me about the Ministry so I'd know what part of town to avoid. So, I went there. I told them I'd trade them information. The story I gave them is that my father is a military attaché—new, so even if they have lists of Americans working in the West, they won't be able to check right away on him."

The Brown-Jacket Man dipped his chin, maybe approving.

Max continued. "And I've gotten this far. They gave me a mission today. I have to complete the operation or the girl is as good as dead. I need to go to the Zoo to prove I can be at a certain place at a certain time. Then I'll cross at Checkpoint Charlie and they'll release Elsa."

The man made a "hmmph" sound.

"After they let us both go—"

Another "hmmph" from the man—

"They'll give us an assignment. Maybe when I get back across with her I could make myself useful to the West? And Elsa. She could work for them—us, I mean—too. She knows the East. She could be a double-agent for the Americans."

"I never said I worked for the Americans."

Max thought for a minute and was going to respond, but they had arrived across the street on the west side of the Zoologischer Garten Berlin—the city zoo.

"We're here," the man said before Max said anything, "and you've got a tail."

Max registered this and then continued. "Look, I have it all worked out. She and I cross tonight. We'll make our way to the Mission, if you don't find me before then. Keep an eye on the Wall near Bernauer Strasse—that's where..." Max trailed off. *No one in my shoes should know anything about the tunnels. I already probably messed up about knowing where the Stasi HQ is—I'm really just piling on the unbelievable stuff.*

"How are you going to cross?"

"I'll find a way."

"You'll find a way to get yourself killed."

"No. You can help us. A contact, maybe." He checked his watch. 7:40. *Fifteen minutes til I'm due at the Animal Park—they expect me to have to lose a tail, too. 9:15 is far away—I can make something out of this—turn it to my advantage.*

"No," the man said. "You're talking too much. I can't help you any more than what I've already told you—and I got you here. Get out of the car. Go complete your mission for the Stasi, Max—or whatever your name is."

"No." *If I'm going to get help out of this guy, it's now or never. Whomever he works for... he was in the East yesterday, and the American at Glienicke told me he was one of theirs. He's gotta have contacts on both sides of the Wall.* "By the end of today, the Stasi will trust me at least enough to give me an assignment with Elsa. That's the plan. It's worked so far. Whoever you really are, you can help us. I need a contact in East Berlin."

The Brown-Jacket Man contemplated, chewing his lip.

He has people there. I have to get him to a place where he's willing to help.

"I know some people, boy. But if I do this for you, you'll need to help me with something. A quid pro quo. You know what that is?"

"I know. What do you want me to do?" *I can't take pictures. I can't wear a recording device. I can't even carry a message the Stasi themselves don't give me.* "I can't wear anything. I can't carry anything other than this compass and the papers they gave me"—he patted his pocket. "They'll search me the second I'm back in their hands." *How many different espionage missions am I going to be working on at the same time? There's my mission to help Elsa, the one for the Stasi... this will be the third I'm getting roped into.*

"You don't need to wear anything. No camera—nothing. It is only a verbal message."

"To whom?"

"Erich Mielke."

"Uh... You want me to deliver a message to the head of the Stasi for you?"

"Yes."

Max raised his eyebrows.

"Well, not directly, as I'm sure you won't come across him. And it won't do you or me any good to deliver the message personally. It's more of a symbolic act, actually, then a verbal message."

"You said it was a verbal message. Stop talking in circles. Hurry up and be clear. Tell me what you want me to do, and I'll tell you if I can do it. I only have 'til 10:05 to get to Checkpoint Charlie, and I have to get into the zoo to pick something up. So cut the crap." Max spoke quickly, words pouring out in an annoyed tirade. "And if I really do have someone following me, watching us, then this is already looking suspicious. Every minute you waste makes it worse for both of us, I'm sure."

"Stop talking, then, and I'll explain," the Brown Jacket Man said.

Max shut up.

The driver continued: "There's a church in the East. Zionskirche. Do you know it?"

"Yes," Max answered.

"If they really do release you today—and if they don't arrange for you to have an accident"—emphasis on the word "accident"—"go there directly. Tell them that 'Michael' sent you. Tell them Michael says to proceed."

"That's it?"

"That's it."

"And you're going to tell me that they'll know what the message means."

"I'm not going to tell you anything about it. Take my lead if you want to stay alive much longer. The people you're trifling with are not going to put up with you if they find out what you're up to." His eyes darted as he scanned from one area of the street to another.

At this time of day—before sunrise, even—very few people were out and about—but in West Berlin, it wasn't quite so desolate as compared with the East, and not so locked down. There were some out for morning walks with babies or with dogs, and a few whose evening festivities were somehow only now wrapping up.

"Before you go, let me offer you some advice, free of charge."

Great, more advice from strangers.

"Stop telling lies you can't back up at least with appearances. Your appearance means more than you think. While your outfit today is better than yesterday's, you will stand out if you wander around looking for secret signs in as obvious a manner I have a feeling you will. You've got to look like you belong, wherever you go."

"Ja, Ja, I know, okay." Without thinking, Max borrowed a phrase from 2021 German.

This earned him a quizzical look and then shake of the head.

Back to the church. I can do this, maybe, if I get Elsa to come with me after they let us go. I'm sure she'll know where it is, anyhow. But what do we get from him? Max was getting used to not knowing the full story about much of anything people said. "And how will you help us in return?"

"You'll have to trust me now. I'll see what I can do, and then you'll see how I will help you."

Trust him, he says. Max weighed things. *I have no idea how we're going to cross. If he can't help, I'm no worse off than I am right now. But if he can, well—that'll be better.* "Alright," he said. "I'll take your message to the people at the church. One last thing—Who are you?"

"Who I am is not important. What I can do for you is the only thing that matters. My help may make the difference between your living and dying—or between escaping the East and being trapped there forever. I've already helped in ways you cannot know." With this, the man nodded toward the door handle.

Max used it and stepped into the street.

The man pulled away in the Fiat with purpose but absent conspicuous hurry. For the second time in two days, Max's encounter with the Brown Jacket Man had ended as abruptly as it had begun.

TWENTY-SIX

DRY CLEANING

Max saw them now.

Two men in an Opel—a brand of car he'd seen in modern Germany. Four cars back, pulled over on the side of the empty road astride the animal park.

Are they following me or the Brown Jacket Man? Max pulled his shirt collar up around his neck, wishing he'd had a proper jacket to bear the brunt of the chilly air. He crossed the street away from the gates where he'd eventually be looking for a marking on the wall.

Get away, he thought as he crossed. *Lose the tail. I expect the Stasi to follow me. If they are, that's fine, seeing how I'm an East German asset. It would not be okay at this point if I'm being followed by the BND or by American Army Intelligence. But how do I know if those guys are Stasi or westerners? Would it matter? I've gotta lose these guys.*

Max rounded a corner onto the next avenue and ducked into a bar called "Cafe Orange". He chose Cafe Orange because—A, it was open—and B, the entrance was down a few steps, set into a building's basement. *Easier to disappear down here.*

He descended four steps to a heavy, stained-glass-inlaid door.

As Max entered the darkened space, and the barkeeper looked up from behind a long and narrow mahogany bar top. Although unsure of what he had expected, Max was surprised at the man's appearance: long hair, for the era—below the ears—and a beard to match.

Weird. Some kind of West German hippie.

The man smiled, at first, and said something in German that Max didn't understand.

I guess I'm not supposed to understand this bit? The whole English-German language barrier in his time travel still didn't make any sense. He used what little German he knew to request a glass of water.

The man grimaced but he complied. He filled a glass with water from the tap, grunted as he set it on the counter, and turned to cleaning something in the back of the bar. He made no effort to hide that he was planning to ignore this non-paying customer, which suited Max just fine.

The rest of the barroom—maybe 50 feet long by 15 feet wide, and with a low, pressed-tin ceiling—was empty. Max chose a booth toward the back and sat against the wall facing the door.

Catch your breath. Think through what happens next. 7:55am. I can hole up here for a while. Maybe I should find an exit out back in case someone saw me come in here and is sitting out front waiting for me.

It was not a complete surprise that the bar didn't remain empty for long. *The more people the better.*

A man wearing a proper hat—the kind Max had seen in old photographs of American cities—entered the bar alone. He also wore a burgundy scarf wrapped around his neck and tucked neatly into a brown, buttoned-up peacoat. Through a gap in the curtain, Max saw him rub his hands together for warmth, say something to the bartender, and receive a beer. The man dropped some coins on the bar.

Beer at 8am. This guy could be my fictional father—he might have a problem... he turned his mind away from the man to figure a way of losing a tail if he were to have to leave by way of the front door instead of the back.

The man with the beer bee-lined for Max's booth.

Max busied himself with his hands, scrunching his face in consternation and trying to figure out how to disappear without leaving the booth. *Don't look, don't look.* He was not successful. The intruder sat down with a groan across the table from the boy. There was no finesse in the way the man moved. He presented as a tough man with no time to muck about. Sharp chin, dark eyes, and clean-shaven. He didn't bother to remove his hat.

"What did you say to him, Maximilian?"

German accent. Great. That really narrows it down.

"Who are you?"

"I know who you are. That is enough." The stranger was not in a sharing mood.

"For you, maybe, but I don't know who you're working for. Are you a Stasi agent? Are you BND? Who you are makes a big differ-ence to me."

"Why? Have you not been honest with us?" *So he is Stasi. Maybe? If the Brown Jacket Man was with the West, then it's possible "us" means the West. He could be with either.*

"Us? Tell me who you are, or I'm not going to say another word. I don't owe you anything."

"Max. You have—" the man checked his watch—"two hours six minutes to get to the checkpoint, which is plenty of time. So, you know, there's no harm in sidetracking somewhat first. You might take a brief detour for an interview..." he looked around as though disgusted, "elsewhere."

I'm not going anywhere with this guy. He knows the timing of the mission. That makes him Stasi, right? I should disengage in any case, get on to where I'm supposed to go.

Distracted, Max almost didn't notice the front door open again. Nor did he note a voice telling—not asking—the bartender to take a ten-minute walk. So intent was Max on his own conversation he only barely registered the barkeeper passing the table and scurrying out of the rear door—out into the cold. If Max had been paying attention, he'd have seen that the West German hippie didn't argue for even a second with the demand that he abandon his business.

"What?" Max said. "No. I know my timing. I won't be discussing anything with you. Thank you for the suggestion."

"It wasn't a suggestion, Max."

I'm out of here.

Max slid from the wooden booth to leave the bar. The bartender was gone from view, and a second man in a long coat—no hat—was seated at the last stool. This man had positioned himself between Max and the exit. Max froze, a step away from the booth where he'd been hiding.

The man at the end of the bar spoke with a clear American English accent: "Let's go for a walk, Max." The man did not smile.

TWENTY-SEVEN
THE AMERICANS

Max turned toward the booth he'd left and the narrow hallway in the rear of the bar. The man in the hat stepped out of the booth and blocked Max's egress. He spoke, this time with a calming tenor, encouraging Max to comply: "We only want to know about the girl and your deal with the Stasi, Max. Then you can carry on. They won't find out. Trust us on this—we know how these things work."

Trust us.

So these men work for the BND or the Americans—or both. But how do they know the timing of the mission?

It was crystal clear that Max wasn't going to be permitted to leave on his own terms, and he wasn't about to take on two full-grown men, so he acquiesced. "Okay," he conceded. "Where to?"

The man from Max's table gestured, fingertips down, toward the rear exit: "The courtyard out back. You'll be fine, Max. We want to talk to you. The bartender went that way, and he'll be coming back around to the front again in a moment. Plus, the bar isn't closed. We cannot talk here."

"Fine. Let's go, then."

The man in the hat led the way, and the other followed behind

Max in a scene echoing those from time with Sam and Ernst at Ministry headquarters.

As he stepped into daylight, Max checked his watch. 8:04am.

Taking in the courtyard, he observed the space was quiet and private. All of the windows were shut to the cold, November air. The central yard pulled double-duty, divided in half, as a concrete parking lot and gardening area. In between ran a narrow driveway of cobblestones from an underpass that opened up to the avenue in front of the building that now surrounded them. On the edge of the community garden was a wooden bench. On the bench sat a woman. She watched Max with knowing and curious intensity.

She spoke: "I hope Jake and Henrick there didn't spook you too much. It's tough to avoid, seeing as that's what they are called sometimes, and for some reason or another, it suits them. Spooks. You know the term?"

"C.I.A.?"

"Yeah. That's what people call them sometimes. Of course," she continued, "I can't confirm that we work with the Agency—I'm just repeating what some other people say. Come," she invited him with a wave, "have a seat here. You're in no danger with us. I'm here to talk. That's all."

Seeing no real alternative while Jake and Henrick flanked him, Max walked to the center of the courtyard. The four-story walls enclosing the space blocked most of the morning's light. He did his best to exude calm self-control. He sat, keeping a forward lean in his posture so that he could at least attempt to escape by running if he decided he had to try.

"You can call me 'Judy,' the woman said as Max posted himself on the edge of the bench.

Keep an eye on your surroundings, Max. "Okay, Judy. Well, you know me already. I'm Max Fredericks."

Judy nodded. She had trustworthy eyes—hazel, like Max's own— and curly hair pulled back and tied back in a way that struck Max as not fitting the rest of her approach, which was definitively stern. She wore a light-blue blouse and a brown corduroy skirt.

Max didn't have time to take in any other details, as the woman wasted no time in getting to the point: "I understand that you're to complete some task or another for the Stasi—it doesn't really matter what—and then return to Checkpoint Charlie for crossing at 10:05. I know that you were picked up from Glienicke bridge by a man in a brown jacket, and I know that it wasn't the first time you've seen that man, either."

Is she guessing about me seeing the Brown Jacket Man yesterday, or does she know?

"We need your help in completing the picture we already have. If you haven't already abandoned your country—you're obviously an American—then you can do some good here. Quite a lot, actually, if you get one of our assets out of East Germany today."

Maybe this asset works for the CIA. From what the woman said, there was no telling. Max made an effort to clear his mind. He'd pretend. *The best lies are the ones I believe, so I need to will this to be true. I don't know anything. I can't offer anything.*

He also tried his best to work out how much she knew. *What she's said so far could have come from the Brown Jacket Man, but it could be some other source...*

"Max?" Her impatience showed. "Just like you, we don't have all day. I need you to fill in some gaps. You can assume that you won't be able to complete your task here in West Berlin without being monitored—but we'll keep a distance sufficient to stop the Stasi from knowing we're watching. Likewise, we won't interfere with your mission. We just want some basic information."

Something about the woman's approach rendered Max more pliant than he had been with Sam, Ernst, the Brown Jacket Man, or the two characters who had stopped him in the bar and were now watching from the southern exit of the courtyard. *Maybe there's something I can tell them that will get a friendly reaction—something that will get me some information I can use as well.* "What is it that you want to know, exactly?" he asked.

"Well, I'll tell you what we don't need, first. We don't need any operational details. We have those already, thanks to our source. What I want to know is whom you saw or to whom you've spoken. And we want to know where you came from."

What difference could it make if I say who I saw at the Ministry? Or where I've come from? I can just tell them about some stuff that's probably true about Utah and get these people off my back. So, Max told her, keeping the lie about his father and the plastics job opportunity.

"I crossed with my Dad yesterday morning and was sorta wandering East Berlin while he had an interview. I saw someone get kidnapped and wanted to help her. I went to the Ministry for State Security headquarters—"

Judy's eyes widened.

—"and told them that I'd help them in exchange for releasing that person. They told me to come to the West to pick up some kind of intelligence from a contact here. A physical object—a half-dollar. I need to pick it up soon—" he looked at his watch. "Then I cross back at Checkpoint Charlie at 10:05."

"We already know all this, Max. You're leaving out what I'm asking you for. You may not know this, but offering details I haven't asked for makes it tough to believe much of anything you say. It sounds as though you've thought through these particular answers before I asked the question, which is something people do when they're lying. I'll say again: to whom did you speak during your night at MfS?"

"Okay. Sorry." *If she thinks I'm lying, I'll get nothing out of her to help.* "I talked to some guy who called himself Sam—probably a fake name—and someone working with him. The second guy was an operations officer named Ernst. Oh, and Markus Wolf."

"Wolf?! You spoke to the second in command of the Stasi?" The tone she'd used here was the one people use when they're incredulous and they want you to know that they're incredulous.

"Well, we didn't talk long. He stopped me in the hallway and wished me luck."

"He wished you... luck?" Judy puttered, aghast.

"Yeah. I mean, he was okay to me. I know he is not a good guy. He probably was just trying to get me to trust him. There's a lot of that going around..." Max broke off.

"What did he look like? No one has any photos of him. We know his name from documents, but that's it. No one working for us has been able to provide a detailed description of his actual appearance." Her eyes widened, and slight wrinkles appeared above her eyebrows.

Max thought for a moment, remembering some old cowboy movies he'd seen back home. Some of those had been made in the sixties. An image struck him.

"Do you know who Clint Eastwood is?"

"The actor?" This time, a head tilt communicated some of her confusion.

"Yeah. Think about him, but, like, a bit older. Double-chin, but not a large guy. Balding a bit, but nicely combed over." Judy nodded along.

"Okay," she said. "And that's it? Did you speak to anyone else since your father left you yesterday for his interview?"

He hesitated.

"Max. Who did you speak to?"

"Well, I talked to the guy who picked me up this morning—the Brown Jacket Man."

"Oh right, that's Weissman. We know him already."

"The Brown Jacket Man is Weissman?"

"I mean, you can call him what you want. We know him as 'Weissman.'"

"Okay, so Weissman the Brown Jacket Man. Got it." He began to lean on his right arm to get up from the bench, saying, "Well, if there's nothing else..."

She interrupted him: "Oh! And I almost forgot. There's one more thing."

Always 'one more thing.' He straightened to stand the rest of the way.

Judy rose to stand in front of him and continued, "What do you know about the young woman you're doing all of this to help?"

"Not much, I gotta admit. She was taken by the Stasi off a public street next to the Volkspark yesterday at around 10 am. That's all, really. She seemed... well, she seemed terrified."

"Okay. Well, we are quite concerned about her well-being, so it's important that you are successful with the rest of your mission. If they don't let her go, she could be a risk to us. You'll be doing us a favor if you do get her out, and I want you to know that your country will be grateful."

"Wait, you know who she is?"

"Yes. We can't tell you why, or that would make you almost as dangerous to us as she is, and it already seems like you know too much for a kid your age—you know who Markus Wolf is, for one thing. Quite frankly, that's bizarre. It's inexplicable. But we'll get to that in your after-action briefing."

She's right. I messed up going on about Wolf. There is no explaining away that knowledge. I could just play it like I didn't know him before he introduced himself... it's too late for that, though. Change the subject.

"Can you help me get back to the West?"

Judy answered, "I'm sure they've worked that out at MfS, right?"

"I guess. I mean, they said that I'd get across, but they didn't say how."

"Well, we monitor the border crossings, so I'll be alerted if you're spotted at checkpoints Alpha through Delta. If you come by way of... unofficial means... I'm afraid I can't be much use to you."

I told the Brown Jacket Man—Weissman—I might be looking to find a way near Bernauerstrasse. I'd better quit talking to Judy. Who knows if the CIA wants to help me or will use my location to get rid of a loose end with Elsa...

Time check: 8:21am. *Under an hour to get to the drop, and this is without even knowing which option I'll have to follow.*

"Look, this has been real nice and all—*"It hasn't been"*—but I gotta go. I need to do some things before I walk back to the border crossing."

"Of course. It was pleasant meeting you, Max." She shook his hand. "I hope you make it so that we might talk again soon."

Jeez. Judy, you're a real confidence-booster. He nodded and made his way toward the corridor that would take him to the main street. Turning, he saw Judy sit back down.

"We'll wait for you to clear before we go anywhere, Max. Don't worry. We know how to do this." The two men were already gone, in fact.

Max shrugged and hurried out and turned right onto the sidewalk, away from the bar and toward the Zoologischer Garten Berlin. He thought, *if I hurry, I can get there by 8:30. But...* he stopped.

I should make like I'm losing a tail... wander the neighborhood for fifteen or twenty minutes, maybe. He doubled back past the bar and headed away from the park to do some neighborhood loops.

The Sun had risen in the east while he'd been inside that bar. It glimmered off of windows on taller buildings that counted in '65 as modern and chic anywhere—and downright scandalous in inefficiency to the easterners when compared with anything they had built for the workers.

The morning foot traffic picked up, which helped him to blend into the neighborhood activity somewhat. Unfortunately, it also hid from Max the operative following behind at a hundred paces distance —a late-aged woman in a light-blue formal cap and dress, covered with a shapeless, navy frock, somehow keeping up. She stayed hidden all the way to where she paused across from the park entrance, all the while maintaining an air of an inconspicuous matron out for a morning stroll.

TWENTY-EIGHT

MISSED SIGNALS

8:47am, and Max was crossing the street on a flashing signal back toward the park. *Someone is following me,* he thought and turned as he reached the east side of the crossing. A woman with a brown package sat on a bench at a bus stop directly across from the Zoologischer Garten Berlin. Two young men in business dress were walking along the road on that same side. Another woman, older and less steady on her feet, stood waiting at the crosswalk for the next green "walk" signal. She hugged her navy jacket around her blue outfit with one hand and held her cap on her head to spite the breeze with the other.

Who is the most likely to be following me? He thought, remembering Brady's words... *They all are,* he concluded. *Be safe. Assume they're all observing.*

He turned toward the entrance to the Zoo, examining the wall to the left of the wrought-iron entrance gates for markings. The Brown Jacket Man's words of advice played at the top of his mind, reminding him not to be so damned obvious about the whole thing. *You're waiting for someone. You check your watch. 8:50am. Stand there. Appear to grow impatient. Are they watching?* He glanced across the street. The two men were gone, but the young woman was still on the bench clutching her package, and the older woman was crossing eastward across the boulevard now. Not one of the people nearby appeared to be watching him.

Assume they are watching anyway. Now—now glance back at the wall, turning as though to see if your friend is waiting inside. Max moved as if to lean against the heavy-stone, dark wall, doing his best to look half-frustrated and half-bored. *There! The mark. It's okay. Whoever has something to drop is inside the park.*

With no one in sight to watch turnstile violators, Max slipped in without paying the 1 West Mark fee, ducking under with ease and proceeding into the park. He kept near the left-hand side of a brick-edged, concrete walkway.

The older woman who'd just completed her arduous street-crossing didn't call out his transgression. Max would have recognized her silence as uncharacteristic of the rule-following Berliners—even the raucous bunch in the West. He'd been keeping his eyes front, trying to look like he belonged exactly where he was headed. So he'd missed it.

Max marched past two green benches, counting off a hundred paces, and approached the next bench he saw. He sat and made as though to stretch, reaching above his head and yawning, then reaching down to his feet. As he did this, he scanned the area.

Nothing. There's nothing.

He was early, though. 8:55. *No. I screwed it up. The person dropping the intel is probably still walking around, losing a tail—what I should be doing right now.* At this realization, Max's throat closed somewhat, and his chest tightened. His breath came in shorter gasps, and, though he didn't notice it, he began to sweat. He leapt in a jolt to his feet and looked both ways—back from where he came and eastward further into the zoo. No one.

Maybe I'm too late? What am I missing? He began to walk back toward the zoo's entrance, cursing himself for his rush to get to the drop spot.

The tree. The mark on the tree! He'd forgotten a critical step in the Stasi's procedure. Deciding on a solution quickly, he doubled back toward the bench, passed it, and hung a left at the next intersection— *Get clear as quickly as you can. What if the person with the intel just walked right by that walkway and avoided the drop at the bench because I was sitting there? I would've caused them to miss me.* Anxiety washed over him as he thought of the myriad ways he probably just caused everything to go south.

He did a large circle around the zoo's city block and took an unplanned tour of zoological features—the hippopotamus house between him and the bench meant that he couldn't see anyone at that location, nor could anyone at the drop spot have seen him. *Did my thoughtless cost Elsa her life—or me my life?*

As he came back around, he noticed an older woman loitering near the entrance of the park. It was the woman from across the street. She seemed to spot him at the same time, and she turned and began to walk eastward on the path toward the bench. She was on the other side of a U-shaped bend in the path that crossed the entrance as he turned south and then east to follow her.

She's been watching me.

As he now tailed the woman in the frock coat, about fifty feet removed, and keeping apace. *Pretty lithe for an old lady.*

Two West German-uniformed military men passed him on the sidewalk walking in the opposite direction. He didn't meet their eyes, and they didn't stop him. *I guess the clothes worked. Is it weird that I'm here at the zoo immediately after opening? Shouldn't they ask me for my papers or something? Maybe that's not a thing in West Berlin. No, no it's not.*

You're getting paranoid, Max.

He was glad to put the West Berlin police behind him as he turned a corner at the southwest edge of the walkway. While the same could not have been said in the East, where he was suspected criminal behavior, he was engaged in truly anti-state activities in the West.

9:10am as he passed the bench again, forgetting to look for the mark on the tree once more. *Still early. And I keep getting distracted. I am not that great at this spy thing...* He did another loop, this time to the right—the south—and through the ape house. It was a low building, its rooms each a miniature Coliseum of Rome, complete with archways and open-air spaces, and built from ugly, orange bricks.

He paused to watch a few apes, and the beasts watch him with pensive, thoughtful looks on their human-like faces. *What are you thinking?*

Out and on the other side of the building, he checked his six o'clock and turned east to make his way back to the tree with the signal mark.

Do rotten forebodings of morning cloud cover and frost still count as forebodings when the ill fate is already unfolding? Asking for a friend.

This time, Max did not forget. He looked for the tree with the marking. *Don't miss the tree. Left side.* There were trees everywhere there wasn't a footpath. Big leafy trees camouflaging the exhibits to the north and south of this east-west path. Smaller trees held together in tight groups of planters at the path's center line.

Stay focused. He slowed to a snail's pace, checking his watch again: 9:21am.

There. A mark on a sycamore standing out among walnut trees. *Three marks. Option three. No bench.* Max scoured his brain for memory of the three options. *Option one, bench. Option two, lamppost. Option three means a physical handoff. Slash would mean cancel and go to safe house... but three marks—that's option three.* He kept moving. *Don't telegraph what I'm looking at,* he thought. *Keep moving forward. Find the southernmost exit. Find a map to get me there. Head south. Go go go.*

The zoo was a maze.

9:35 and running out of time. Five minutes to get moving from the drop if I'm going to stay on track. Did I screw up the handoff timing? How will the contact get it to me? He thought of all the brush pass staples he'd read about or seen in documentaries—newspapers, coins, envelopes full of cash... *they said a coin—the handoff will probably be the same. If I can even find the person.*

Max paralleled the external fencing and facing away from the aquarium building that housed a bit of the zoo recently rebuilt from war damage. While he followed the "escape the maze by hugging the edges of a wall and holding to it," he checked his corners with slight tilts of the head, keeping his shoulders forward, as Brady taught him in 2021 Alexanderplatz.

No followers.

He permitted his mind to wander. An image of him and Elsa trying to climb the Wall in the middle of the night crept in. He could almost see the moon overhead, shrouded in billowing white clouds. The pair crept along looking for a place where he expected to find a rope, but there was none. In this scene, he grew more panicked, while Elsa, meanwhile, had a look of growing satisfaction.

Pop! pop! Loud, staccato gunfire bursts brought Max back to the Zoo and to real violence. *Gunfire at the Wall. Do people get used to that? How frequent is it, really?*

Where is this handoff supposed to happen? The rifle shots added to his anxiety, and he began to panic in reality, just like in his fantasy. *I'm not going to make it. I will never find my way.*

TWENTY-NINE
OUT OF TIME

I know. A map. Max quickened his pace and shook off the distractions. He found a park map in less than a minute.

The southern exit is behind me. Through the aquarium. Max hurried as he snaked his way through paths. He almost skipped past defunct fountains, over slight hills leading to narrow and shallow waterways, a tiger pit without tigers, and other winterized zoo attractions.

Tourists had begun to filter through the grounds. He passed people walking with friends or taking their children out for walks in large-wheeled carriages. They might have been following morning routines. They might have been people assigned to those spots to keep an eye on him. There was no way of telling the difference.

The leaves in the trees surrounding the pathway had all fallen in the autumn, but naked branches creaked, jostled for position, and contributed their soundtrack to his solitary walk.

Hurry. Which way am I facing? Where am I going? I have to get west! He had lost all sense of direction when a voice came from behind.

"You seem lost, comrade." The voice had a distinctly Russian accent.

Max spun to face the voice out of defensive instinct, despite his head screaming at him not to turn.

The man seated there closed a book he'd been pretending to read and smiled jovially. He wore a whitish-beige collared shirt without a tie and leaned casually, placing one thick arm over the back of the bench. "Don't worry, friend. I believe you're looking for the next path down." He tipped his cap and gestured in the direction Max had been heading. The man then went back to his book and ignored Max as though he hadn't just spoken to him directly.

Max took off. He halted his jog at the broad avenue running north-to-south through the zoo as he cleared the forested, narrower path, nervous to leave behind its partial cover. He turned south. A few men in suits seemed to be hanging around the southern edge of the Tiergarten as he finally—*finally!*—approached the aquarium. In a moment, he was through to the southern exit.

Where am I supposed to meet this person? He searched his memory once more, trying to picture sitting with Ernst, walking through the operation. *"Southernmost edge of the park, nearest the exit,"* he had said. A sinking feeling overtook Max. *Oh, no. I screwed this up again.* He had left the park—he wasn't "near the southern edge"—he was beyond it! Frantic, now, he turned toward the exit, which was also an entrance, and he contemplated vaulting the turnstile to break back into the zoo. *More people now. I have to do this. I have to do this.*

He was psyching himself up for it, hoping against reasonable hope that he would be even luckier now than he had been at the western entrance when he ducked into the park without paying. He waited for a break in pedestrians crossing the street—when it seemed that no one was watching him directly. *If I time it right, they'll notice, sure, but I'll be inside and can get out of sight before I'm identified.* He took a step toward the pinwheel gate.

As he did this, the very same older woman he had seen and

followed briefly earlier exited the park through the gate through which he was about to launch himself. He stopped short. *What the...* he was flabbergasted. *Is this the end of my mission, or...?*

She gave him a direct look, silently speaking volumes: "Stay there and do not move," the stare said.

I'll stay here. I won't move. As he followed her unspoken commands. the woman approached as though passing by without thought and seemed to trip over a crack in the sidewalk.

Instinctively, he reached out and grabbed her arm to steady her. "Are you okay?" he asked.

"Why yes, danke," she answered. In another moment, she was gone, crossing the street away from him.

Max's hand was balled up in nervous tension. He opened it slowly, revealing an American half-dollar. *Yes!* Elation plus relief. He tried not to show it and turned immediately to the south, parallel to the Wall running south of the Brandenburg Gate. He set a constant pace on Kurfürstenstrasse, a busy thoroughfare where he hoped he could disappear again.

Somehow, she made that work—not me. That was something.

A briefcase-carrying man passed him on the same side of this street, and Max noticed the man turn and lean as he passed Max. *Probably some kind of camera in that briefcase,* he thought. He was definitely catching onto a few things that would have gone without notice twenty-four hours before.

9:50am. Fifteen more minutes to reach the border checkpoint. He picked up the pace, snaking through crowds coming from the Kaufhaus des Westerns—that glitzy shopping mall west of a small intersection where he turned to the east—at Keithstrasse.

After bumping into several people, Max realized he was going to attract more attention racing through the crowd than keeping the same pace as the flow of foot traffic, and he adjusted accordingly. He stopped to check the date on a newspaper at a small magazine kiosk. November 30th, 1965. *So a day has passed. I wonder what day it is back home?*

A woman in a heavy fur coat stood awkwardly close to him, picked up the same newspaper he was examining, and paid the man in the kiosk in West German Marks. "Such times," she remarked in accented English—half to him and half to no one in particular. "One must be very careful."

A cold feeling threaded through Max, and he turned away, ducked between several passersby, and kept up once more with the crowd. Risking a glance behind him, he saw the woman put the paper down where she stood—*Not a good sign*—and she fell in with the train of pedestrians.

The sky darkened and it began to rain.

9:55am. It has to be over a half an hour to get to the checkpoint from here if I don't hurry. He began to jog once more. *Anyone following will have to be obvious about it. I can't risk not making it— gotta get there. Ten minutes to get there, there's no way...*

As these thoughts pummeled him, each one increasing his anxiety exponentially, a screech on the street beside him jerked away all his attention—along with the notice of every person on that side street.

It was the two-seater Fiat. Weissman, the Brown Jacket Man, waved to Max. Not in so many words, he signaled to the locals, "We're only tourists!" The people on the street got back to whatever they were up to, and Max positively leapt to get into the car. It sped off through the city toward the border crossing.

THIRTY

CHECKPOINT CHARLIE

"What are you doing here?" Max was breathing heavily. He was short of breath from worry and from the surprise of seeing Weismann again.

Instinctively, he reached for a seat belt. *Right. No seat belts in this car, either.*

The man responded: "I'm here to help, Max. I told you this."

"No, actually—that's what I told you I was doing. I have no idea what you're doing." A pause. "I don't believe you want to help out of the goodness of your heart, so what do you get out of it?"

The man grimaced and then forced a pursed-lip smile. "Well, I guess you've got me. Somewhat. You're not wrong, at least. I need you to deliver the message to the young people at Zionskirche. If you don't make it to the checkpoint when you said you needed to—10:05 —" Weissman checked his watch—"eight minutes from now, you won't be able to deliver the message. If the Stasi decide that you've jumped ship, gone AWOL, switched sides... they may not let you back in the East."

"Can't you deliver the message yourself? You were in the East, too, right? I smacked right into you yesterday morning. You could go back however you got there before."

"I was there to deliver the message myself when I ran into you. After watching my run-in with a suspicious person, you—" he punched this word for emphasis, "in the park, I had to assume they had me on their radar. I must also assume I'd be followed in the East if were I to return today, tomorrow, or anytime soon. My cover is blown, or it may as well be. So I need someone they trust—at least that they trust more than me."

"That doesn't make any sense. They'll be following me, especially if I have Elsa with me. What are you talking about?"

"They'll be following you, maybe. Here's the thing, and I'm giving it to you in exchange for nothing: you can make them an offer they can't refuse."

"Again, I don't follow what you're saying. I would lead them right to the church."

"Exactly. They already know where the church is, and that it's a hotbed of subversive activity. There's no problem there. It's not that they'd follow you that's the problem. They won't follow you *inside* the church, and they won't hear you delivering my message. If I were to deliver the message myself, and if they were to follow me, they would either raid the place while I was delivering the message or would arrest me as soon as I leave the church. Either one would be a disaster for the movement."

"And why is it any different for me?" Max was not buying it.

"It's different because they already have you under their thumb, in their eyes. They won't pick you up and arrest you afterward because they'll have just released you specifically to gather intelligence on this group. They won't raid the place while you're there because you're going to be working for them. That's what you can offer them. It will also help your case in getting out of there once they pick you up again from Checkpoint Charlie."

"What can I offer?"

"Offer to do what you already are doing. Offer to spy for them.

The young people in the movement will trust you more easily than me. Hell, they've met me, either. Anything you say is automatically more believable than anything I have to say, on account of your age. Plus, you're going to ask them to get you out. That might build trust, too."

"Out?"

"Yeah, out. You thought you'd figured it all out, but have you forgotten how you'll get back to the West yet after you've gone and rescued your princess?"

"She's not... I'm not." His delusion had been pegged. *I was imagining myself a hero... and he's right about the other thing, too. I need help getting back to the West. Back home.*

"So, you'll probably need the movement at the church to get you out," Weissman continued. "Probably through a tunnel, but who knows—maybe some other way. And you can kill two birds with the same stone. When you tell the Stasi that you'll help them gather details about who is participating at the church, what they have stashed in there, it'll be an added incentive to let you go. But once they hear that they might be able to crush some escape attempts—to find out where the tunnels are, they'll happily agree to send you off to do more of their bidding. They can't refuse this offer because their duty to stop those fleeing from the DDR demands it.

Then you can do whatever you want. Help them, don't help them. You'll be over the Wall, right? And you can deliver my message in the meantime. Two birds. One stone. We help each other."

"How do I know this isn't a setup—that you're not working for the Stasi? They told me a contact would pick me up at the bridge crossing, and you showed up."

"I never said I don't work with the Stasi."

Max digested this.

"Wait, so you work for the Stasi, but you want me to deliver a message to an anti-Stasi movement or group of some kind?"

"You're quicker than you look, kid. Something is different about you today."

"A night in a Stasi holding cell will do that, I guess."

The man grunted.

"So you work for the Stasi," Max said.

"I might do some things with them, but I didn't say I work for them, either."

"So which is it—do you work for the Americans or the East Germans? Whose side are you on?"

"I told you not to trust anyone, and I'm going to remind you of that: Don't trust anyone. It's a cliche to say, 'I'm on my own side,' but it has the virtue of being true. I am trying to survive, just like you. If you haven't noticed, you're working with the Stasi, too."

"Yeah, but..."

"Yeah, but nothing. You're working for them in a limited capacity. You have your own goals apart from theirs. Well, I have my own goals, too. I'm helping them, but I'm helping myself in the process."

"What's going to happen to the movement in the church?"

"The same thing that was going to happen anyway. They're going to get arrested, and they're going to be sent to prison, to a reeducation camp, or they'll be executed as traitors."

I can't be a part of that, Max thought. *What good does it do to save one person if I sacrifice ten or twenty others in the process? There's no way I'm going to sell these people out. If they're against the Stasi, I'm on their side.* He made the promise and kept it to himself.

Max's turn to grunt.

"You got a problem with that, then don't do it. But you'll have to give them something to sweeten the pot. Better to dirty your hands with something that would have happened with or without you."

We'll see, Max thought at the man. He checked the time: 10:02. *Three minutes.* He looked around but didn't recognize the surroundings. "Are we almost there?"

"I'm moving as quick as we can, okay? Two minutes."

"I only have three minutes, so I have to get there now."

Max turned to watch the streets go by. Less traffic here than nearer the shopping mall. *We must be getting close. Not a lot of street traffic at the checkpoint.*

The car turned to the left, and Max checked for road signs. Friedrichstrasse. *That's it. Checkpoint Charlie.*

A small, wooden guard booth sat in the middle of the street. Glass allowed guards to observe those approaching, and a jeep was parked sideways out front. There were sandbags, as well, protecting the building. Above the hut, a white placard sign announced, "Allied Checkpoint." They closed their distance to the building.

"Wait," Max hesitated, eyes narrowing in recognition of an impending threat. "You can't let me out there. If they see you and see me, they'll wonder what went wrong. You weren't supposed to pick me up to get me here—you were supposed to meet me this morning. That's it. If they see us together again, they'll know something is off..."

At this, the man checked his mirrors more carefully. "You're right." He made a U-turn in the center of the road and pulled the car into a spot whose line of sight was blocked by another, larger vehicle. They stopped about 150 yards from the checkpoint.

As almost an afterthought, Max took a moment to collect the Kennedy half-dollar from his pocket. He breathed as though steeling himself for a fight, and he reached down with his right hand. He was careful not to show the coin as he slipped it into his sock. He felt it drop between his shoe and his ankle, pressed there by his body weight, and he was immediately uncomfortable. *No way of shifting it now,* he thought. *I'm out of time.*

10:04.

Max didn't say a word. He yanked at the handle and bolted from the car.

THIRTY-ONE
ANOTHER ABDUCTION

This isn't going to look right. He walked instead of ran. *So I'll be a few minutes late. What can they do, arrest me?* He couldn't manage a chuckle at his own sarcasm. He looked back. The Brown Jacket Man and his Fiat were gone.

Turning again to Checkpoint Charlie, Max noticed the three flags of the Western Allies—American, French, and British—had been painted above the black words telling him he was approaching the Allied Checkpoint. A smaller sign was posted on the right-hand side of the street, announcing—in case it wasn't somehow obvious—"You are now leaving the American Sector." It was written in Russian beneath the English, and the French and German translations were beneath that. It's not as though the words themselves were threatening, but rather that they'd need the sign at all. It was like he'd seen in photos at the exhibits he visited in 2021, only much scarier in ʼ65.

When I cross that line, he thought, *the Stasi will be in complete control again. I could just not go back—stay here on the American side and have a walking tour.*

It was no use, though.

I can't leave Elsa. I can't. I'm not a hero saving a damsel, but I'm a human who can help another human. And maybe I can help those people in the church if I'm the one who decides what the Stasi will find out or not. And if I get back to 2021 before I meet with them after seeing the movement's headquarters, all the better.

Not going back the the East wasn't a real option. He kept walking.

I'm late. 10:07.

He approached the crossing from the American side, looking at the soldier but not engaging. He noticed a .50 caliber machine gun positioned on the left-hand side of the American post.

The man outside the guard house made a move to stop Max, shouting, "Hey! You are about to cross to Russian territory! Wait!"

It's not a closed border, Max reminded himself. *I can cross here.* He carried on. "I know," Max said as he passed the man, adding, "I'll be fine." He marched on into the neutral zone between the checkpoints on the American and on the East German—effectively, the Soviet side of the city.

The American soldier shrugged. Probably dumbfounded, he didn't make a move to stop Max.

This is it. Back into enemy territory.

The East German border guard most definitely cared that Max was approaching the border. Max counted eight DDR border guards standing around the post on the other side of the neutral zone, with one out in the main lane checking motor vehicles. Whether or not these German border guards understood what the Allied soldier had said to Max, a pair of them awaited his arrival and checked his progress.

A short man in a long, Russian-styled, military overcoat spoke first: "Papers." Just as had been the case in the Stasi headquarters, this wasn't a question.

"I'm Max Fredericks." He removed his entry pass and handed them over.

"What's this?"

Two more guards came over to investigate the disturbance.

"Look," he appealed. "I'm Max Fredericks. You should be expecting me. I'm supposed to be here. I can't say why, but I am supposed to be here."

"We don't care who you are. Have you applied for a visa? Have you declared your destinations?"

"What? No. I didn't, because..." His pulse quickened. "The papers I have, they should..."

The paper was gone—into someone's pocket, maybe.

At this critical moment, Max ran out of ideas.

There were now four guards surrounding Max. One called back to the guard post, and a fifth came to join the group as a sixth ducked inside the building. A seventh and eighth stopped paying mind to anything else and faced Max. Max himself faced seven Stasi-trained border guards, not knowing what to say. He said nothing.

At that moment, a van pulled into the checkpoint area. Someone threw open its side door. The same men Max had seen the morning prior hopped out, their nimbleness again surprising for men of their size. They approached Max as the guards, those who had previously been intent on stopping Max from going anywhere, stepped aside without a word.

Max nodded at the two from the van, and they grabbed him under his elbows, dragging him. "You're coming with us, you Western stooge," one of them growled.

"Guys, guys—you don't have to drag me. I'll come along."

They released somewhat but still guided him firmly. He kicked at the ground to get his footing, and they were dragging him once more.

"Please, let me walk. I'll walk." His eyes widened in fear. "I'll walk, I'll walk, I'll walk," he pleaded. *What are they doing? Why are they doing this?* He looked back just in time to see the American guard he'd passed on the other side shake his head and turn away. He also noticed nearby East German border guards smiling and laughing, one clapping another on the shoulder as though he'd just told a hilarious joke.

He faced the open maw of the van door, the small compartment inside the van, the tiny seat in the dark closet. Max was being crammed inside. For a moment, he felt as though he weren't himself but were instead watching what was happening to him. He watched himself being shoved into the holding spot inside the van, being shut in there, and the sliding door slamming closed. The diesel engine sputtered and tires squealed as the van lurched into motion.

THIRTY-TWO
HOHENSCHÖNHAUSEN

Max faced the rear of the van in his mobile prison cell. Although a bit of screen let air inside, terror overtook Max. *I can't breathe in here. I can't see. I can't breathe.* He reached in front of him to touch the wall. He had about half the space one gets in a coach seat on a super-saver airliner, except that the seat in front of him was a solid wall, and his own seat was made of metal and wood. His knees pressed into his gut. *How could an adult fit in here? Don't panic. Stay okay. Stay okay. Breathe the bad stuff out and inhale the good feelings in.* Except that there was nothing good to inhale. It was all bad air.

"Hey, could you open the door?" He tried. "It's too small. I can't breathe."

"Shut up. We'll be there soon."

"Where's 'there'?" He dropped his guard, overcome by true fear. *I want to go back home. I don't want to be here anymore.* He said it aloud, "I want to go back."

The Stasi men didn't reply.

What Max got was not a return to his own time or a sympathetic noise from the guard stationed outside his door. Apart from the loud bumps and shifts in the van itself, there was nothing. Nothing. No response, and no hope for release.

Max felt a tear mix with the sweat on his face. He wiped it with the back of his hand. *No. Everything can still be alright. I'm going to get Elsa, and they'll let me go. I did what they asked.*

Focus on something I can know something about. Calm down. Where are we going? There were a lot of turns and a lot of straight-aways. The drive seemed to last forever. He counted to sixty to try to slow down his mind and gain some perspective on how much time was actually passing.

There's no use, Max thought, remembering the stories of the Stasi driving prisoners around for hours to keep them confused about where in the GDR they were being taken. *I could be going to the Ministry HQ in Friedrichshain, or to Hohenschönhausen north of that, or... I guess I could be going to Bautzen, but I've never seen that place —with the time travel thing, can I even go to a place I've never seen? They have holding facilities and prisons all over the East. I could be going to Russia for all I know. I could be going to a gulag.* The panic rose as a lump in his throat once more. He shook his head violently to shake the feeling and thinking. *This is doing me no good. I have to wait to see.*

It didn't take forever, though it felt to Max as though it did. A long stop and some clanking told Max they were, well, wherever they were going. *Must be a gate.* Then a turn to the left—and a right, then a quick left. The driver cut the ignition as a rolling garage door slammed closed.

What happened next became something of a blur: The vehicle's sliding door opened. Max's inner cage door opened. He began to clamor out on his own but was grabbed again. Held firmly by the arms, Max was pulled out and into the garage inside the prison. An iron-gated doorway connected the room he was in with the rest of the building.

Someone inside the hallway on the other side of that gate activated the release on the door, and as it unlocked a red light illuminated above the door. "Move, now, and don't say anything," one of the two men commanded, pointing at the doorway. The two men who'd taken him from the checkpoint remained with the vehicle, and Max was met at the hallway by a uniformed guard.

The grey-uniformed guard shoved Max along and into a small room on the left-hand side of the hallway. Once inside, the man told Max to hold still. He searched Max, ankles to shoulders, and came up empty. The man left him alone facing the wall opposite the door.

The half-dollar that woman handed off to me. He didn't check my shoes—he didn't notice it. Is this some kind of trap? What am I supposed to do? Should I tell them they missed it?

Before he'd figured out what to do, no choice at all became his choice by default. A different man entered and told him to turn around. He faced the voice. The man had glasses and a round face. He smiled at Max, but Max knew this man was no kinder than the guard who'd been so curt and who'd gripped Max's arm so tightly a moment earlier. The smile on his face did not hide its iron. "Face me," was all he said.

The man in the glasses snapped a photo. "Turn to the side." He snapped another. "Here," he said, handing Max a set of scratchy clothes. Max took them, thinking, *Prisoner's clothes.*

The man did not pause for Max to think about the significance of the clothes—that they meant he'd probably be staying for an indeterminate amount of time. "Put those on when you get to your cell, and hand your clothes through the door to the guard who comes to collect them. Keep your shoes, for now. Your number is six. Do you understand?"

"I'm not a number. My name is Max." He didn't know what to say.

"From now on, you are Number Six, and that is all. If you use your name, no one will know who you're talking about. You will be called Number Six and nothing else. Here." He picked up from the desk and handed Max a glass of water that until then Max hadn't noticed. "We don't need you passing out from dehydration. You'll get a meal later in your cell."

"Later? When can I see Ernst or Sam?"

"I don't have a clue as to whom you're referring."

"What about Markus Wolf? Can I see him?"

The guard scoffed. "It may be awhile before you see anyone. You'll see who wishes to see you and will answer their questions. That is all. We are in control now."

Max thought on his feet as best he could: "I know you're in control. You're totally in charge. I just know that Markus Wolf and Ernst—the operations officer—and Sam, his superior officer—they all would want to know that I'm here."

"Look. If someone wants to know that you're here, they'll know. It'll all be sorted out later after your questioning."

"My questioning?" *Interrogation.*

"Yes. You should admit what you've done. It'll make everything easier and simpler."

"I haven't done anything."

"Well, you won't get anywhere with that attitude. Honesty is best, really," he advised. He knocked twice on the white, steel-plate door. It took a few seconds before the door was unlocked and opened, during which time the man looked squarely at Max as though trying to figure out what the boy was doing in his country.

Like I'm an invader. He really believes I'm a criminal.

As an afterthought, the man in glasses offered: "Maybe there's something you can offer to help the State. Maybe you know someone who is a threat that it wouldn't harm you to tell us about. Think about it. It would help. Show that you care about the people. Think about it," he repeated himself. The door swung open, and he pointed to it.

The guard who had brought him to the photography room awaited Max in the hallway and steered him through another metal gate between passages. They passed underneath another red light.

The guard took him to his cell—remarkably similar to the cell in the MfS—and shut him inside. The steel door closing behind him must have echoed for miles. He sat down on the wooden bed and began to cry.

THIRTY-THREE
ZERO SUM

Simply put, the situation was hopeless. Max thought of the myriad ways in which things were hopeless: *The people at this prison don't know Sam or Ernst. They don't care that I mentioned them, or Wolf, and they aren't listening to me. These are Stasi who just so happened to arrest a suspicious person at the border, and now I'm here. I live here now. There's no getting out. I barely made it to Checkpoint Charlie—I was late, actually.*

His thoughts had begun spinning out of control.

Yeah ,a few minutes late, but that might have made the difference between succeeding and failing. And why didn't I make a better deal —Elsa should have been there when they picked me up—they never should've thrown me in the back of a van. They should have met me at the border and let her go. I wish I could go back... He lost the thread there.

A moment later, he was back to thinking of other ways things were messed up: *Once I picked up that intelligence for Ernst, he has no reason to keep his end of the bargain. What am I going to do about it if he doesn't?* He stopped dead in his thinking tracks.

What if this was the plan all along?

An eternity passed, and Max marinated on that thought. *I did a favor for them, and they disappeared me.*

There has to be some way...

He remembered the half-dollar, feeling it pressing against the side of his foot. He unlaced his right shoe and removed it. Reaching into his sock, he pinched and removed the object. He examined it. *A normal coin. It's not hollowed out—there's no place to pry it open. This is nothing special.* He added it to the list of ways plans had gone awry. *I've been played.*

Absentmindedly, Max began playing with the half-dollar. He tossed it in the air, and he caught it. He did it again. *Something is off.*

He flipped it again, paying close attention to its sound and feel. *I don't know much about these half-dollars, but this is wrong. The weight is wrong. It sounds wrong when it comes off my finger. This is not a regular coin.* He looked with care at the ridged edge....

And that's how the guard found Max when he peeked through the peephole from the other side of the cell door: one shoe off, squinting at a coin he held between two fingers, turning it over slowly. Max froze at the sound of metal on metal and could just make out the man's eye and part of his face.

Max heard the keys jingle and the lock slide into the "open" position. The door swung slowly open. It was Ernst. Ernst stepped inside and nodded at another man in the hall. The door shut and was locked once more.

"Well, Max," Ernst said, looking at the boy as one might expect someone to look at someone with one shoe off and leaning into the light to squint at a coin. "Looks like you've got the item. May I inspect it?"

Without any other option, Max handed the half-dollar to Ernst.

"Thank you, Max." He flipped the coin, turning an ear toward its sound. He smiled and put the coin in his pocket. Max stood there, shoeless on one foot, in front of him.

Hopeful, now that Ernst was here and had what he wanted, Max tried, "So I collected the intelligence. I met my end of the bargain."

"Well, now, you know that's not quite true, Max." The smile was gone, now. His lips pressed tightly together in dissatisfaction.

"What do you mean?" Max threw up his hands in frustration. "I went to the West, met the contact, lost any tails, and came to the border crossing at 10:05. That was the deal. Now you need to let me go, and Elsa with me." He took a step back.

Ernst shook his head. "It was 10:07, not 10:05, Max. Espionage is a careful business. We warned you about the stakes." Max blanched at this, the color draining from his face. *But...* After a pause long enough to give Max space to sweat, he qualified what he'd said: "Now look. We are reasonable. We know that not everything comes off as planned. 'Contact with the enemy' and all that."

"Right, of course. I did what you asked."

"But there's a worry we do have: we still don't know whether or not we can trust you, Herr Fredericks." Ernst tilted his head and narrowed his eyes somewhat.

"What do you mean? I followed the operational instructions."

"You disappeared, Max."

Max's heart sank into his stomach. Not entirely in control of his reaction, he looked down at his feet.

"You disappeared for 40 minutes. From 7:52 to 8:32, you were not in view."

I'm caught, Max "You were there?"

"We are everywhere, Max. You didn't think you'd be seen? Now, let's see how honest you can be. What were you doing for those forty minutes?"

He thought—maybe six or ten seconds passed—but even that pause felt like far too long to hesitate. Max answered, "I was doing what you asked. I lost a tail. If the tail were State Security, I had no way of knowing it."

"Hmm." The man looked Max dead in the eye and waited for more. Max didn't offer anything else. "I suppose that may be true." He chuckled. "But let's get more precise. Tell me more. Tell me everything you think I should know as your handler."

This open-ended way of asking was a major problem for Max. *If I short him any info that he already has, he'll know I'm lying. If I tell him more than he knows, I'll be helping the Stasi. These people are no better than the Gestapo.* Ten seconds passed this time. He sighed deeply.

"I was meeting with a woman who called herself 'Judy'. She claimed to work for the American intelligence agency." He waited, but Ernst offered nothing.

The overheads flickered for an instant. Maybe two or three flashes. Ernst was still as stone. His eyes bored into Max.

"She seemed to know about my mission for the Stasi. I told them that I'd tell them more about the East when I return to the West with Elsa."

"So, you admit to espionage against the DDR?"

"No." Max was firm. *I got this,* he coached himself.

"What do you mean, 'No'?" Ernst was surprised.

"I can tell them whatever you want me to tell them. I do want to help the workers' state. I want to help the DDR. Capitalists are all about money. It's not right. I can still do exactly what you think is best. " *Please, please buy it.* "This is even better than before because the CIA thinks they can trust me. You feed them whatever misinformation you want.

"Ah ha." Ernst though, breaking eye contact for the first time since he had asked Max what he was doing for those missing forty minutes. "I see."

Max exhaled. *I think it's working...* "So tell me what to say, and when I go back, I'll tell them."

"I'll consider that. What is your intention if we allow you to leave here?"

Max heard the word "if" loudest. "What do you mean 'if'? You made a deal. I did my best, and I succeeded. I have been honest. I've made an offer to run ongoing counterintelligence for you with the CIA. I have been compliant. I have been straightforward, and—I can't stress this enough—I have been honest."

"I will take it up with Sam and Wolf. I'll run this fresh idea by them. You'll wait here, in the meantime. I may see you later today." He turned to leave.

Max knew right then that it wasn't enough. But he had more to offer. He'd acquired more. From Weissman. The Brown Jacket Man. He had the activists at the church, Zionskirche. Before Ernst could knock to be let out of the room, Max called, trying not to let the desperation in his heart creep into his voice: "Wait! Wait. Just wait."

Ernst waited.

"I can do something else for you, but you have to let me out today for it to work."

"I'm listening."

"First," Max asked, "What time is it?"

Ernst checked his leather strap, silver watch. *That's a lot nicer than the ones they give their field agents...* "Almost 12:15."

"Good. Well, I have to get to Zionskirche before sundown, which should be around 5pm. I have to speak to the people there today. I have a message to relay."

Ernst's raised eyebrows belied feigned disinterest. He stepped back toward the center of the room where Max remained—it was only a few feet. He leaned in until his face was mere inches from Max's face. "Max." He spoke slowly: "What's the message?"

From Ernst's behavior, Max understood: *He doesn't know what the message is. I can say anything. What should I tell him?*

THIRTY-FOUR

MAX AND ERNST

One hundred and twenty minutes later, Ernst had opened Number Six's cell in the Stasi's Hohenschönhausen Prison in East Berlin and was standing with the captive once more. Prisoner of the State, Number Six, had been waiting without knowing how much time was passing. He'd put his shoe back on his right foot, and he had paced back and forth in the compartment that counted as his lodgings for the foreseeable future.

Max had given his all to the mission of getting Elsa out of there, and then he'd given even more to save himself. He'd done what he had to do. Weissman, the Brown Jacket Man, had been right.

Over the last two hours, Max had oscillated between *It has to work* and *It will never work*, between *They have to accept this* and *This is too good to let go* and *I will never be allowed to see the outside world again unless it's to be shot or transported to a gulag in Siberia.*

He was in a mild state of shock while Ernst stood in front of his open cell door explaining, "She's being transported to this location now. When she arrives, we will release both of you. You will be transported to the Volkspark in Friedrichshain. You know it, right? I will expect your report in person tomorrow morning at the cafe you mentioned. In the western sector."

"I'll be there."

"If you don't appear as you say you will, we will fulfill our promise."

"I understand."

"To be clear: if the anti-state action is not thwarted, the State Security Service will hold you personally responsible. You will not be able to move freely anywhere as long as our socialist paradise exists."

Max nodded. *With any luck, I'll be gone by tomorrow, Elsa will be safe, and your "socialist paradise" is doomed. Let's see what you can do about my decisions in 2021.*

"Come with me, Max." Ernst led Max from the room down the hallway and back to the garage.

THIRTY-FIVE
ELSA

Ernst and Max waited together. They waited for a long time. There was an analog clock on the wall in this room. When the garage door cranked open from the outside, the hands on the clock read 3:00. The van entered—the same van as had abducted Elsa a day earlier and, Max could tell from its sound, the one he'd ridden in just a few hours prior. A brown, boxcar-shaped cargo truck, small like other German vehicles, parked beside the van disguised as a flower delivery vehicle. The driver killed the engine.

The door to the dull brown van slid open, and one of the toughs that had grabbed Max stepped out. He leaned back into the van to unlock and open the cabinet inside the vehicle. The man stepped back. Ernst signaled to him, and he turned and left the garage, pulling the garage door closed behind him.

Elsa climbed out, squinting somewhat at the light. She stopped and stood in front of Max and Ernst.

"Well, Max, Elsa's here. This is what you worked for."

How awkward.

"Hi," Max said, trying his best to make and keep eye contact. *Show certainty.* "You're getting out of here."

She looked at him, head cocked to the left, and asked, "Who are you?"

"I'm sure you don't remember me, but I was there at the park yesterday. The Volkspark. When you were taken."

"That was yesterday? Oh, god," she groaned.

"I know how it is being inside, locked up. I was there, too. I made a deal to get us out. Both of us."

Elsa looked worried, her eyes widening as Max spoke. She looked to Ernst with uncertainty, then back to Max with the same look. "Who do you work for?" she asked.

"I'm helping the DDR, but I'm helping you in the process." He turned to Ernst. "So, can we go?"

"Yes, Max. In fact, you need to hurry. Sunset is inside one hour from now. Get in the truck." He gestured to the white truck that looked somewhat like a refrigerator on wheels. Max began walking.

"Why should I trust you?" Elsa asked, not moving anywhere.

"You don't have to," Max replied, not skipping a beat. "But your alternative is to stay here with them." He looked toward Ernst. "I mean the prison."

Ernst understood. He looked at Elsa, saying, "Max is right. You don't have to trust him any more than it takes to get in that truck and be released at the Volkspark twenty-five minutes from now. And you'll need to go with him to the Wall, though I expect he'll explain the details to you when we drop you off. Let's go."

Ernst led the way to the white truck. Silver lettering displayed "Barkas B 1 0 0 0" on the front quarter-panel.

The Stasi man opened its side-rear door, revealing two holding boxes similar to those in the flower van, if a few inches taller inside. They stood open and waiting, each its own compartment of a hearse.

Max looked at Elsa. "Come on," he said, and he moved to climb in the back of the Stasi van. "Let's go, Elsa."

She was obviously conflicted, but she must have decided to follow him because she followed Max into the disguised van. As they boarded, they found there were—somehow—three holding cells in the truck. They took mobile compartments next to one another, and each sat in the tight and enclosed, upright-coffin-shaped boxes.

Ernst shut the van's rear doors. This not only secured them inside but also blocked their view out.

The driver honked once and started the engine.

It was tough to hear outside or tell from the motion of the van what was going on, but Max could tell someone—probably Ernst— was riding in the front of truck with the driver. The garage door opened, and the vehicle was put into reverse, and then they were moving. Max could further make out they were stopping at the front gate, were being checked out by the guards, and were turning right on the street outside that gate. From there, they turned left, and at the end of that street, another left. He heard the sound of a streetcar.

After that, everything blended together. They made a series of turns in broad, 360-degree patterns. They made doubling-back patterns. The driver's job, in part, was to cause the passengers to lose their sense of direction and, with it, all sense of where they were in the city. This way, even if the captives were paying attention, they wouldn't be able to make it to or from the prison from what they could remember.

Not that Max wanted to return to Hohenschönhausen anytime soon, but this driver didn't know that the old "get the passengers lost by driving in circles" routine wouldn't work on Max, who had visited the prison back in 2021 after this man had lost his job and the DDR had collapsed.

Max didn't know that Ernst was right about it taking 25 minutes to get to the park. When they came to a stop at the park, it was 3:30 in the afternoon. The clouds had cleared, and the Sun made an appearance. For now.

The driver stopped the van, and Ernst opened the side door, stepped out, and allowed Max and Elsa to step out on their own. He didn't speak to them. He nodded as they stepped out. He didn't look back but instead got back in the van, which tore off down the brick road.

THIRTY-SIX
YOU AMERICANS

Max knew he wasn't free of the Stasi, but he breathed deeply in relief nonetheless. He started toward the same entrance the Brown Jacket Man had pulled him into a day earlier. He motioned to Elsa to follow him into the park, and when she did, he returned to that same bench on which he'd sat under the steady gaze of concrete Lenin. Elsa followed, hesitating in keeping up. He sat, and she sat beside him.

This second 1965 visit to the Volkspark was different from his first. This time, Max assumed he was being watched. He checked the windows around the plaza. He looked for the cars doing laps around the park. He did not look at Elsa but kept his eye on his surroundings, knowing a potential risk could be in every window.

"Okay. You got us out of there," Elsa said. "Now, where are we going?" She seemed... annoyed.

Max couldn't help but to wonder at this way of beginning this conversation. *No "Thank you, Max, for freeing me from prison and for saving my life?" Maybe she wants to get out of the East before she thanks me.*

Max attempted confidence: "We're going West tonight. I have to deliver something, and then we can both cross over," he replied.

Elsa radiated skepticism. "They're not going to let us just waltz through Checkpoint Charlie, you know? We won't be permitted."

"I know. We're not going that way."

"So which way are you planning on us going to get across? You thought this through?" Max detected more sarcasm in Elsa's tone.

"Of course I have a plan..." He hesitated. "I don't know every detail, yet."

Elsa stood. "You don't. Know. The details." She annunciated each bit of this sentence with derision.

"I have a contact who can get us to the West. I think."

"You *think* you have a contact? You? Who is the contact?"

Max knew she was exasperated, and he was losing grip on himself, too. He didn't respond but instead looked at his feet.

Elsa began walking away. Before she reached the exit, she turned back and came to where Max still sat. She crossed her arms. "Okay. So you don't know who the contact is, but you have one. Where is this contact?"

Max hesitated. He looked at his Stasi-provided watch. 3:40. *Sunset is close.*

Elsa read his wavering attitude but said nothing.

I'm running out of time. And you're why I'm here. He couldn't well blame Elsa for his choices so far in this misadventure. *I've come this far, and now you're standing right in front of me, waiting for me to explain how I'm going to get us both out of danger. Should I say I'm not sure about it, now that we're here?* His experiences in the last thirty or so hours had evinced in him a growing sense of caution.

Should I tell her everything? Should I go on my own? She seems perfectly happy to be left alone right now. But what was all of this worth if I don't follow through? I don't even know who this girl is. He knew he was running out of time for his escape, whether or not he trusted Elsa.

"Let's walk, and I'll tell you The Plan as we go."

She could hear the capital letters in his intonation.

Max continued. "But I have some questions for you, first. I got you out, and I think you should answer them for me."

"Okay," was her response.

Max stood, and they headed for the park exit.

Elsa wore her shoulder-length brown hair pulled back, and her darting, bloodshot eyes spoke of the worries of a day-and-a-half in Stasi interrogation and little-to-no sleep.

Everyone I know, except maybe Mom or Dad, would have collapsed under the weight of the Stasi boot. The pressures of round-the-clock questioning, sleep deprivation, and bright lights weren't not to be dismissed or scoffed at. The Stasi didn't torture people outright, but the standard treatment they gave was close enough to draw out from almost anyone a confession of any act, real or imagined. The pressure to turn on one's friends and loved ones was calculated, and turn people it did.

Elsa looked unharmed by what Max assumed was a vicious ordeal. *She's strong. I could never handle that.* Max nodded and turned to leave the park.

And so they began walking toward the Zionskirche to the west of the Volkspark, keeping a quick pace and glad to be putting more space between them and Hohenschönhausen and the MfS. The whole of East Berlin was a bigger Hohenschönhausen, yes, but being inside the Stasi prison proper felt different. It was safe to say all of Elsa's and Max's hopes were pinned on never returning.

Only a few seconds had passed when Elsa answered Max's question. "What do you want to know?"

"Let's start with who we are. I'm Max." He put out his hand.

"I'm Elsa." She didn't shake hands—she kept marching, looking straight ahead.

"I know." He paused. "Yesterday morning. Why did they take you off the street like that?"

"What do you know about it?"

"I saw it. You didn't notice me?"

She shook her head

"You looked right at me." *Maybe the ordeal was so intense she didn't see me even though we were looking right at each other.*

A shrug.

"I saw the whole thing," Max said. "I want to know why they picked you up."

"Why do they arrest anyone? 'Subversive activities'." The noise Elsa made along with this explanation told Max she didn't believe she was doing anything subversive.

That's a good sign, he thought. "What are you supposed to have done?"

"They said I was conspiring to help someone escape."

"Were you?"

"Well, yeah. The Stasi just happened to know about it."

They seem to know everything people do around here, Max thought. *I don't think I got that through my head until it was about me.* "What sort of conspiracy were you involved with?" he wondered aloud.

Elsa puffed up her chest and raised her chin adamantly. "Look, I don't know who you are. I'm not telling you anything more than I told them: a neighbor and I have been talking about getting out since we were twelve, when the Wall went up."

So you're sixteen. Elsa's story is kind of like that book—A Night Divided.

She continued, "And someone approached me in the Volkspark the very morning I was taken, asking if I'd like to go to the West. I said that I'd think about it."

"I thought you would have jumped at a chance to get out. If you were planning it for years..."

"I do. But you don't go plotting and planning with people you don't know." She eyed him.

Now I'm one of those people, Max deduced. *She doesn't trust me. Of course. Even after I've got her out of holding, she doesn't know if I'm helping her or if I am working for the Stasi. They have a way of doing that to people. Even if someone were to save my life, I'd have to wonder if I can trust them or if it's part of a bigger plot.*

Just thinking through this bit made Elsa's attitude more understandable. His sense of empathy kicked in. He'd probably have the same reaction to being arrested for agreeing "to think about" helping or being helped by someone who gets people to the West.

"I see," he said.

"Do you?"

"Well, you have been tricked before, and you were duped yesterday. So now you're wondering if I'm working for the Ministry and got you out of there to get you to trust me." He didn't await a response. "Well I'm not, you know? I'm an American. I saw you get abducted, and I decided that I should help you. I risked my life for you."

"You're an American. So that's supposed to explain everything? All of the American boys are just looking for someone to rescue. Perhaps you don't know this: not everyone needs or wants to be rescued. A girl can rescue herself, you know? They'd have let me go, eventually." She sighed and began walking back the way they'd come. "I'm from here. I can handle this on my own."

THIRTY-SEVEN
ZIONSKIRCHE

This isn't working. I got her wrong. Why would they have let her go? How does she know they wouldn't keep her forever—or send her to a gulag? Max caught up. "Would they have?" he asked.

"Eventually, yes. They'd try to turn me into an informant, and of course I'd agree."

"What?" Max was incredulous.

"It doesn't do any good to fight them—not directly, anyhow. But I could feed them whatever information suited me. I could gain favor, maybe some trust. Maybe they'd even send me to infiltrate an organization. I could use their support of my mission to get access to a way of escaping. I could work for the West, or I could cut hair, or hitchhike—whatever people do over there."

Dream big.

She continued. "I've heard it's a lawless place, but too few laws is probably better than too many."

This is what people in the East think about the West. That it's chaotic and dangerous. They think this because the DDR tells them that's how it is, and even the people who don't trust their own government believe some of what they hear. They got nothing else to go on. "You're telling me more than you told them, I think." He tried to keep up, but Elsa's pace quickened. The street was far from empty, at this hour.

"No," she said. "I told them this, too. I told them most of this plan because if the Ministry leaders think they can use me in the West, they might let me go. They have thousands of spies there. If the higher up people believe that I'll tell them everything, they'll trust me to infiltrate a disruptive group."

"And you could disappear in the West."

She didn't respond.

"Okay." *She's playing a long game. Jeez. It's hard to track.* Max changed the subject. "So how come you speak English so well?"

She shrugged. "A lot of Germans have learned English since the War ended. I grew up in Frankfurt. My father worked for the Americans. They de-Nazified West Germany. He took a contract with them to make announcements at theaters before the films about Nazi atrocities they'd show at the local movie screens. So I had to go to school with your country's army brats. I spent ten hours a day with Americans and Brits from when I was four until I was eleven. Then my aunt Sofia wrote to my father from East Berlin. She said that she needed him." Elsa scowled.

Elsa blames her aunt.

"She was sick, and he couldn't say no to her. We applied for an apartment in Friedrichshain; he applied for a job. The government gave him one. They're always happy to get converts from the West instead of leaking workers the other direction."

Max knew about that, of course. *Her dad was a gift from the West. He worked with the British and American armies, the West German government probably...*

She continued: "He's an officer with the *grenztruppen*—the border guard—all checked out and run by the Ministry for State Security Service."

"He's Stasi?!" Max shout-whispered at her.

Elsa whirled, looking in every direction for listeners. She gave Max a withering look and shoved him.

He checked his volume and reaction. "Sorry, jeez."

"Shut up! Of course he is. The Stasi control the borders in the East. He speaks English. He knows some things about the American and British Armed Forces. About westerners. And he seemed an idealogical convert to the DDR's cause—those people are usually its best defenders. So in a lot of ways, my father is useful to them. They give us a comfortable apartment in exchange. Better than most people get. Some extra food and alcohol." She paused. "I don't care about that stuff."

I get it. Your father betrayed you, got you stuck in the East, for more comforts. "So you're going to leave him behind here?"

"And why not?" She was indignant. "He's abandoned me by taking this job. Why do you think the Stasi were watching me? I'm sure my father turned me in. He wants me out of his hair. My behavior puts his career at risk. His comforts." She sneered as she said that word—comforts—balling her fists in resentment.

"So you want to leave."

"Yes, of course. I don't want this life. State-controlled socialism is a lie. It ignores the greed that the leaders of the revolution have in their hearts. It ignores the plight of the actual workers and revolutionaries. As long as they're reserving nice apartments and extra food for people who will turn in their own daughters..." she trailed off.

Does she hate communism or just the East German version of it?

They walked in silence, and Max thought about the complaints seeming to drive Elsa. They crossed one main boulevard and moved as fast as they could to the next narrow side street. Neither one wanted to put them under whatever prying eyes were surely watching an open space, ready to make a phone call at the first sign of something out of place. Max and Elsa were out of place in deed as well as in thought.

"Okay. I can help, I think. Honest." He checked the watch once more. "It's three-fifty. I need to get to Zionskirche. Now. I have a message for some people there."

She perked up at the mention of the group at Zionskirche. She followed up, saying, "And then what? We stroll out of the East?"

"I'm hoping that someone there can help us get out."

"That's a lot to hope for, Max."

That was the first time she'd addressed him by name, and he stood a little straighter. A little taller. She knew how to parcel out signs of respect. He said, "I know someone in the West who asked me to deliver a particular message. The man said that in exchange, they might be able to help us. That they might have a way out of here that he didn't know about."

"Okay. When are you supposed to be there?"

"Well, I don't know. I mean, I know..." He tried again: "The Brown-Jacket Man—"this way of thinking of him didn't seem as silly as it did upon his uttering it aloud"—told me to go as soon as I left Hohenschönhausen and to get there before sunset. I think we're pushing it."

Elsa stopped walking. "They'll be there," she said with the certainty of someone who knows more than they're saying.

"How do you know?"

"That's the group that the Stasi told me in my—uh, interviews—to infiltrate."

"Oh, man." Max exhaled. "I'm bringing a spy into the place the Stasi want to bring down? That's just great. Just my luck." *Uhh, two spies, if I'm being honest—but who is, around here?*

They reversed course.

"Look, I'm not a spy," Elsa said. "I'm trying to get to the West. I don't plan to turn anyone over to the Stasi. I hate the goddamned Stasi. They surveilled me, set me up, threw me in the back of their van, locked me in a tiny cell, and they only let me out to interrogate and humiliate me. I have no affection for the Ministry. Say otherwise again and I'll punch you."

Whoa. Touched a nerve. "Okay," Max said.

Metzer Strasse crossed Schonhauser Allee, a main avenue still deserted at this early hour, where it then became Schwedter Strasse. They turned south on Kastanienallee. Three forty-five.

They approached Zionskirche from the street to its east. A single, weak spotlight highlighted the single, large tower above eighteen-foot-tall wooden double-doors. The building, set back from the cobblestone avenues on all four sides, showed wear and disuse, having never been fixed up after the war and with religion as good as outlawed in the East. Buckets and wheelbarrows sat amidst hedges and weeds in a homegrown restoration project on the southwest side of the building.

They came to a stop before reaching the front doors near a tree beside the approach sidewalk. Max looked at Elsa, and she continued to look straight ahead. He approached and pushed on the imposing front doors. "We're heading inside to pray," he said aloud to no one.

It didn't take much. The great door expelled a creak as it opened. The cavernous interior was darkening with the departing light of day, but amber and opaque-white stained-glass windows filtered light from the sunset into reds and oranges that spread across the pews in the church's open spaces. Before him stretched a long, empty rectangle of about sixty rows of parallel pews under what maybe ten stories of empty space and an arched ceiling.

It was deserted.

"Now what?" Max asked aloud, made nervous by the slight echo from even soft-spoken words.

"You haven't prepared at all for this, have you? You don't just march up to the front door of these places and expect to find a clandestine anti-government action group. A key you'll want to remember is that secret groups operate in secret. They think they do, anyhow. This town's got a heart. Let's poke around."

They walked up the center aisle toward the altar at the far end of the church. The ceiling was highest there, and Max couldn't help but to stare up as he ascended four steps. He stood in the center of the raised space and looked right and left. No movement anywhere. No sounds except for their breathing.

As they turned away from the altar at the heart of the building and began moving back toward the doorway they'd used, a tiny shuffling sound caught both Max and Elsa's attention, and they turned together toward its source. Against the wall on one side of the church and behind a spiral set of stairs that led to a raised rostrum, and partially obscured by shadow, a woman peered out of a door.

This must be a door to the basement or some kind of back hallway system.

Max looked at Elsa, eyebrows raised, but she continued avoiding his looks. He said nothing, having learned when to keep his mouth shut.

They moved cautiously toward the woman into the shadow and toward the doorway leading deeper into the church. Max stepped in front of Elsa before she could say anything, and he said to the gatekeeper: "Michael sent me. I have a message."

The woman, maybe twenty years of age, eyed him and evaluated the threat he and Elsa might have represented. After a few seconds, she must have decided that they didn't pose much threat at all, as she nodded and moved aside.

It was dark as pitch inside the narrow hallway, which ran to the right and left along the whole left side of the church until the woman shut the door and brought a wooden beam down to lock it. At first, they heard the woman place the beam in position, hearing the same scuffling sound they had heard from the center of the church. Then, they saw that's what it was when their guide-turned-captor switched on a handheld flashlight.

The woman fiddled with something outside the visible penumbra of light. An instant later, in the glow of the flashlight, Max watched the woman point a pistol. She motioned down the hall. "Move. That way. Now."

THIRTY-EIGHT
THE CHURCH BASEMENT

This time, Elsa did look at Max. Visible at the place where light met shadow, her lips pursed and a cheek muscle under her eye twitched.

Max smiled meekly but didn't turn from the woman with the gun to walk as she'd instructed. Rather, he faced her and the gun.

"Go," the woman repeated. "I won't repeat the instruction."

He held up his hands. "Didn't you hear? I have a message. I'm here to help."

"Explain that to Freddie downstairs."

"I don't know what good you think I can do you if you keep threatening us with that. What if you shoot us by mistake? Can't we at least have that thing put away, and we'll go wherever you want us to go. We came to you, after all. You don't have to force us to walk to wherever we can sit down in peace and talk with you, or Freddie, or anyone else who wants to talk to us." This little speech was ineffectual.

"I'll decide what to do with the gun." She didn't repeat what she'd said, but she motioned again for the pair to turn around and face the other direction.

They edged forward. As they took a few steps forward toward the darker end of the hallway, she spoke again. "I'll tell you where to go, and you go there."

This time, Max obeyed, and Elsa followed suit. *I tried,* Max thought.

As they walked, the woman with the gun explained, "I get that you might be here to help—but you might be here to hurt, too." They passed three doors on the right and one more on the left that must have led back out into the congregants' space. "Or both."

"I get it," Max remarked. *Don't upset her. We just do what she says, talk to the guy in the meeting room or whatever, and convince them to give us their help to escape the West. They'll help after I deliver Weissman's message.*

"Down the stairs," the voice from behind commanded.

The stairwell to their right was the last opening prior to the last door in this long hallway. *That one probably leads back out to the wider section around the altar area of the church. Last chance.*

"Okay..." he said.

Elsa and Max felt their way down the stairs. The air smelled like the musty basement at his uncle's place by the lake, except that it reeked of instant coffee and felt even damper than it smelled. As they descended, a light from a large open room rendered the flashlight unnecessary, and at the bottom of the staircase their host switched it off with an audible "click."

Weird. Flashlights were louder back in the day.

The room must have stretched the length of the church hall above, with hanging light bulbs illuminating a central strip of stone floor running end-to-end. A small group of young people huddled at a table under the last light bulb at the end of the room that must've been under the entry alcove of the church. All of them faced the intruders at the base of the stairwell, though at that distance, Max couldn't make out anything beyond the fact that there were three of them. One was leaning against the table facing the stairs, and the others were seated at the table, maybe playing cards or messing with leaflets or something.

Max looked back at their captor.

"Go on," her nod told him.

They edged forward toward the group, approaching like they were Alice about to meet the Red Queen.

"That's close enough," barked one of the blobs of light and shadow at the table.

Max and Elsa stopped under a bulb a few feet from the wooden table. A scrape accompanied the movement of a chair moving. The person who had been leaning back on the table, half-sitting, stood to meet Max and Elsa.

"No problem, no problem," Max hurried to be reassuring in tone. *Be agreeable. Do what they ask.* He kept his hands in front of him, trying not to move.

"I'm Freda." The blond-haired woman put out her hand. "They call me Freddie, but you will call me Freda." Elsa shook her hand, and Max followed her lead.

"I'm Elsa. This is Max. He's an American."

"Of course he is."

"What? Is it that obvious?" Max was no less taken aback in the basement of the Zionskirche than when Weissamn, the Brown Jacket Man, had called him out all the way back in the Volkspark the prior morning.

Freda ignored him, looking behind the infiltrators. "Thanks for checking on them, Sophie."

The woman who had led them down the stairwell shifted to stand behind Freda. Whereas Sophie looked to be about twenty, Freda was at least a few years older—maybe twenty-five or twenty-six.

The natural leader of this group.

The two who still sat at the table were closer to boys than men at maybe eighteen or nineteen years of age. Both had close-cropped brown hair and, like Sophie, looked to Freda for cues.

"You know you two make noises like elephants up there, right? The door, the heavy footsteps, all of that?" She shook her head in disbelief. "Good thing you're not crossing the death strip or anything." She looked back at her three compatriots. "They'd be dead in twelve seconds, right?" Then, she added, "Some spies." Nods around the table.

Max responded: "We're not spies. I am a messenger, and I brought you a message..." he trailed off. "And we might need to cross the death strip." He swallowed.

"What?"

"We need to get to the West today."

"I hope you have it all set up already," one of the two boys spoke up. "That is not going to go well. Not well at all."

"It will not be possible," said the other. "Not possible—"

Freda interrupted, "Before we get into the hows and whys of you dying in the death strip, you might as well know who you're speaking to. That's Emil over there,"—she pointed with her thumb over her left shoulder to the boy at her eight o'clock—"and the other one is Jacob." She didn't look at Jacob but instead tilted her head to the right.

She kept her attention on Max and Elsa. "You already met Sophie, and I told you to call me Freda. You're Elsa, and the American is Max. You're working for whom—the Americans? The Stasi?"

"Actually, we're not working for anyone," Max said. "We're trying to help. We're trying to help and to get help from you."

"And you planned to offer us something."

"Yeah, of course," Max picked up the thread as if he had intended to continue on to this anyhow. "We can tell you what we know about the Stasi. We sorta know how they work." Elsa looked sharply at Max.

"You what?"

Honesty. Show them you're honest. Just tell them about the Stasi. You can be useful to them. "Oh, yeah. We were both captured." Max couldn't see, but Elsa's eyes widened at this revelation.

"Moron," she whispered under her breath.

He carried on. "We were interrogated and everything. But I got us out."

"You got out. You got both of you out of the grasp of the Stasi?" Freda sized up Max. She crossed her arms. "I see. Please, I need a moment to confer with my colleagues." She chuckled as she turned.

"Of course," Max said.

She looked back. "You can take a few steps that way." This was not an offer but a specification of where Max and Elsa were to move.

They did.

Freda back to her comrades, and the four of them huddled around the table. Their voices did not carry.

While they did that, Max noticed some items against the wall that he hadn't noticed before because of the hanging lights and how the crew at the table had drawn his attention. Bookshelves. He couldn't read the titles, but they were stocked with at least thirty or forty books.

Beside the bookcase sat a white refrigerator that must have come from the West. "General Electric," he read across the silver strip on the fridge door. The machine was shorter than Max—really small. It was a banned item in the DDR, and the East German people would've counted it as a miracle of modern science. A sign was painted across a sheet above the bookcases and fridge, and Max strained to read it: "Memory gives force to the present." *What...*

Elsa interrupted Max's musing, whispering, "You are not even half as bright as you look, which is not all that bright, if I'm being honest."

"What do you know? What's the problem with what I said?"

"You talk too much," Elsa replied. "You put your foot in your mouth so much that I wonder what in the world you said to that Stasi agent to get us out of there. It's suspicious, Max. You are either too honest or too dumb to be an effective spy—maybe both.

I don't even know how we wound up here. You should have left me with them. I could've gotten myself out."

Max was almost speechless. "I wanted to help," he said, eyes downcast in her shadow. It was all he could think to say, and he was getting tired of hearing himself say it. *I can't come right out and tell you I'm from the future and that I already know how this story ends for the DDR. What can I say?* He hadn't the time to come up with anything.

Freda was marching back toward them. She wasted no time in getting to the point: "There are several difficulties we find here, Max and Elsa. Problem one. You were in the hands of the Stasi. So was she. If you"—she looked at Max—"got you two out, it means you traded something. We don't know what you traded. How do we know you didn't promise to make contact with *us* to become an informant for the Stasi?

They let people out all the time, but they don't let people out without getting what they want. Offering to make a trade was the first thing you did with us, so it stands to reason that you did the same with the Stasi.

That leads me to my second point. You want to trade with us to get our help, so you have a strong motive to tell us whatever you think we want to hear." She was placid, but there was menace buried in her tone, too.

"And though these other concerns," she said, "practical and important though they may be, this third reason is perhaps more special to us. Third of all is the principle of this thing. You think you can come in here and trade for our support? The thing that puts us off the most is that you're exactly like them—you reek of Stasi. This is not a marketplace, and we will not sell ourselves for a promise of some information. We stand for freedom here. The smartest thing for us to do right now is to show you the door."

Emil spoke up from behind her: "I still think we shouldn't let them leave at all. Look, they've seen the books. They can just turn us in for having Western books and Western goods, Freddie. They have enough to go on already."

Sophie chimed in, "Freddie, we can't let them go." She lifted the muzzle of the gun from where it had been resting on the table.

"And what'll we do with the bodies, huh?" Freda snapped at Sophie and Emil. "No."

Jacob had a solution. "There's a furnace in this basement," he said quietly.

Sophie stood, gun in a tightening grip.

"Good and hot," Jacob said.

Oh, no. Out of the frying pan... okay, that's a little too on-the-nose. Max checked his gallows humor. *This is real, and we are about to be killed. Think of something. You got out of the Stasi prison, but you're going to be killed by the anti-communists. Go figure.* "But–" Max stammered. "But, I didn't even give you the message."

"Well, out with it," Sophie spat.

"Michael says to go ahead with the plan."

Freda locked eyes with Max. "Michael sent a message to go ahead?"

"Yeah. That's all I know. He sent me to tell you that. That's why I'm here. The Stasi didn't send me. Michael did."

"Shit." Sophie sat down.

"That's good, that's good," Freda said, palms downward in a "calm down" motion. "Now that's a horse of a different color."

Sensing opportunity, Elsa spoke up: "Look, we know you need funds. Back in the West, East Marks are cheap. We can get you what you need there and send it back."

"They check every piece of mail from the West," Jacob intervened from his place at the table. "That won't work. You can't send us currency. It'll never get here."

"They won't smash a cuckoo clock. They'll look inside, but we'll stuff the money into the the timing mechanism weights. We can fit at least four or five bills in each weight, and we can send two clocks. That's six weights, twenty-five or thirty bills of whatever denomination we can get. That will help. You could buy whatever you need on the black market with that, right?"

Freda didn't answer, which Max took as a good sign.

She's thinking about it.

True to form as decisive leader, Freda didn't think for long. "Okay. Elsa here is onto something that we need. We have our principles, of course, as I said. But you've brought us the message we were waiting for, and she's not mistaken. We need the money to begin the movement. Eventually, you know, we'll buy a typewriter for our ideas, and we will open a library where ideas can be exchanged freely. We can't do that without the money." She paused as if drawing a final conclusion. She turned to face the three others. "We will help them." She looked at Jacob, Emil, and then Sophie.

They each nodded in turn.

Freda checked her watch. "It's five. Mostly dark already. You can leave now and go to the tunnel we've set up at Bernauer Strasse. Go to Schönholzer Strasse. Look for the two broken street lamps. At number 21A—the basement entrance—knock with three quick and quiet taps on the door. Our man there will let you in and will get you across under the death strip tonight.

You have to hurry, though. You'll need to leave right now." She ushered Max and Elsa with her hands, suddenly concerned about their timing and safety. She said to Sophie, "Take them. Get them back to the surface and point them in the right direction," adding, "and leave the gun here."

Sophie rose to take them back upstairs through the stairwell, grabbing her flashlight again and leaving the gun on the table.

Max relaxed somewhat. *No gun equals no coded instruction to kill us.*

Jacob remained seated, but Emil stood to see them off. He offered his hand, and they shook it in turn. He smiled. "Thanks, both of you. I know we're a bit rough at the edges, but we have to be. Good luck. I hope you make it. The tunnel gives you a good shot. We just reopened it after an informant scare."

"Thank you," Elsa said. "I'll see you again." She smiled at Emil.

"Thanks Freda," Max offered as he shook the group leader's hand. She did not smile.

"Gute Nacht," she said, "und viel Glück."

Max turned to leave, striding under the hanging lights behind Sophie and her flashlight.

I know those German words. "Good night, and good luck."

THIRTY-NINE

ORIENTEERING

As frightening a place as East Berlin was for Max and Elsa before their descent at gunpoint into the basement of the Zionskirche, it was scarier to leave that church in the dark. Thunder rumbled in the distance as they stepped into a darker and closer version of East Berlin outside the brick church. By comparison, the dank basement felt safe.

Sophie had accompanied them to a rear door and deposited them outside without speaking. This way of leaving was better than how they'd entered, as it was a small door leading to a gravel pathway between hedge rows.

Much better than the squeaky front door leading to a wide-open space, Max thought. Sophie had checked that the coast was clear and then opened the door long enough for Max and Elsa to slip away. After it closed, it was as if the doorway disappeared into a solid wall, so quiet and unobtrusive it was. *It's like it's always been closed, and there's nothing in there. All for the better.*

They set out together like two explorers taking their first steps out into the deserted salt flats of Utah, where it was said that there was so much nothing for so long an uninterrupted distance that one could see the curvature of the Earth in the vacant flatness. In 1965 Berlin, a curfew had emptied the streets, and like the desert creatures who scurried underground in the heat of the day, it was hard to believe that anyone here had ever lived their lives out in the open.

Despite everything in Max's body telling him not to do it, he and Elsa would have to cross the emptiness to move 1 km to the northeast to 21A Schönholzer Strasse and their tunnel to freedom. Max hoped he could save himself and he and his partner would survive.

He and Elsa met one another's looks of discomfort with a shared sense of purpose, and they set off together from the protective shadow of the church out to the street. A lamp hanging from a wire strung from one side of the street to the other lit the crosswalk area, and they didn't need to say anything about it to know that they had to avoid that and any other well-lit area. They crossed in the darkness.

I've learned a few things in the last thirty-six hours, Max thought to himself.

"We're being watched." Elsa vocalized what they were both thinking as they edged along a building in that first block from the church.

A man in a mustard green Trabant 601 was sitting parked across the street from the church and near the block they had gone down. He didn't appear to be hiding the fact that he was keeping an eye on them.

Max nodded.

"Come on," Elsa hissed.

Max followed, keeping an eye out for other watchers. As he followed her between buildings and down an alleyway angling away from their destination, he caught movement in the apartment behind across from the entry to that narrow passage. He did a double-take at the thought of seeing motion. The lights were off in the room where he'd thought he'd seen something. *Is there someone there?*

He turned and kept moving. *I'm starting to lose my cool. Just because there is a person in an apartment doesn't mean the person is spying on us. There are normal people here. Not everyone is a Stasi informant.* His anxiety increased with every turn, and every rustled curtain shook him. It seemed to him that the person's shadow along with every closing or opening shutter, and even the fluttering of birds escaping maple trees to soar upward and over the wall—all of it was closing in on him. All of it strengthened his nightmare.

Knowing better at this point than to try decide every duck into a crevice and turn down an alley, Max trusted Elsa to lead the way to the tunnel house.

Hiding, dodging being spotted by Stasi patrol cars, and keeping out of any lighted areas, the walk took on the aspect of a terrifying obstacle course, and as such it lasted a lot longer than it would have had they been out for a casual and direct stroll. Eventually, they reached Schönholzer Strasse no worse for the wear.

They paused at the corner of Brunnenstrasse and Schönholzer Strasse, a few hundred meters from the wall. They could see it, over three meters tall and capped with a grab-proof, rounded, and glass-shard-bedecked. Just shy of that structure lay a strip about the width of an American football field. Constant patrols crisscrossed the strip on foot and in vehicles, raking it regularly so footprints would show. The vehicles kept to a small road at the edge of the death strip, and those patrolling on foot knew where the land mines were buried. They also knew where the trip wires and automatic machine guns were, and border troops had no need to avoid the searchlights operated by men in nearby towers.

Those in the towers were trained to kill anyone trying to escape from the East, and they weren't even allowed to serve more than a night or two at a time together for fear of pairs of them developing agreements not to shoot escapees. They would fire. They had done it dozens of times before and would do it again if they spotted this pair.

Fortunately, they had no need to cross the death strip, and they had no need to try climbing the wall separating East from West Berlin. *Thank goodness for the people in that church basement.*

Max took all this in standing at that corner for maybe twenty seconds. As he counted his blessings, Elsa grabbed his arm and motioned for him to follow her onto the block they'd been seeking. A quick glance at his wristwatch in what little light remained told him that it was almost half-past five. Dusk had passed, and the early darkness of late-autumn nighttime hid much of their movement now.

It began to rain, storm clouds contributed to the general gloom, and thunder shook Max from heart to head, as he repeatedly mistook the sound for gunfire.

They walked past the address, 21A, and hurried across the street to check it out from there. Together, they ducked behind a rusted car on flat tires near a bombed-out, crumbling building a few doors down. Elsa pointed at the windows on both sides of the street. No lights. Max eyed the smooth concrete walls of the apartments that were still standing and facing the Wall.

Can they see into the West from there? They can at least see the death strip. I'll bet those people could get favors by turning in suspicious people breaking curfew and wandering so close to the Wall.

Lights flashed along the center of the road and swooped from side to side. They emanated from the end of the street they'd just left. No words were needed. Elsa and Max scurried to the opposite side of the broken car to put it between them and the sources of light. Voices followed lights. *Those aren't search lights—they're flashlights.* Four grenztruppen appeared behind the light, and they weren't stationary. They were moving down the center of the street toward Max and Elsa's position behind the busted Trabi.

Elsa grabbed at Max's shirt.

I don't know what to do! he thought at her.

But Elsa didn't need Max to tell her what to do. She tugged on his shirtsleeve again, harder, and got his attention.

He pleaded with wide eyes.

Elsa's eyes weren't as flooded with fear, and she indicated he should get low, gesturing flat—parallel to the ground.

He did crouched as low as he could.

She held up one finger for, 'hold on," and she pointed at the rubble that had been an apartment before the War, holding up the finger again and widening her eyes with a curt nod.

He understood, and he waited for her signal to move.

She picked up something from the ground and, without moving from behind the car but leaning backward for leverage and throwing space, heaved it back in the direction of the intersection. Panic took over, and Max began to move before the stone even found its target. Elsa yanked him down, hard, catching him on his left leg before he could stand to full height and give them both away.

Elsa's shot was well-placed. *Crack!* It struck a window near the end of the street. The Grenztruppen whirled to investigate, and their lights turned with them.

Elsa signaled, and she tugged Max along with her behind the half-wall across the sidewalk on their side of the street. The men were jogging now toward the sound of broken glass, and Elsa threw Max into stone and dust. He went down hard.

Max caught Elsa's expression in a flash of lightning, and with determination written all over her face, Max learned that it was possible for a person to be simultaneously terrified and relieved. The border guard was fixated on the broken glass, and a light, dim but there, flashed on and then off in 2 1 A across the street. They had been spotted, but not by the guards.

"Let's go," urged Max. "Now, before they come back. We can get in there..."

"Shhht," Elsa corrected him.

Max became silent.

"This isn't good," She said. "Those officers are looking for us, or for the tunnel, or both. We need another way. This is not going to work. Come on."

"But..." Max protested.

"No. You know your thing about how to talk us out of prison, and I know my thing. This is a setup. We need to disappear."

Okay. Good points. I trust you. "Okay," he said. "You got me this far. Where do we go, though?"

"Well, we can't just stand here. They'll find us."

"Okay."

"Come on," she breathed, "and do not make another sound."

A little tricky with climbing through this rubble.

She ducked under a collapsed archway and headed deeper into the wreckage of the building. Max followed, cautious. Elsa grabbed his hand and guided him to stay closer behind her. She felt her way along a collapsing wall toward the rear of the building.

There's a skill that many children in Utah learn, if only on a rudimentary level: orienteering. When a person practices this skill, that person uses a compass and a map, usually a map with topographical lines on it, to find one's way out, down, or home. At this moment, Elsa demonstrated a master level of orienteering—in the dark, in a horrific and dangerous passageway with uncertain footing and without light —to get them both to an alternate exit. Terror at their circumstances, elation of her rescuing him, and a spreading warmth that seemed wholly inappropriate at the time from her grabbing his hand all meshed in an overpowering emotional maelstrom. In moments, they stumbled into the alleyway behind the building together.

From the next block over, they heard the grenztruppen banging on a door, shouting, "Open the door. You are all under arrest!" and then "Halt!" followed by a gunshot. They dashed northward and found another narrow space between buildings one more block over where they disappeared together to wait for the danger of the moment to pass.

FORTY

HELP ON THE WAY

Bright spotlights emanated from towers some three hundred meters apart and swept the grey concrete surface, right to left and then back again. They swung down and across the death strip, showing smooth sand free of footprints. Erratic overlapping spotlight patterns made predicting their path impossible. In the West, platforms high enough to allow people to peek over the wall were visible. Here and there, people gawked into the East, waiting for some action. Some even held binoculars, though they wouldn't do much good in the dark.

Have these people been there all day? Is this what tourism looks like in 1965 West Berlin?

"The best place to make a run for it is halfway between the two towers," Elsa was saying to Max as they huddled low in shadow out of view even of direct spotlight approaches.

He snapped out of it. *Get your head in the game,* he chastised himself. Max replied, "Okay, so when we get to the base, we're going to throw stones to the other side. Someone there will hear us and will throw rope over. They have that and ladders ready to go over there, right?" He steeled himself to make a break for it. *I'll have to run faster than I ever have.* Elsa didn't answer as he prepared, leaning down and digging his foot into the dirt for a push-off. "On three," Max announced...

Then she broke in, interrupting before he could begin the countdown, grabbing his shoulder. "Look, I don't know if they'll be there. I don't know at all. It was your idea." Max faltered, withdrew from his starting-block position, and faced Elsa.

"Well, what should we do? I can't think of anything else." *This plan sucks.*

"This is a bad plan," Elsa said, echoing his thinking.

"I know it is. We can't do it this way," Max responded.

"Come on. We have to get out of this spot." Elsa led him back across the street. When they'd settled somewhat against a stairwell leading up to an apartment building's entrance, she took charge again. "Hang on—wait a minute. I'm thinking." She looked like she was thinking hard. She closed her eyes and furrowed her brow.

Come on, Max thought. *Please think faster.* He began to get the feeling he was running out of time in a way he hadn't felt before. *This isn't the same as running out of time on a clock the Stasi set for me, or losing time to get Elsa out of jail...* This felt different, though, like he was being pulled home.

Max smelled smoke and dust, as though he were crouched in an active construction site. *It's too real,* he thought to himself, sweating terror. Just few feet from where he and Elsa crouched together, paralleling the length of the concrete wall, he could make out in the dark a line of barbed wire. *I definitely don't belong here.* For the first time since arriving in 1965, Max got the feeling that if he stayed too long, he might not be able to return.

But things couldn't be left the way they were. He had to make sure things were *right.* He'd set out to Do the Right Thing, and he wasn't finished, yet.

They both saw what happened next and turned to look at one another, smiling. A group of would-be escapees crossed the street toward the row of buildings nearer to the Wall three doors down from where Max and Elsa were stumping themselves trying to plan a last-minute escape from a city holding them captive. They exchanged hopeful looks and held their breath to see where the three were going. A sudden noise from the direction of the wall turned everyone's head. For half a second, everyone in both groups—all five people—were certain they were caught.

Border guard?

No. The noise was from a party in a flat across the border in the West. Someone had switched on a record player at a volume probably sufficient to upset neighbors. Max recognized the twanging tune of a Beatles song, "Help". *That fits*, Max thought.

The defectors, Max, and Elsa all recognized they were in the clear. They all exhaled sighs of collective relief.

Thunder and a harder falling rain drowned out the sound temporarily.

The refugees and the escaping spies recognized one another's presence at the same time, and Max and Elsa ran to meet the escape artists. Soaking wet, they reached the group without making a noticeable sound. The rain helped. The pair looked up into the faces of the three, a woman and two men. All three Easterners wore the same expression of fear and hope. This was an emotional composition Max had never felt in his whole life before Cold War Berlin but that he was coming to know quite well.

Introductions went around with haste:

"Elsa."

"Max."

"Sabine." She had short hair, and even the way she said her name spoke volumes of her determined attitude.

"Stefan." Stefan was softer-spoken than Sabine, but his fierce eyes belied a deeper anger directing his choices than his voice alone suggested. He, like the westerners, had a pair of binoculars hanging around his neck.

Fat lot of good they're going to do us in this weather. Oh well, people probably want to bring all sorts of strange little things with them when they cross.

"Thomas." The third member of their clan was taller than the other two, had a close-cropped, military styled haircut, and seemed distracted.

Alert, rather.

Stefan, Sabine, and Thomas weren't wearing what one might recognize as escape clothes. They weren't dressed in black turtlenecks, wearing face masks, or anything like that. The thing is, the kind of grays most common in an everyday East German wardrobe didn't really stick out and shine as modern clothing would have. They were dressed, probably, in whatever they'd been wearing all day. They may as well have been part of the walls around them or the sky above them.

Not wasting any time, they approached a door on the west side of the street, nearest the death strip and the Wall, and they entered without so much as a knock.

Do they live here?

It appeared no one lived in this building. It was empty, and some leftover scaffolding suggested someone was amid a renovation job.

Thomas explained breathlessly as they stepped into the building foyer: "Two weeks ago, the Stasi came through and cleared everyone out. We got a letter first—everyone in the building—telling us the state required our living spaces 'for the purpose of securing the homeland against potential fascist incursions.' That's code for 'We need your apartment to use as a Stasi and border guard observation post.' See? They've knocked down most of the non-load-bearing walls on the ground floor already. I'm sure they will do the same upstairs. We'll have to see. It may even make our plan go easier than we had thought," he added.

How Thomas dared to be hopeful Max couldn't say.

Stefan added, "They told us we would have new living quarters at the edge of Friedrichshain, but this was the last straw. They can't just take our apartments."

"I lived below these two," Sabine offered. "Thankfully, they trusted me enough to tell me about their plan to get out."

"I hope your plan is better than his," Elsa said, indicating Max.

Max shrugged. "I'm open to new ideas."

Sabine answered for the group, "Come on, we'll show you. It'll work. It has to."

Max and Elsa followed as Thomas, Stefan, and Sabine hurried up the stairs. Before he started, Thomas warned, "Stick to the edges, or we'll make such a racket with these stairs the storm won't cover up the noise."

Max chose his footing carefully as he clamored upward four stories on narrow stairs. Each floor was like the bottom one. Each was emptied of furniture, and building and painting supplies spread strategically, tarps and similar objects arranged mid-project. Non load-bearing walls were gone.

Each set of stairs was situated directly above the last, and between wooden banisters and walls Max could make out a slotted opening allowing him to look down past all of the levels below. Occasional lightning flashes and ambient light from the street illuminated the space through the hallway windows.

The fourth floor had not been altered and was not under construction. At the top of that last set of twenty stairs, the five of them stopped dead in their tracks. Through the tumult of the storm, a loud creak in a floorboard under Thomas's foot triggered an overwhelming fear response in all members of the escape party. Thomas turned as though to run, and Stefan steadied him with a firm grasp on his forearm. Stefan shook his head violently.

Don't move, Max thought in agreement.

This floor was undisturbed by the ongoing work below, and it looked as it must have appeared when these three were shoved out. No sound from the party across the border made it through the storm and inside this building. Also, the hall itself had one lonely window. Unlike those stories below this, this wasn't a freshly opened area with windows at the edges of former apartments. As a consequence, no echoes reverberated through the fourth floor except those that could be heard faintly from the lower levels. The rain hammered away at the roof, but its eaves meant that no raindrops pattered against the hallway's single-paned glass.

There was almost no sound. In the hallway were four apartment doors. One was at the top of the stairs, mere feet away from where they'd all held fast in silence, and three more ran the right-hand side of the narrow corridor, the stairwell opening taking up the opposite side against the brick edge of this side-by-side building's neighbor.

Another loud creak. This one came from behind one of the three heavy wooden doors to their right.

They stood as statues, and Max heard two distinct sounds: the crackle of voices from a speaker and the squeaking of a chair. Max pictured a man behind the first apartment door to his right in the hall. The man would be sitting forward in a chair on wheels, listening to and recording a live conversation, and taking notes. He'd be hearing a private bedroom discussion from a couple none the wiser in the apartment sharing a wall with the room where he sat.

"Come on," Max whispered at a volume barely above inaudible. "Where to now?"

"Our apartment," Thomas mouthed.

FORTY-ONE
DON'T LOOK UP

Where the sound had seemed to disappear moments ago, it was back full force, and Max heard every exhalation. The rain droplets were individual bombs exploding onto tile roofing above.

Sabine leaned close to Max's ear—so close that he could feel her breath. "The attic access panel is in there. We don't know if there's another one."

Max thought for a moment and breathed back, "Let's go, then. We can brain him and get to it."

"No. He'll have time to call for help. If he's on a radio call with the ministry to report, he doesn't even have to dial a number..."

No luck there.

"What then?"

Elsa had an answer: "Let's check the other apartments. If there was access from one..." she left the rest of her thought unspoken, for another loud creak interrupted her. Quiet as they were being, the risk was too much. Everyone in the group of five stared at the door.

Max's internal dialogue narrated what the five each were think-ing, though each heard a personal, internal voice: *We can't say anything else. If that guy doesn't have headphones on, he will hear almost any sound we make.*

Elsa leaned to her left, crept closer to the brick wall, and tried the door opposite the top of the stairs. On it, a copper #41 picked up and reflected the minimal light from the window on the other side of the stairwell. The doorknob was as silent as everything else, but it didn't budge.

Locked. Crestfallen, Max began to slump into a sitting position. Elsa grabbed him under the arm and steadied him, shaking her head. For an instant, she flashed a mild smile at him.

He felt the impact of that look at the core of his being. *We can do this. We aren't beaten yet.*

Stefan made the next move, bearing close against the edge of the wall closest to the doors—

It must be quieter that way, but he's closer to the Stasi agent, too.

He passed the threshold of #42 to #43 and stood with each of his feet pressed against that door frame as he tried the knob.

Max realized he was holding his breath. *Come on.* He allowed himself to exhale in a measured and yoga-like breath.

The knob turned in Stefan's hand. He held it in place as he pushed the door, holding it carefully to take pressure off the hinges. A tiny squeak escaped those, and he stopped. Everything stopped.

The click-clack of rain on clay tiles of the roof above the attic became louder, and there was no change in sound from Stefan's and Thomas' apartment. Still the static and muffled voices carried through the door and walls. No one moved.

Nothing. There's nothing. We are okay.

Stefan stepped into the apartment beside his old one, and he disappeared.

Max counted seconds and breaths.

Sabine, just behind Stefan, did not follow but instead waited to see that the coast was clear. When it took time for Stefan to return, Thomas got impatient and began moving in that direction, tripping forward over Sabine's foot, which had been outstretched at an odd angle because of where she'd stopped walking. He pitched forward in slow motion, but Sabine caught him. Only, she didn't catch all of him. He tumbled sideways and fell in a heap on the floor. The sound was tremendous.

From inside #42, the voices and static stopped. The chair shifted. Then, silence again. Another squeak from the chair.

Elsa was first to act. She pulled Max and gave him a push. Sabine and Thomas barreled into the apartment beside the one occupied by the Stasi and his listening station. Footsteps crossed #41 toward the hallway door, closing on the group.

At the last second, they all managed to skitter inside and maintain composure and quiet. Elsa held her hands over her own mouth to stifle the noise of heavy breathing. Thomas turned the doorknob and lock only after he managed to close the door behind the group. As he slid the lock home, Stefan and Thomas heard the door from their former apartment open. Max pictured the Stasi agent, dressed in plain clothes, peering into the hallway and down the stairs.

They all five hid inside their neighbor's apartment. It had been emptied of most of the furniture except for a wooden kitchen table and benches that were built into the wall, as they were for every other apartment in this building. Soot and ash fogged over and rendered semi-opaque the kitchen and living area windows, but flashes of lightning lit the rooms. They could see around them in staccato bursts.

Finding a passage up to the attic was easier than they had worried it might be. Stefan found it. He had the head start into the apartment, and he had forgotten to come back to get the group when he realized it was safe to have a look around. He'd then begun searching, creeping room to room, and the other four found him standing still in the center of the apartment, looking up at a trapdoor in the ceiling.

He motioned to it as the others joined him after their close call with the Stasi. It wasn't a warm night, but every one of them was sweating.

Thomas and Stefan joined their hands for Sabine, who climbed up, grappling Thomas' right shoulder and Stefan's left shoulder.

They lifted, and Sabine was able to reach up to unlatch the door. She fiddled with something, and the trapdoor swung down and then outward with speed. It came loose and fell.

Somehow, Sabine caught it, saving it from crashing to the floor.

That would have been it.

The two men hoisted Sabine further upward, and she grabbed the frame of the trapdoor, pulling herself up into the dark attic. She was gone for a moment, and then her face appeared again. She was smiling, but tension showed, too.

As everyone's attention was focused on Sabine climbing up into the very top of this building, something dropped from Elsa's pocket from inside her slacks onto the floor. It was a small something, but it would be a giveaway to anyone hoping to track her. It was a Kennedy half-dollar. She immediately stepped on it with her shoe, so it didn't make the sound you'd expect a coin to make if one were to drop it onto a wooden floor. No one noticed.

Thomas motioned for Elsa to go next, and she did what Sabine had done.

I don't know...

Stefan waved at Max to do the same, and he followed Sabine and Elsa's example. The final hoist up into the attic was so difficult, Max wasn't sure that he could have done it without Elsa and Sabine pulling to get him the rest of the way up. But he made it.

Now, Thomas used his hands to boost Stefan. Last was Thomas. He was in the empty room on his own, with no one to lift him. They practiced this part, too, apparently.

Stefan hung down from the opening, bracing himself against its frame, and, in an act just shy of impossible, Thomas took two steps and launched himself as high as he could get. Stefan caught him. Max, Elsa, and Sabine all three held onto Stefan's legs and waist. Thomas used Stefan as a ladder, climbing up his shoulders. Meanwhile, Sabine let go of Stefan and helped by grabbing Thomas' forearms and pulling him up into the attic. Then they grasped Stefan's feet and legs, steadying him as he did a push-up back into the room.

All five of them lay on the rough wooden surface, staring up at beams and roofing above them, out of breath.

For as quiet as they'd hoped to be, absolute silence wasn't possible for what they'd just gone through to get up to the alcove above the apartments.

As it was, they'd gotten the Stasi man's attention. Not fifteen seconds after they all had clamored up above the ceiling of #42, the front door burst open. He'd found a key and had raced to the scene. They lay in a row on their backs—Stefan, Thomas, Sabine, Max, and Elsa—clenching their jaws shut and imploring the heavens to keep the agent from finding them.

After the plainclothes officer searched the other two rooms in the apartment, he stepped directly to the center of the room, right under the trapdoor. The room was dark, though, and he wasn't looking up at the ceiling. He grumbled something to himself and turned away from their hiding place. The rain must have hidden the sound of their breathing, and the man left the room without further incident.

Max noted the agent didn't close the apartment door on his way out and back to his post.

They heard the Stasi man again, through the floor this time, take his seat and turn up the listening device's volume. They picked themselves up, and Max and Elsa followed the original three refugees over to the window on the Wall-facing side of the building. Sabine looked at Elsa and said, "We have some friends who are expecting us." She opened the window to the stormy Berlin night.

FORTY-TWO

INTO THE STORM

"Thomas?" Sabine looked back to him inside the room. He pulled the binoculars from around his neck and handed them over.

What... Max still didn't know what she could use them for, in this darkness. She took the field glasses and, rather than holding them up to her face, held them at an angle, moving them this way and that, adjusting them in the darkness. Everyone in the group's senses already heightened, a flash of lightning and subsequent explosion in the sky frightened all of them.

Max thought through the scene. Relative to the pitched roof the window opened upward at 45-degrees and protected Sabine from the rain. More importantly, the roof and window angles worked together, keeping the rain from the attic floor. *If the open window doesn't get the agent's attention, water pattering onto and draining through the ceiling over his head surely would.*

He sneaked up beside Sabine and peered out of the window.

The death strip is right below this building, and that's only a football field long. Maybe it's a hundred, hundred-fifty yards to the other side. The West is a lot closer than I'd thought when we were down on the street and couldn't see over the Wall. It seemed a world away. But it's not so far... That's probably why they want the Stasi in these buildings.

The question remained. *How are we getting from here to there?*

They stood at a window in an attic five stories up from street level 100 yards from the Berlin Wall with no clear way across. He half expected to see purpose-built hang gliders stashed in this attic, but he hadn't spotted any yet, and he had no idea how to work one of those.

A flash in the distance that wasn't lightning. It was a pinpoint in a black canvas. It took him an agonizing and full minute, but Max realized what Sabine was doing with the binoculars when he saw the signal. She had been signaling, and someone was returning the call.

Did the guards in the towers see it? They don't face the West, so the other flash probably wasn't seen. But did they see ours? Five stories up and sitting in the middle of a thunderstorm—he hoped they hadn't been spotted.

"Okay," Sabine whispered to the group. "Take cover, just in case."

"What? Take cover?!" Elsa and Max both whispered back in a unified, raspy, whisper. Sabine waved them away from the window and back down onto the floor. They did what they were told to do.

What is going on? Max couldn't get out of his head as flattened himself against the floor.

Seconds later, a loud *TINK!* was distinguishable in the bedlam of the storm. Something had struck the tile roof. Thomas, Stefan, and Sabine gave no signs that whatever had been attempted was successful. Fifteen or twenty seconds more, and a *THWACK* reverberated but was overtaken by the boom of a fortuitous thunderclap. Thomas and Stefan jumped up and wrestled with something in the frame of the window. They pulled hard, eventually coming away with a kind of bolt attached to a tightly wound cable. It was thinner than one of those Max had seen back home attached to telephone poles.

Stefan grasped the cable's end, wound the first two feet of it around his arm to keep it from dragging, and walked it across the room. Meanwhile, Thomas stabilized it and kept it off the tile on the edge of the roof, the frame of the window, and the attic floor. Sabine, Max, and Elsa worked at that, too, still maintaining silence best they could. There must have been an attachment on the framing inside the attic, for Stefan attached the cable to something and pulled on it to test its grip. No movement. It pulled taut from the other side, as well.

"Are we zip-lining out of there?" Max asked aloud.

"Are we what?" Sabine answered. "We're climbing. Go. You first. We're getting out of here. We'll be right behind you."

"But how am I supposed to...?"

"Wrap yourself around that cable good and tight, and shimmy across," Elsa instructed.

"Alright." But it was not alright. He began to tiptoe toward the window, running his hand along and so testing the cable as he went.

"Wait!" Thomas hissed, placing a finger against his lips. He pointed down toward the floor.

No.

The speaker the Stasi agent was listening to had been turned off. When that had happened, no one in the group could have said.

Thomas risked one more whisper: "We have to go. All of us. Right now."

Max stood, went to the window, and—without allowing himself to fixate any longer on the terror coursing through his body—he grabbed the cable. *Head or feet first?* He led with his head first, thinking, *Better to see whatever's coming.* He looped an arm around the cable, swung his feet up, and he wrapped his legs around the cable. Max began maneuvering, and within mere seconds, he was outside the house, holding onto a metal cable, and realizing that had he thought about it at all beforehand, he never would have agreed to do any of this.

He reached, one hand at a time, and pulled, while he did his best to push by locking his legs around the cable and using his shoes to grab it and push from behind. The rain made the cable slick and nearly impossible to hold onto. The going was more than tough. Six or eight feet from the window, Max made the mistake of looking down. His stomach turned, but he didn't dare stop his climb toward the West.

He tried tilting his head at the chin and looking down the cable, but the rain obscured his target. He couldn't very well look behind him, either, as he saw the ground when he was doing that, and he lost track of his hands. He could hear Elsa—he thought it was Elsa, anyhow—crawling behind him. The blackness of the sky above him opened up, and flashes of lightning illuminated the emptiness of the world outside of him, his body, and the cable that suspended him. He was alone and would have to make it on his own, whether or not his co-conspirators were behind him on the line.

Shouldn't I have a harness or something?

Yes. He should have had a harness—or something. But he didn't.

Lightning flashed again as Max approached the fifty-yard mark—about a third of the way across and nearly precisely over the center of the death strip. He realized where he was because he spotted two of the five guard towers along Bernauer Strasse, one over his right shoulder and one over his left shoulder. He was right between them.

Not that it makes a difference because I'd die from the fall, but if I fall here, I might be blown up by a mine, trip a spring-loaded machine gun, or be attacked by dogs before a quick arrest and beating.

He tried to stop thinking about it, but one more thought plagued him. *If I don't fall but instead I'm spotted on this wire, I'll be target practice for both sides.*

Once he got to the West, though, the guards might not fire into that territory, so he'd be okay. Probably. Possibly.

The wire quaked in the wind and from the weight they'd put on it. Lightning raged. Max realized: *I'm holding a metal cable sixty feet in the air in the middle of a lightning storm.*

Max knew that Elsa, Thomas, Sabine, and Stefan were all spread along the wire behind him. The others went head first like Max. Stefan, the closest to the fifth floor of the building they'd come from, made it 20 feet from the window when the agent appeared there. Max knew it was the agent because he heard a shout.

"Stop! Halt! Return immediately or I will fire!"

Of course, no one stopped when the guard shouted. Instead, all five picked up their pace. Max was passing the guard towers as he heard the guard's shouts fade into the wind. The men in the tower to Max's right had heard something and were all out on the balcony of that post. Local sirens began blaring, sounding like the air raid sirens Max had heard in World War Two movies, but he knew these were to alert every grenztruppe in all directions to come to this spot. The guards in the towers moved searchlights wildly across the groomed sand of the death strip, back and forth, up the wall and down it. Max assumed they'd point the light at him next, but maybe they couldn't.

In the wind, he couldn't make out the alarmed shouts from the apartment building, and neither could the guards beneath him.

Can he cut the line? Can he unfasten it? Max pictured himself swinging downward against the Wall, a target in its center, or losing his grip completely as the cable dropped seventy-five feet at one end, sending him crashing into the wall and knocking off his partners into the mine field around it.

He kept shimmying. A morsel of one shout made it through the wind and rain, and Max heard it as well as everyone else: "Up!"

No.

Frantic now, Max yanked himself forward on the line, a few feet from crossing the path of the wall. His muscles burned, and he was blind from sweat mixed with raindrops pouring into his eyes. *Go. Just go.*

A gunshot. The rain doused the sound. A second. A spotlight swung past the group once, twice, and then it hovered on the center of their line. More gunshots. Max heard a scream. An awful scream, and a few seconds later, a crumpling sound.

Another gunshot rang out as the light moved back toward the east end of the line. *They're not going to shoot me. They can't fire into the West.* Max got almost no relief from the realization that as long as he held on, he'd make it. There were no more gunshots, though he could hear the guards in the tower shouting for the escapees to stop where they were and to come back.

Max looked along the line in front of him at at the balcony in the West. He saw them—people reaching out for him, shouting encouragement.

Then he looked down. He'd crossed the demarcation line the wall cut into the landscape. A massive trampoline, maybe 30 feet across, was stretched beneath him. *Fat lot of good that'll do with sixty feet below me. Keep going. Don't look down.*

Hand over hand. Pull. Hand over hand. Pull. Five more crossovers.

Four more.

Three more.

Then he slipped. Max heard a scream from behind him as well as in front—now above him—as he fell. He landed hard on canvas, rubber, or something else... but he landed on the stretched-out trampoline surface in place for just such a case. Someone grabbed his shoe and then his foot to pull him off the surface to clear the landing, moving him to a curb.

Before he was much aware of what was happening around him,

he felt a shiver in the landscape, and he shut his eyes on reflex. He felt dizzy.

As if waking from a hundred-year slumber, Max came around in a slowing drizzle, forcing open his eyes. His body was drained of its energy, exhausted from effort and the steady terrors of the last fifteen minutes. He sat on a curb across from a graffiti-covered concrete wall. He was back in 2021.

FORTY-FOUR
S-BAHN

Early the next day, a Sunday, Max and his father rode the S-Bahn to the new Brandenburg Airport. He recognized now that Schönefeld was Terminal Five in this new structure. As Max sat on the jostling but modern elevated commuter train, he stared out of the window, wondering if he'd return to Berlin. *I think I'm done with hanging out in Cold War East Berlin*, though. *I'm good on that. Do I get to choose where and when I go?* He spent the first twenty minutes of the ride wearing a kind of focused stupor on his face, and his father didn't interfere.

He wondered what had happened to Elsa and the other asylum-seekers. Did one of them die on the way across? He hadn't been able to see and hadn't dared to take his focus off of his own escape. Had they all made it? Some of them? None of them? Whether or not the events were real enough to be captured in historical records was another thing he thought about. Not every escape was captured on film or in print, so even if what he'd done had really happened—had made a real difference—he might not be able to find it with web searches or even deep dives in print archives.

It sounds like something Max's grandmother would say, but the best description of how he'd slept after he'd returned to the hostel the night before was that he'd slept like the dead. His head had hit the pillow, and it was lights-out for Max. That was, it was lights-out until the blaring alarm shocked him into bolting upright and hitting his head on the underside of the top bunk in his room. He'd mistook the alarm clock for an escape alert from the Wall. *How long will it take to get over that,* he wondered, *and how much worse was it for people who actually lived in East Berlin? Could people really get used to any of it?* It was as though Big Brother had come to life in the city, straight out of that Orwell book he'd actually read when required to do so back in the eighth grade.

"So, how was your day yesterday on your own? How was Friday?"

"Uh, it was cool. I learned more about the Stasi and the Wall." He thought, and he added, "I learned some stuff that I wish weren't true."

"Real life isn't like a story. It's stranger than fiction—that's what they say, right?"

"Huh?"

"They say that. So don't you want to know how things went for me on my overnight in Cologne?"

"Yeah, sure. How did it go?"

"Well, I have an interview to consult with a company that operates out of a small town on the Rhine River—but not 'til next month. You into that idea? You can come. No tutor needed. Unless you want me to try to get Brady to come out there." He was talking to himself but speaking aloud, saying, "We probably can't afford it, though. The company is paying my airfare, but I'll be staying in a hostel again." He looked at Max again, "I think we could get back over here. You'd have to miss a few days of school, though."

"I'm in. Don't even need to think about it, Dad."

"Awesome."

"Wait, where is it, exactly?"

"Well, they operate out of Braubach, south of Cologne. We'd fly into Frankfurt. They also have offices in Rome and in Paris, though, so things could change..."

"Any of those is fine, Dad."

"Okay. I'll set it up when we get back home."

They rode the rest of the way to the airport in relative silence. Max listened to the train wheels on the rails beneath their car and wondered about where and when he'd go next.

Mr. Fredericks looked over his meeting notes. Incidentally, that meeting took place about 200 kilometers from the very spot where, 2,010 years earlier, a Roman legion had disappeared in a forest deep in enemy territory. It was also a mere 100 kilometers east of a spot where Belgians had held off a monster of an invading German army, turning a lightning war to a grinding, entrenched grudge match. Cologne was also only a few hundred kilometers where the people of France had seized the King and Queen, removed their heads, and the launchpad from which they took a million-man army a-conquering across the entire continent of Europe. A lot could happen on a return trip.

FORTY-FIVE

THE MYSTERIOUS PACKAGE

On January 20th, 2022, Max turned eighteen. It turned out to be a long day for Max, but it began like any other day off school. Because of the timing of the holiday commemorating the memory of Dr. Martin Luther King, Max didn't have to go to school on his birthday, so he slept in. The weather was warmer than usual for that time of year—fifty-five degrees for the high temperature. The basement always felt chilly, though.

A private carrier service delivered the mysterious package to the Fredericks' front porch at 9:15am. The mail carrier was off that day, and special deliveries for his mom or dad always came early in the day because their house was first on that route. When his mother received the thick envelope upstairs, Max was in his new basement bedroom just coming out of another dream-filled night of heavy sleep. He rubbed his eyes, bringing himself back to the world of the real. His mother, Jeanne, knocked twice at the top of the stairs and then descended into his basement kingdom.

"Good morning, World Traveler." She'd been calling him that since his Thanksgiving trip with his father. "Got something today in the mail. Dunno what it is. No return address, but the postage here is weird. Check it out." She handed him the envelope.

It wasn't heavy, but it had post markings from another country and stamps with something he recognized on the top right corner. *The Brandenburg Gate!* It was from Germany. He opened it carefully while his mother stood waiting for a report.

There were some clean pages inside, but on top of those was a brief, handwritten letter in what he now knew better as Brady's scrawl: "Sorry to have missed you that Friday in Berlin. I got caught up with an early-morning appointment at the documentation center at the old MfS headquarters and never made it to our meeting in the park. I left a note, and the bartender told me he gave it to you, so you must have been completely surprised when I didn't show—I'm quite sorry about that."

Jeanne Fredericks remained standing on the area rug beside Max's timber bed, waiting for some explanation.

"It's from Brady, Mom. No big deal."

"Hmm? Anything interesting? Anything you care to share?"

"He is just saying 'hi,' I think. I'll see you upstairs for breakfast, Mom."

Jeanne Fredericks shrugged, said something about bagels and cream cheese, and headed upstairs. He could hear her at the top of the stairs saying, "Hun, tell Dad to drop his work and come have bagels. They're fresh."

He heard the door close, and he continued reading:

"But what I found at MfS was something I think you'd want to see. I was going to email you that same weekend with an apology and a note about how I'd found myself in the records, but that Saturday I came across something that took the next two months to sort through. I had to push for access. The documentation center at the MfS museum was only letting me see the files that mentioned me. I have my ways, though, and I was able to get copies of some other material. I think you'll be interested.

I have to say, something about you struck me when we met and spent those eight hours in tutoring sessions, but it was hard to recall. All of it happened so long ago, and what I was thinking was so improbable that I couldn't believe it. Then, I found this. I can't explain it, but it's real. I didn't know what else to do but to send it to you."

Max flipped to the next page. His hands began shaking as he read.

FORTY-SIX
[REDACTED]

Council of Ministers of the German Democratic Republic
    Ministry for State Security
    Main Department / Department / Divi-
sion __Main Directorate for Reconnais-
sance, HV A__
    Regional Administration / Administra-
tion __East Berlin__
    Case Officer __Gen. Richter__
    Telephone __7826__

Observation Report
    Subject __Max Fredericks__
    Address __unknown—high priority__
    Code Name __Kleiner Spatz__
    For the period from __29 Nov. to __30
Nov., 1965__

Note: Concerning report of 1 December 1965, person of suspicion "Kleiner Spatz" active in East and West Berlin. Assembled reports follow.

<u>Personal description:</u>
  Sex: Male
  Height: ca. 1.58 m [62 in., 5 ft 2 in]
  Age: ca. 12 - 14 yrs
  Build: unimpressive - average
  Hair: brown, cut short in military style
  Shape of head: rectangular
  Face: cheekbones and orbitals notice-able; face somewhat thin
  Forehead: prominent due to haircut
  Neck: short
  Eyebrows: straight, not bushy
  Nose: angular, downturned
  Arms: thin, long
  Hands: average—not stubby, not long
  Walk: short strides, shoulders back
  Clothing: stands out, jeans and maroon jacket; white short-sleeve tee
  Special features: none
  Particulars: Unknown. High priority to follow up and discover. Claimed connection with U.S. Embassy in Bonn, West Germany and mayor in W. Berlin.

29 Nov. 1965
  As of
  10:01 Note young person of suspicion

observing "Kaninchen" being collected at southwest corner of Volkspark in Friedrichshain. [This person of suspicion code name "Kleiner Spatz" inserted henceforth for continuity in reporting.] "Kleiner Spatz" standing streetside edge of park on sidewalk. Appears careful to observing surroundings. Possible drunken youth. Suspicious behavior. Clothing stands out. Western jeans. Possible espionage activity.

10:15 "Weißer Hase" in Vehicle #5 begins moving northward. At this instant: "Kleiner Spatz" begins to run along sidewalk—appears to be following Vehicle #5. Possible connection to "Weißer Hase". Proceeding under presumed orders to observe and report on "Kleiner Spatz".

10:16 "Kleiner Spatz" is assessed to be reckless, not circumspect. Progress halted by "Mantel" and steered into Volkspark. Conversation between the pair is animated. "Kleiner Spatz" appears to be upset and nervous. "Mantel" appears to be trying to dissuade "Kleiner Spatz" from something. Perhaps "Mantel" attempting to assess whether or not "Kleiner Spatz" would take action against the state. Suspicious. Note: Can "Mantel" be trusted? Recommend assign agent to determine threat level.

10:24 "Kleiner Spatz" leaves the other person-of-interest ("Mantel") and moves eastward through Volkspark. Lost sight of target from position over west side of Volkspark.

10:27 Telephoning MfS with report outline.

The report went on like this, page after page—switching perspectives between different observing Stasi agents in various locations, some stationary and some mobile, some in East Berlin and others in West Berlin. He skipped forward to the page containing his orders from Ernst and Sam. It was identical to the sheet of paper they'd shown him as he sat in an interrogation room in 1965. Except one thing had changed: where Elsa's name would have been were the German words "Weißer Hase". He skipped forward again, rifling through pages until he found what he was looking for.

30 Nov. 1965

Agent in Observation Post XV, 4th fl, assigned to observe ----------- family, notes the following:
    As of
    18:05 Loud sound downstairs. Phone call received to be on notice for Weißer

Hase leading Kleiner Spatz. Other persons of interest observed entering location housing new observation post. Group moves upstairs. Passes my location and at 18:11 and enters attic space.

18:15 Group makes contact w Western agitators. Escape attempt in progress.

Grenztruppen in Tower 27 observe 4th floor window open. Report after action as follows:

as of

18:14 Kleiner Spatz first out of window on cable fired by crossbow from West to East. Weißer Hase follows. Persons of interest 1, 2, 3 behind. Weißer Hase stalls long enough for Agent ---- to catch up, but not close enough to stop them—he is unarmed. Signals to us at 18:16.

18:16 We call for escape group to halt. Open fire. Avoid possible asset Kleiner Spatz and asset Weißer Hase. Persons of interest 1, 2, 3 escape attempt halted successfully.

Final Report: Weißer Hase cannot make contact w Kleiner Spatz on West side of Anti-Fascist Defensive Barrier. Presumed escape. Western assets cannot locate. Weißer Hase proceeds with successful interruption of Zionskirche subversive elements. Their activities halted,

```
leaders imprisoned for the security of
the State.
```

The papers fell from Max's hands. He'd lost his appetite.

MAX WILL RETURN...

You've reached the conclusion of this episode, but Max Fredericks will be back! Keep in touch.

There is so much to learn about German history in general and about the Cold War in particular. A lot goes into writing a book like this. In addition to many personal visits and conversations with average East Germans, a former inmate and associated experts at the Hohenschönhausen Prison, and current residents and citizens of a unified German Federal Republic, some of my sources and inspirations follow in the pages following my "about the author" note.

If you'd like to know more, feel free to contact me at stevecaponejrauthor at gmail dot com, on TikTok @steve_capone_jr_author, or find my author's web page on Facebook at www.facebook.com/SteveCaponeJr. I also run a website at www.stevecaponejr.com, and if you're interested in the travel that inspired this book, that's where you can find a lot of my public diaries from traveling Europe.

ABOUT THE AUTHOR

A multi-genre, Utah-based writer hailing from the Rust Belt, Steve Capone Jr debuted his YA historical/espionage fiction novel *Max in the Capital of Spies: A Max Fredericks Story* in March 2024 following a successful Kickstarter campaign.

In 2026, Gibbs Smith's True Fiction Press will distribute his next scheduled release nationwide. Working title: *Jimmy vs. Communism*—a McCarthy-era story of censorship and mob thinking set in the steel town of Homestead, PA.

You can find his short fiction anthologies such as *We Are Dangerous* (LUW Press, 2023) and *This Isn't the Place* (Timber Ghost Press 2024, forthcoming).

Steve is a long-time teacher of students from second grade through college. He's also worked as an editor and researcher. He's an unpaid pizza advocate and hopeful dog rescuer (props to Arctic Rescue in Utah). A member of the League of Utah Writers and the Horror Writers Association, his literary dream is to write a [good] book in every genre.

SELECTED RESEARCH MATERIALS

<u>Nonfiction Books</u>

Andrew, Christopher and Mitrokhin, Vasili. *The Mitrokhin Archive: The KGB in Europe and the West.*

Donovan, James. *Strangers on the Bridge: The Case of Colonel Abel and Francis Gary Powers.*

Funder, Anna. *Stasiland.*

Gaddis, John Lewis. *The Cold War: A New History.*

Gieseke, Jens. *The History of the Stasi: East Germany's Secret Police 1945-1990.*

Keegan, John. *Intelligence in War.*

Kempe, Frederick. *Berlin 1961: Kennedy, Khrushchev, and the Most Dangerous Place on Earth.*

Koehler, Jason. *Stasi: The Untold Story of the East German Secret Police.*

Larson, Erik. *In the Garden of Beasts.*

Verlag, Jason. *The Prohibited District: The Stasi Restricted Area Berlin-Hohenschönhausen.*

Whittell, Giles. *Bridge of Spies.*

Willner, Nina. *Forty Autumns.*

<u>Works of Fiction</u>

Le Carré, John. *The Spy Who Came In from the Cold.*

Nielsen, Jennifer. *A Night Divided.*

Yelchin, Eugene. *Spy Runner.*

<u>Podcasts</u>

Spycast, produced by the International Spy Museum in Washington, D.C. (a museum I recommend that you visit— it's a lot fun!)

<u>Maps and Other Tools</u>

In addition to using Google Maps almost every day of my process, I acquired several copies of a map of East Berlin circa 1968, reprinted, available at the Gedenkstätte Berlin-Hohenschönhausen bookstore (I could find these nowhere else in Germany or online). I also accessed some useful maps at German History in Documents and

Images, accessible as of 31 July 2020 at https://ghdi.ghi-dc.org/ and at Berlin Wall Map, also accessible as of 31 July 2020 at https://berlinwallmap.info/map.

Another helpful tool was Professor Marcuse's currency calculator, which was also accessible as of 31 July 2020 at http://marcuse.faculty.history.ucsb.edu/projects/currency.htm.

<u>Journal Articles</u>

Andrews, Molly. "One Hundred Miles of Lives: The Stasi Files as a People's History of East Germany." *Oral History* 26, no. 1 (1998): 24-31.

Fulbrook, Mary. "Popular Dissent and Political Activism in the GDR." *Contemporary European History* Vol. 2, No. 3 (Nov., 1993), pp. 265-282.

Galanova, Olga. "The Ambivalence of Detail-Documenting Wiretapped Phone Conversations by the State Security Service of the former German Democratic Republic." *Discourse and Society* 30, No. 3 (2019): 248-263.

Macrakis, Kristie. "Science and the Stasi: the acquisition of scientific and technological secrets was at the heart of East Germany's foreign espionage operations before the fall of the Berlin Wall." *Nature* (Vol. 461, Issue 7264): Oct. 2009.

<u>News Articles and Other Periodicals</u>

Bennhold, Katrin. "The Fall of the Berlin Wall in Photos: An Accident of History That Changed the World." *New York Times*. 8 November 2021. Accessed on 31 July 2020 at https://www.nytimes.com/2019/11/09/world/berlin-wall-photos-30-year-anniversary.html.

Central Intelligence Agency. "The East German Refugees." Accessed 31 July 2020 at https://www.cia.gov/library/readingroom/docs/1961-08-10a.pdf.

Central Intelligence Agency. "The Family Jewels." Accessed 31 July, 2020 at https://www.cia.gov/library/readingroom/docs/DOC_0001451843.pdf.

Central Intelligence Agency. "The SSD Agents' Center". December 1961. Accessed 31 July 2020 at https://www.cia.gov/library/readingroom/docs/DOC_0000202719.pdf.

Chronik der Mauer archive. *Bundeszentrale für Politische Bildung*. Accessed 31 July 2020 at https://www.chronik-der-mauer.de/.

Citizens Committee of Leipzig. Museum in der "Runden Ecke" mit dem Museum im Stasi-Bunker. Accessed 31 July 2020 at http://www.runde-ecke-leipzig.de/index.php?id=76&L=1.

Colitt, Leslie. "Lord of the Spies." *The Independent*. 15 September 1996. Accessed 31 July 2020 at https://www.independent.co.uk/arts-entertainment/lord-of-the-spies-1363355.html.

Everts, Sarah. "Over the Wall: Six Stories from East Germany." *Science History Institute: Distillations*. 15 January 2013. Accessed 31 July 2020 at https://www.

chemheritage.org/distillations/magazine/over-the-wall-six-stories-from-east-germany

"Fatality: H. Holger." Chronik der Mauer. Accessed 31 July 2020 at https://www.chronik-der-mauer.de/todesopfer/171343/h-holger?n.

Fisher, Mark."Ex-East German Spymaster is Barred from U.S.." Washington Post. 12 March 2006. Accessed 31 July 2020 at https://www.washingtonpost.com/archive/politics/1996/03/12/ex-east-german-spymaster-is-barred-from-us/9626308a-039c-464a-bda8-53752277c838/.

"The Founding of the Ministry for State Security." Federal Commissioner for the Records of the State Security Service of the Former German Democratic Republic, Accessed 31 July, 2020 at https://www.bstu.de/en/the-stasi/the-founding-of-the-mfs/.

History of Zion Church accessed 31 July 2020 at http://zionskirche-berlin.de/english. (Author's Note: The underground pro-democracy group as depicted in this novel wasn't active in Zionskirche church building until the 1980s. Its activities were mostly related to the publication and circulation of anti-communist screeds. The activity in the book is to be considered a fictionalized composite of real groups and activities fitted for narrative purpose.)

Hollersen, Wiebke. "Stasi Headquarters Provide Headache for Berlin." *Der Spiegel*. June 3, 2010. Accessed 31 July 2020 at http://www.spiegel.de/international/germany/fighting-over-the-past-former-stasi-headquarters-provide-headache-for-berlin-a-698267.html.

Hopkins, Robert. "A Glimpse of Life Behind the Berlin Wall." *Telegraph*. 16 May 2015. Accessed 31 July 2020 at http://www.telegraph.co.uk/expat/expatlife/11570669/A-glimpse-of-life-behind-the-Berlin-Wall.html

Independent Editorial Staff. "Markus Wolf." *The Independent*. 10 November 2006. Accessed 31 July 2020 at https://www.independent.co.uk/news/obituaries/markus-wolf-423686.html.

Kelly, Erin. "33 Vintage Photos that Provide a Peak into Life in East Germany." *All That is Interesting*. 9 January 2018. Accessed 31 July 2020 at http://all-that-is-interesting.com/east-germany-photos.

New York Times Editorial Staff. "They Came in From the Cold War." *New York Times*. 12 Nov, 2006. Accessed 31 July 2020 at https://www.nytimes.com/2006/11/12/weekinreview/12cxcerpts.html.

Paterson, Tony. "Why Berlin Cannot Forget the Stasi." *The Independent*. June 17, 2010. Accessed 31 July 2020 at http://www.independent.co.uk/news/world/europe/why-berlin-cannot-forget-the-stasi-2002600.html.

Pakenham, Michael. "The Saga of the Berlin Wall: The Tale of Communism's End." *The Baltimore Sun*. 21 March 2004. Accessed 31 July 2020 at https://www.baltimoresun.com/news/bs-xpm-2004-03-21-0403210471-story.html.

Schuler, CJ. "History of the Berlin Wall through Maps." *Here 360*. 6 November 2014. Accessed 31 July 2020 at https://360.here.com/2014/11/06/fall-wall-missing-pieces/.

Smale, Alison. "On Berlin Wall Anniversary, Somber Notes Amid Revelry." 8

November 2014. Accessed 31 July 2020 at https://www.nytimes.com/2014/11/09/world/on-berlin-wall-anniversary-somber-notes-amid-revelry.html.

Stasi Museum website. Accessed 31 July 2020 at http://www.stasi-museum.de/enenausstellung.htm.

Stasi observation report. Accessed 31 July 2020 at https://www.documentcloud.org/documents/705180-stasi-observation-report.

Sturdee, Simon. "Fighting to be Fashionable in Communist East Germany." *The Sydney Morning Harold*. 25 July 2009. Accessed 31 July 2020 at https://www.smh.com.au/world/fighting-to-be-fashionable-in-communist-east-germany-20090725-dwex.html.

Taylor, Alan. "World War II: After the War." *The Atlantic*. 30 October, 2011. Accessed 31 July 2020 at https://www.theatlantic.com/photo/2011/10/world-war-ii-after-the-war/100180/.

Walsh, Mary Williams. "Ex-Chief of East German Secret Police Freed: Europe: Court Releases from Erich Mielke. He Served Time for 1931 Killings - But Not for Any Crime from the Communist Era." *Los Angeles Times*. 2 August 1995. Accessed 31 July 2020 at https://www.latimes.com/archives/la-xpm-1995-08-02-mn-30656-story.html.

War History Online Editorial Staff. "War Zone Zoo: Remarkable Story of the Berlin Zoo in WW2." *War History Online*. 20 July 2018. Accessed 31 July 2020 at https://www.warhistoryonline.com/instant-articles/war-zone-zoo-berlin-zoo.html.

"The Watchtowers of East Berlin." *Digital Cosmonaut*. 2 November 2015. Accessed 31 July 2020 at https://digitalcosmonaut.com/2015/the-watchtowers-of-east-berlin/.

Wilson Center Digital Archive – International History Declassified (Aug 24, 1984 notes accessible as of 31 July 2020 at https://digitalarchive.wilsoncenter.org/document/115721.

<u>Videos</u>

"A Spinning Coin Explained." CSIRO. Accessed 31 July 2020 at https://www.youtube.com/watch?v=Sm96UC6O8Kw.

"Memories of a Former Stasi Prisoner." euronews (in English). Accessed 31 July at https://www.youtube.com/watch?v=Y3le69-Daok.

"Targeted by the Stasi." DW Documentary. Accessed 31 July 2020 at https://www.youtube.com/watch?v=bArtnedm3eQ.

ACKNOWLEDGMENTS

While writing is work completed in solitude, that's never the whole story. One must make one's way in and through the world first.

I would like to acknowledge for continued support and real-life inspiration two dear friends, Edward Simon and Derek Illar, as well as my brothers, Dan Capone and Andrew Capone. Deserving of gratitude also is my friend and Italian host Michele di Cesare. Always encouraging my efforts are my college advisors turned adult friends, Arlan Hess, who offered me my first platform to read from my book in her shop—City Books in Pittsburgh—and Lauryn Mayer, who never let me off the hook in my college years.

Travel was at the heart of my developing this book. I appreciate lengthy chats with the staff and travelers at U-Inn Berlin Hostel in Friedrichshain, specifically my brother from another mother, Thomas de Block. Also deserving of a mention are hosts Madaela and Spiro and visiting travelers staying at the Sunrock Hostel in Corfu, Greece (I recommend it! Their family-style meals were experiences I cherish). Atlantis Books in Oia, Santorini provided me a sun deck with an incomparable view on which to work on my first draft, though they didn't know it at the time. I hope to return for a visit and to work on another book on their rooftop patio. Other bookstores that contributed to my sense of wonder while I developed this book include the renowned Shakespeare & Co. and the wondrous Abbey Bookshop in Paris as well as St. George's English Bookstore in Prenzlauer Berg, Berlin.

I wish to thank from the bottom of my heart the volunteers and staff at The Berlin-Hohenschönhausen Memorial, the former Stasi prison in Friedrichshain; along with those working to keep the former Ministry headquarters open to the public and its associated documentation center open to those who have been victimized by the Stasi; and those working at the memorial at the former prison in Dresden and the Museum in der Runde Ecke in Leipzig, Germany.

I also would be remiss not to express gratitude overflowing to my present and former students and colleagues—especially Heather Novotny, an impassioned librarian who taught me the most important thing I know about books (there's a book for every reader).

Beta readers offered valuable comments and helped me to get an impression of what my audience might be thinking while they're reading. Beta readers included Ruth Wagner, Alex Muzio, Abby "Frankie" Kissell (my first enthusiastic endorser), Alicia Thompson, Nance Morris Adler, Dr. Lyndi King, Owen Edmonds, Lori Jennings Matthews, Gage Lazar, and Michelle Lazar.

Other supporters, readers, and interlocutors also include my friends and colleagues Katherine Cance and Matthew Berk along with my family.

My parents, Sharon Capone and Stephen Capone Sr., had so much to do with this book becoming a real thing.

My brother, Andrew Capone, graciously allowed me to name a character after him.

My mother-in-law Ruth Wagner has also encouraged me from the first and has always been honest with me.

My family has always supported my writing interests and taken me seriously as a person of creative ability, which is more than I can say even of myself.

Author and local bookstore proprietor Aaron Cance (The Printed Garden of Sandy, UT), fellow author Creed Archibald, and colleague Heather Novotny all read early drafts of an early chapter, and all offered substantive feedback that proved helpful. I thank Tom Lonero and Katie Powell for comments on what became chapters three and four. Thanks also to Sean McTigue and Josh Leland for some quick research assistance regarding Kennedy half-dollars and to Justin Barbour for technical assistance.

Thanks to the Eisenman family for welcoming my family to their guest house in Torrey, Utah for a weeklong respite from our pandemic-constrained world at home. In solitude at that desert abode, which I called my Writer's Residence in the Summer of 2020, I edited at least a third of this book.

Also deserving praise are my critique group partners, Lee Tucker and John Meehan, who offered frank and perspicacious advice—always constructive—on several chapters. Their feedback shaped how I edited the rest of the work, whether or not they commented on those sections directly. John and Lee, I cannot thank you both enough.

The members of the Salt Lake Writers' Group and the Salt City Genre Writers (both chapters of the League of Utah Writers) deserve praise, as well, and I am grateful to members of both. Those in the SLWG stayed with Max and me for a year without much pause, and they helped me to find places where Max disappeared and Steve took charge of the narrative. Without a doubt, there are more corrections to be discovered, and the SLWG would have found them all, given the time—but what's that they say about works of art? I've decided it is complete.

The shortcomings of this book are of my own devising and are not the fault of any whom I'm thanking.

Thank you to anyone who's read this far in the book. I appreciate you.

I owe a timeless and incalculable debt to my best childhood friend, Ari, who helped me to grow my imagination and creative energy when we were young and free. We made countless imaginary karate-themed movies in our backyards as kids growing up near Braddock, PA (where I have since learned some amazing history took place). I want to note for all reading that addiction is a condition that can take any of us at any point; help exists even for those who feel hopeless. He left us in 2010, and it took me two years to delete his number from my phone. As I write this during edits on New Years Day in 2024, I still miss him every day and hang out with him in my dreams on a weekly basis.

I also want to thank Ron Cambest, without whom I would never have written a single word of this book. Also, you called while I was editing today, and you were cool with it when I told you that I needed to go. Thank you.

I leave for last the most important and influential people in my adult life: Sara Capone, my darling wife and the mother of Rylee Capone and Aidyn Capone, who have welcomed me without reservation into their lives—the companionship of all three are the greatest gifts of my life. They all set aside innumerable hikes, breakfasts, and board games with me so that I might direct attention to my writing.

Thanks to the pups Quinn, Nova, and Odin the Survivor, whose love I didn't know I needed.

I am so very grateful.